CW00868264

COLD
LIKE ASH

COLD LIKE ASH

Max Deacon

Cold Like Ash is a work of fiction. Names, characters, places, and incidents either are the product of the author's imagination or are used fictitiously. Any resemblance to actual persons, living or dead, events, or locales is entirely coincidental.

Copyright © 2022 by Max Deacon

All rights reserved. No part of this book may be reproduced or used in any manner without written permission of the copyright owner except for the use of quotations in a book review.

Book design by Ross Ingielewicz

978-1-7397258-0-8 (paperback)

978-1-7397258-1-5 (ebook)

Published by Milk Tooth Press 2022

For Mum and Dad

One

"Oh, it looks fine," Mum said, though I could tell she was unconvinced.

The room was a squat rectangle, blank and box-like, with a bed against one wall and a desk against the other. There was a tall bookcase in the corner and two flimsy-looking cupboards, as well as a window half-covered by an ugly, yellow curtain. In a recess beside the door there was a sink and a cracked mirror. Water dripped from a crusted tap.

"It looks like a prison cell," I said, putting down the bags I'd been carrying and closing the door behind us. "Even prisoners get their own toilet."

"Oh, don't start. It just needs a bit of sprucing up. It'll look much nicer once we've put all your things away. Come on, give me a hand."

I nodded but said nothing. I didn't want to seem ungrateful after how much she'd helped with my application, but a whole year stuck in this room? I wondered how hard it would be to get a transfer into different halls, but Mum was already fussing with the décor.

"Well, don't just stand there," she said, pulling the new bedsheets from their packaging. "Let's make this place more cosy, shall we?"

There was something hopeful in her voice that almost made me want to cry. I distracted myself by unpacking, putting my course books on the bookcase, hanging my clothes in the built-in wardrobe. It only took about half an hour, and as usual, Mum was right. The bedding I'd picked out – a black and gold Aztec design – broke up the blankness of the walls and made the whole room less depressing. She'd insisted on buying a new lampshade and she'd been right about that too. It softened the harsh lighting, diffusing it down to a pinkish glow.

"I brought this for you as well," she said. "I didn't think you'd want to forget it."

She reached into her pocket and pulled out a tiny action figure of *Xena: Warrior Princess*, the one from my bedroom back at home. This was the evil Xena of the past, her plastic limbs wrapped in a huge fur coat. It seemed to look up at me impassively.

"You brought this?" I said, confused. "I thought you said I was too old for dolls."

"I know, but maybe she can be your good luck charm." She smiled encouragingly, passing it to me and closing her hand around mine. "Or maybe she'll remind you of home."

I wanted to roll my eyes but something in her expression told me not to. Mum and I had watched *Xena* every Saturday when I was younger. It was our *thing*. After my dad died it became an easy way for us to spend time together, escaping into a world of legendary heroes, gods, and villains, a world where the good guys always won.

"Thanks, Mum," I said, finding a spot for it on my bookcase.

"Don't mention it," she said, quietly.

She turned away and started fussing with the bedsheets again, pulling them taut at each corner. "How are we looking, Ashley? Are we almost there?"

Ashley. I never understood how my parents could have given me such an awful name. What I'd give to be a John or a Mark or a Michael – a name that was strong, firm, commanding. I always thought Ashley sounded more like a sneeze.

"I think that's nearly everything," I said.

"Really? I assumed we'd be here for hours yet."

"No, it's fine. I can do the rest once you're gone."

It was strange. I didn't want to be alone, but as Mum started adjusting the pillows, I found myself urging her to leave. I was ready to start my new life, to be the person I'd always *wanted* to be, but everywhere she went, she left little reminders of my former self. All my life I'd been the quiet one, the bookish one, the one who faded into the background. I'd never been popular at school, but I'd never been picked on or bullied either. Really, when I thought of the person I'd been, I saw someone who was always searching for something, anything, to help forget what

I'd always known – that I was painfully, embarrassingly normal.

Mum sighed. "You're so lucky. I wish *I* could've gone to uni when I was your age. So many new things to learn, so many new people to meet…"

I stopped her before she started crying. I could tell she was nervous to leave me alone, but I knew she'd be fine if she saw how excited I was, how independent I could be without her. In reality, I was terrified; I had no idea how to fend for myself. Uni had been entirely my own idea, but now I was here, I couldn't help feeling like I'd made a mistake. What if I had?

Once Mum was certain I could take care of everything else, we left the room and made our way back through the halls, following signs towards the carpark. As we went, she nodded approvingly at every boy she passed, particularly those with short haircuts and neat, presentable clothes. She nudged me in the ribs, raised her eyebrows, spoke too loudly.

"Don't you see how good you'd look if you put a bit more care into your appearance? I know it's not *my* place to say, but these boys don't all feel the need to –"

"Jeez! You don't miss a beat, do you?"

"Okay, okay," she said, holding up her hands. "It was only an idea."

I bit my cheeks to stop from smiling. I thought it was best to not encourage her.

"You're the worst," I said, trying to sound serious.

"I know," she said, and grinned.

Out in the carpark, next to her scuffed black car, she launched into a long speech about laundry detergent, the importance of a balanced diet, and the perils of unsafe sex. I nodded in all the right places, but it was a speech I had heard before. When she was done, she put her hands on my shoulders, looked into my face, and exhaled shakily.

"Call me if you need anything, okay? Even if I'm at work." Then, after a long pause, she said, "I'll miss having you at home with me."

I felt the painful stinging of tears in my nose, and when she pulled me into a hug, I was shocked to realise I was crying, my face pressed into her coat, laughing nervously in between sobs. Mum was surprised at this too. We had never been very touchy with each other, but now she pulled me in close, holding me so tightly I couldn't breathe.

"I'm sorry," I said, drawing myself away, wiping my eyes on the back of my hand. "I'm just a bit nervous about being on my own. I mean…what if no one likes me?"

"You'll be fine," she said. "Just be yourself. And remember to be interested in everything and everyone. You'll make loads of friends in no time."

I sniffed. "Do you think so?"

"Of course I do!"

I wiped my eyes again, grateful there was no one around to see. I watched her get in the car and waved her off as she drove away, disappearing through the main gates. Now I was alone, I closed my eyes and took a deep breath, counting to ten, fifteen, twenty. I could feel my lip quivering, but before I gave in to the feeling completely, I thought of the little six-inch Xena clutching her sword, standing defiantly on my bookcase. Giving up her evil ways, Xena had shown she could be a better person. Now it was time that I did the same.

When I got back to my room, I saw that an orange flyer had been pushed underneath the door. It was an invitation to a first night party and dinner in the dining hall. Since Queensway was off campus, it was crucial – or so the flyer said – that we build up a community amongst ourselves. There would be a complimentary buffet followed by drinks and then dancing. *Till late!!!* declared the flyer. I started to feel like I was back in Sixth Form.

I checked the time on my phone. I still had a few hours to kill, so I sat at the desk and went through my course manual. I would be studying English Literature, and I made notes about the modules I'd choose and which ones I'd drop later on in the year. I was nervous to see so much Shakespeare, so many Jacobean plays on the course, but then, wasn't that what I was here for? I imagined conversations with my peers in campus cafés, post-lecture and pre-seminar, making jokes about our favourite books. I tried my best to keep that in mind.

When it was almost time for dinner, I flicked absently through my wardrobe, trying to decide how I wanted to look. I'm not entirely sure why I bothered. Most of my clothes were all black and unassuming, and I owned nothing that demanded even the slightest bit of attention. But maybe that was a good thing. It would serve me well to look adaptable, like I was easy to get along with. But how could I do that without disappearing?

I eventually settled on a black turtleneck. I knew it was the safest option really, but then I heard the voice of the new Ash in my head. *"Not safe but simple; chic, effortlessly cool."* It struck me as wishful thinking. My hair was a colourless blonde that never seemed to do what I wanted; my face was round, a little chubby; and there were tiny spots under my chin from all my rushed attempts at shaving. Still, there wasn't much I could do about that now, so I took a deep breath, steadied my nerves, and made my way out to the dining hall.

I was slightly early, so I joined the queue in the main corridor, standing behind a group of girls who were already deep in conversation. I hadn't even had time to check my phone when one of them turned around to face me.

"Hi! I'm Charlotte! What's your name?"

She was pretty and blonde and had freckles all over her nose. On her wrist, she wore a bracelet hung with sharp, silver stars. I wondered how often they stabbed into her.

"Oh, um, hi, I'm Ash," I managed weakly, suddenly flustered.

Charlotte looked me up and down. "Are you gay?"

I winced. I had been out through most of secondary school, and like everything else about me, it hadn't made the smallest bit of difference. I had no problem with anyone knowing I was gay – I was proud of it – but I suddenly sensed she had set a trap.

"Um, yeah, I am," I said, trying not to sound defensive.

"Oh my god, you have to sit with us! I can just tell we'll be best friends. Everyone, this is Ash," she said, waving her hands about. "He's gay!"

The other girls introduced themselves, and so began a whirlwind of giggly questions that seemed to be inching towards an assault. Charlotte, Emily, and Sarah were nice really, and I was grateful for the company, but I'd been hoping to meet people more like *me*. I looked around for another group, but before I could talk to anyone else, the hall doors opened, people cheered, and everyone started to file inside. I'd just have to wait until after dinner.

I'd imagined the dining room to be enormous and

church-like, a place for banquets and formal dances. In truth it looked more like a village hall, with laminate floors, white walls, and rows of shaky, fold-down tables. We sat down in the middle of the room, and though my eyes darted around to the other cliques already forming, my cowardly instinct was to cling to the girls. Maybe they just needed some time to be more comfortable, more relaxed around new people. I heard my mum's advice in my ears. *"Be interested in everyone."*

"So, what are you guys studying?" I asked.

Emily, whose blonde hair had been aggressively straightened, answered first. "Media Arts. I know it won't get me a job after graduation, but all the cutest boys do Media. You should've seen the guys in the department when I came for my interview. Talk about fitties!"

"Emily, you're so bad!" squealed Charlotte.

Sarah, the requisite brunette of the group, shook her head fondly. "You guys crack me up," she said. "You're so random!"

The girls broke into shrieks of delighted laughter, slapping each other's hands and throwing their hair behind their shoulders. *Christ*, I thought, *I have to get out of here.* I could easily see this becoming my life for the next three years – sleepovers watching Disney films, pre-drinking to playlists called *Girl Power!* and *Happy Beats!*, affectionately calling each other *bitch*. I had a sudden, private vision of strangling them all in their sleep.

As we ate, I decided to just indulge them instead, answering whatever questions they wanted to ask me. These were the old favourites – when did you know you were gay? Were you accepted when you came out? Have you ever slept with a woman? Do you think you could if you had to? I could practically answer them all without thinking.

Once dinner was over, it took exactly zero drinks for the girls to be on the dancefloor, jumping up and down excitedly. I declined their offer to join them, standing instead with a plastic cup of beer against the far wall. I'd only ever had the odd shandy back at home, so I reminded myself to take it slow, to know my limits; I didn't want to embarrass myself by getting drunk on the very first night. I made eye contact with a few people as they passed, smiling nervously, but nobody stopped to talk to me. I waited for another few songs, but as I watched the girls' relentless dancing, I figured I had one of two choices. I could either accept my role as the token gay and join them, or I could do what Mum would've told me to do – talk to everybody; don't restrict yourself; be proactive and try to make friends.

That, I reasoned, was the best thing to do, but first I would need to collect my thoughts. I took my beer and went through the dining room, through the adjoining bar, and outside onto the patio. It was only half past seven but it was already getting dark. The sky was studded with stars, just like the rivets on Xena's armour, and the moon was peering out from behind long trails of navy clouds. I pressed my back against the wall and tried to formulate a plan. I would go to the bar to get a drink, and since it was quieter there than in the dining room, I would hang around and find someone to talk to. God, I really *was* pathetic. Why did no one else seem to find it as difficult as *me* to make new friends? Even pre-schoolers could do that.

I was just about to put my plan into action when I saw a guy facing away from me, sitting alone on top of a picnic table. He was noisily smoking a cigarette, the tip a bright, unearthly orange. It reminded me of one of those fish in the deep sea that use a light to lure in prey. I walked over before I could stop myself, before I could find a reason not to.

"Hey. Do you mind if I sit?"

He shrugged, shook his head, blew out another stream of smoke. His face with thin and angular, slightly fox-like, and his hair – short on the sides but longer on top – fell in thick, shaggy curls, a brown so dark it was almost black. He was wearing a leather jacket that looked at least three sizes too big for him, and when he shifted his weight on the bench, I could see a leopard print shirt underneath it. I thought *my* outfit had been cool, but this guy was dressed like a male model. Did I want to kiss him or just *be* him?

"You having fun in there?" he asked.

"I don't know," I said. "I guess?"

11

"Come on, don't lie. It's fucking terrible."

I laughed and sat down next to him, pretending not to be intimidated. "Okay, you're right. It's awful. I'm literally having the worst night of my life."

"Well, that makes two of us," he said.

His voice when he spoke was deep, a little gravelly, but it was slightly posh too; he seemed to be tasting each word in his mouth. He flicked his cigarette onto the grass, then reached for his pack and pulled out another. "Want one?"

"Oh, no, thanks. I don't smoke."

"God, I wish I'd never started. The money I spend on these bloody things."

"I mean, you could always give up," I suggested.

He turned his head and looked at me. His eyes were a golden green, like sunlight glinting on a river. "Yeah, but where's the fun in that?"

He fished a lighter out of his pocket, lit the end of his cigarette, then slammed the lighter on the bench with a clatter. He was noisy and brash, but there was something in the way he gazed off into the middle distance that made him seem sensitive, mysterious. He clicked his tongue, smacked his lips. I noticed his nails were painted silver.

"I'm Ash," I said. "It's nice to meet you."

"Hey, cool name," he said, brightly. "Have you ever seen *The Evil Dead*?"

"Um, no?"

"Oh man, I'll have to show it to you some time. The main character's called Ash too, and he's a total badass. It's fucking great."

He put his cigarette between his teeth and reached out to shake my hand. "I'm Ezra."

His touch made me feel more confident, like he'd given me permission to be myself. I said I was glad to meet someone so interesting.

"Oh, I'm tedious really," he said. "You'll be bored of me before long. Trust me."

I didn't want to tell him how unlikely I thought that seemed, so I asked him the questions I'd normally avoid – where did he come from? What was he studying? What did he do when he wasn't at school? He had just started talking when his phone made a little drumming sound. He apologised airily, then pulled it out and opened Grindr, reading the message he'd just received. I caught a glimpse of oiled, faceless torsos, fresh from the gym and sculpted like statues. I didn't know where to look. I'd never used an app like that in my life.

"Urgh," he scoffed, rolling his eyes and slamming his phone down next to his lighter. "Men are pigs. They're all awful, let me tell you."

I stifled a laugh. "It must be rough being gay if you hate men."

"Tell me about it. Do you use Grindr as well? It's so fucking depressing."

I hadn't expected him to ask me this. "Um, no, I…It's just that, um…I'm…"

"Oh, it's no big deal if you haven't had sex. It's overrated anyway."

I breathed a sigh of relief. I wasn't ashamed to be a virgin, but I didn't want Ezra to think I was as boring as everyone else did. I took another sip of beer.

"If sex is overrated, why do you use Grindr? Isn't that what it's for?"

Ezra shrugged. "Well, technically, but come on. As if I'm gonna go to some random guy's house just to have sex. Not very romantic, is it? Don't I deserve love?"

"Is that what you want?" I asked, laughing.

Ezra blinked at me. "What else is there?"

Two

I spent the next morning obsessing over whether or not I should text him. Ezra was so much cooler than me – even as a friend he was out of my league – and though he'd given me his number, I was pretty sure he was just being polite. I couldn't imagine him wanting to be friends with someone like me, someone with so little to offer, so I figured I'd wait until I saw him around. I didn't want him to think I was desperate.

But just after midday, Ezra came knocking on my door. He was wearing a black shirt patterned with skulls, and his nails were painted the colour of blood.

"So," he said, pushing past me and glancing around my room. "What are we doing today? My only plan is to try not to kill myself from boredom."

I was so surprised to see him that I didn't know what to say. I could barely believe he was in my room. "Um… What do *you* want to do?" I asked.

"Whatever you want, darling. What are you in the mood for?"

I wanted to say that I'd do anything he asked me, but I stopped myself at the last second. I didn't want to seem needy, insecure, like I didn't have anything else to do.

"Well, I was just going to get some reading done."

"That's lame," he said, folding his arms. "Why don't we walk to campus instead? We can look around, get a coffee, see if we can find some cute boys…"

This was what I'd been dreading. Couldn't he see how much it scared me?

"Oh, um…Actually, I'd rather not," I said.

He looked at me blankly, waiting for an explanation.

"It's just that…Well, I don't really know *how* to talk to boys. I've never had to before. Couldn't we just stay here instead?"

Ezra put a hand on my shoulder, consoling me. "Yeah, of course," he said, "but I'm always here if you want advice. I'll teach you everything I know."

I had no idea what that entailed but I laughed anyway. "Thanks, Ez."

"What are friends for?" he said, and smiled.

To my surprise, Ezra and I became inseparable after that. I learned that he lived in Brighton; that his parents were both artists; and that, unlike me, he had been popular back at school. His upbringing, he said, had been painfully middle class, though the details of his family seemed prohibited, off-limits. When I mentioned my mum or I asked about his, he would always shrug or sigh and then quickly change the subject. This constantly surprised me. In all other ways, he was the most open person I'd ever met, often talking about boyfriends, hook ups, embarrassing stories about sex. I let him talk about anything he wanted, and I was glad he seemed happy to share. If I was being completely honest, I was just shocked I had made a friend.

Since Freshers Week meant we had no lectures, we took to hanging out in my room every night. Occasionally we'd venture out to the bar next to the dining hall, though we never spoke to anyone else and soon went back the way we came, drinks in hand, laughing about some joke that Ezra had told me. I even showed him an episode of *Xena* one night. I hadn't wanted to, but once he'd seen the action figure on the shelf, I knew he wouldn't let it go. I tried to think of an episode he might enjoy, something melodramatic but with lots of action. I eventually settled on the one where Xena fights off the Persian army to save her sidekick Gabrielle. He spent the whole time snorting and huffing, fidgeting about on the bed beside me, but when I tried to turn it off, he snapped his head round as if I'd slapped him.

"No!" he protested. "Don't! If you love it, then so do I."

I thought he was being disingenuous, but I soon realised that Ezra – despite all of his apparent confidence – was somewhat needier than I'd predicted. I had no idea why, but he seemed to want me as a friend as much as *I* wanted *him*. I never confronted him about it because I was scared it would put him off, that I'd end up driving him away. And because I didn't mind. I was flattered he thought I was important, that I had become central to his happiness.

On Friday night, we decided to finally venture out of Queensway and go to the Students' Union on campus. We bought tickets the day before, and all through the halls, there was a palpable excitement. This was the first time all the freshers would be together, and there was an unspoken understanding that this night was an important one.

Frankly, I was terrified.

The most exciting part of the night for me was finally seeing Ezra's room, so at seven o'clock – with a bottle of wine tucked under one arm – I went to find which door was his.

I only knocked once but he must've been waiting for me. The door flew open to reveal Ezra, his cheekbones sparkling with gold glitter, his lips a deep, seductive purple. He was wearing a shirt made of black chiffon though I tried my best to avert my eyes. It was so sheer that his entire chest could be seen underneath, throat to collarbone to navel.

"Welcome," he said, bowing dramatically. "Squint as you come in, my darling. The beauty of my room may prove too much for mortal eyes."

"You're ridiculous," I said, stepping past him.

His room was the inverse of mine, like a mirror image, with the sink, bed and window all on the opposite side than I was used to. Blinking fairy lights had been strung up around the window, and he had stuck stills from horror films up on the walls: a zombie with worms crawling out of one eye; a woman in lace being burned at the stake. And above his bed, there was a photo of us. We were sitting on top of the bench where we'd first met, arms slung round each other, me grinning up at the camera while Ezra gazed off to one side. He must've printed it out at reception. I was so touched I could hardly speak.

"You hate it," Ezra said, checking his makeup in the mirror. "It's fine, you can tell me. I won't be offended. It's perfectly alright that you –"

"No! It's just that I can't believe you wouldn't..." I stopped myself and took a breath, pretending I hadn't noticed the photo. "I just don't understand why we've been hanging out at mine so much. Yours doesn't even look like a uni room!"

Ezra grinned and turned to face to me. "Because I had to get it ready, darling. I didn't want you coming in before it was finished now, did I?"

For the second time in half a minute, I was so touched that I thought I might cry. Ezra seemed to sense this and came barrelling towards me.

"Alright," he said, holding up the wine and some plastic cups. "No mushy stuff tonight, please. We're supposed to be having fun."

But Ezra's version of fun was more intense than I was used to. As we drank, we each chose a song to play on Ezra's laptop, explaining why we loved it, what it meant, and who or what it made us think of. He always listened to me in awed silence, even though all my stories were boring. It hardly seemed like a fair exchange when his involved drunk nights out with friends, midnight raves on Brighton Beach, kisses with boys who smelled like Lynx. I found myself wishing, once again, that my life had been more like his.

Once we were sufficiently tipsy, we put on our coats and made our way out to the campus, a twenty minute walk through a series of back alleys. Normally I would've found a walk like this terrifying, but Ezra – singing songs he remembered from adverts – rendered everything hilarious. He kept singing one of them again and again, and in various voices too: *"Flare Pro-Strength is tough on stains, and unblocks drains!"*

By the time we reached campus, I'd been laughing so hard my cheeks hurt. Ezra seemed proud I'd been entertained; he smiled smugly whenever I looked at him.

We joined the queue outside the Union. The other freshers, all dressed up for a night out, were just the same as the ones at Queensway. I didn't know what I'd been expecting.

"Looks like *we're* the only ones who made an effort," said Ezra.

I was literally wearing a shirt from Primark but I was flattered he'd thought to include me. I didn't feel qualified to criticise anyone's clothes, so I just nodded, laughed, agreed.

"Let's find some fit boys tonight," he said.

"Oh, on the lookout, are you?"

"Well, why not? Don't be nervous. I'm an excellent wingman."

I hesitated. "Okay…"

"Look, I know you don't have much experience, but what's the big deal? Isn't that what uni's for? I mean, what would your mate Xena do if *she* were here?"

I couldn't imagine a warrior princess getting drunk on six pound wine from Tesco, but before I could answer, Ezra pulled out his phone and started scrolling through his Instagram.

"Can I see your photos?" I asked.

He nodded and handed me his phone, turning away to look for a cigarette. His account was exactly as I'd expected: an entire grid of arty selfies. First he was standing against a brick wall, sullenly gazing out of frame; next, a close up of his mouth dripping fake blood; next, him topless in a blank room, bathed in the light from an unseen window. Each one was like a work of art, but I was surprised he had so few followers.

"Is this your only account?" I asked.

Ezra puffed away on his cigarette. "Yeah, why?"

"Oh, I just thought…" I paused. "I don't know why you don't have more followers when your photos are so great. I thought you'd be, like, Instagram famous or something."

He looked momentarily stung and I was scared that I'd offended him. He seemed unsure how to respond. After a while, I heard him snicker.

"Clearly no one else has taste," he said.

The people in front shuffled forward, and by the time he'd finished his cigarette, we were both at the front of the queue. We flashed our tickets, walked inside, then checked our coats into the cloakroom. But the Union, it turned out, was the most generic place I could imagine, a perfect combination of every nightclub I'd seen on TV. The floor throbbed with the bass from some forgettable 90s pop song; lights flashed colours like a Year Six disco; and boys and girls stood far apart, trying to look cool in their respective groups.

"Well, this is lame," said Ezra. "Come on, we're gonna need a drink."

At the bar we bought snakebites that stained the insides of our mouths red. We were queueing to buy our second when Ezra grabbed me by the arm. "Let's dance."

"Oh no," I said, throwing up my hands. "I'm not much of a dancer."

"Come on," he whined. "Please?"

"I thought you said this place was lame?"

"It *is* lame!"

"Then why don't we just leave?"

"Are you joking? It's our first night out together! We're going."

I didn't even have time to protest before Ezra grabbed my hand and dragged me out onto the dancefloor. Literally nobody else was dancing. Everyone stared at us from the sides of the room, and for the first time, I felt a bit embarrassed to be seen with him. I'd noticed people looking before at his translucent shirt and purple lipstick, but now I wondered what they thought of *me*, how our friendship must look from the outside. I wanted the earth to swallow me whole but Ezra clutched onto my hands, and before I knew it, we were both dancing like utter lunatics. I didn't know if it was the alcohol or my pent-up nerves, but I suddenly didn't care that I couldn't dance or had no rhythm. I'd never felt so free in my life.

Before the song had even finished, the floor was heaving with people. I couldn't help feeling that I'd had some small role to play, that Ezra and I were partly responsible. I looked up at him. He was singing along at the top of his voice, holding onto me, screaming the lyrics into my face. Nobody else was having as much fun as him, and I wondered why I'd ever cared about what they thought. He was my friend, my *best* friend, and his was the only opinion that mattered. I got the sense I was being a dick. My embarrassment felt like a betrayal.

Eventually Ezra pulled me away from the dancefloor, through the crowds of freshers, and out into the smoking garden. We looked an absolute mess. Our hair was plastered to our foreheads; we were slick with sweat; and Ezra's lipstick was now only a faint, purple smear. As I caught my breath against the railings, Ezra nudged me in the side.

"What about him?" he asked. "Is he cute?"

I looked over. He was staring at a guy with a shaved head standing a few feet away from us. He had a caveman jaw and chiselled forearms, and a shirt so tight it seemed ready to burst. All this was paired with a dopey sort of expression, as if he didn't know where he was. Was this Ezra's type? How could I tell him he looked like a twat?

"Um, he's not for me," I said, "but you go for it."

"Are you kidding? I'm with you tonight, darling."

"Yeah, but it's fine if you see someone you like. Don't let *me* hold you back."

Ezra rolled his eyes. "Oh, relax," he said. "I'm just trying to work out what kind of guys you're into. I know you won't tell me on your own."

"Well, I don't really know. It's just…"

I started to explain but I could see he wasn't listening. His gaze kept going back to the guy with the big arms, hungrily eyeing him up and down.

"Ezra!" I said, teasing.

He snapped his attention back to me.

"I'm only checking out the merchandise! Besides, it's good that we like different guys. It'd be so cliché for us to fall out over some random-ass boy."

"Especially that one," I said.

Ezra arched an eyebrow, but before I could say anything else, he was grabbing my arm and racing back towards the dancefloor. Being his friend was like riding a rollercoaster. It made me feel unsteady, a little sick; but also, in secret, I prayed that it would never stop.

The rest of the night was a blur though I could tell Ezra was drunker than I was. His eyes were red and watery, and his words all ran together, as if his mouth couldn't keep up with his brain. He was more child-like now, more vulnerable. I found I wanted to protect him.

We caught the bus back to Queensway where he annoyed all the passengers by singing from the back row. He was working his way through *The Muppet Christmas Carol* – complete with voices and cockney accents – and then, before I knew it, we were half-naked in his bed. I seemed to come back to my senses then, but when I got up to leave, he wrapped his arms around my chest, dragging his weight on top of mine.

"Please don't go," he whispered, tenderly.

He looked into my eyes and then kissed me on the lips. I froze. He pulled away, looking at my eyes, my mouth, my eyes again. His face was only half an inch from mine, but neither of us moved. Then, just as quickly as it had happened, we both started laughing. We laughed and laughed until tears ran down our faces, until I thought I might throw up.

"God, what are we like?" Ezra wailed, burying his face into the mattress.

This only made us laugh harder, and soon we were clutching onto each other, poking each other like naughty school boys. My whole body was squeezed tight, convulsed; it almost felt like I was crying. We laughed until we heard bangs from the wall beside us. We looked at each other in terror, then started laughing twice as hard, not even stopping when the sun came up, the birds began to sing, and the light outside changed colour – purple to blue, blue to gold.

Three

I woke up at midday. The room was spinning, lurching from side to side, and it took me a while to remember where I was. I tried to sit up and look around, but the backwards configuration of the furniture made me so dizzy I wanted to retch. I rolled onto my side instead and saw that Ezra was already awake, looking up at the ceiling, lost in thought.

"Morning, Ash."

His voice was quiet, small. I barely realised he had spoken.

"God, I feel like shit," I said, rolling onto my back. "I can't believe we drank so much last night! I don't even remember coming home."

Ezra chuckled softly to himself, but then he sighed, cleared his throat. "Can we talk about what happened?" he asked. "You know, when we were in bed?"

"We really don't have to."

"I know, but…I think maybe we should."

I turned onto my side to face him. The sunlight, streaming through the curtains, made his skin look pale, transparent. I'd never seen him move so little before.

"Listen," he whispered, "about the kiss…"

"You don't have to explain anything," I said. "We were both drunk. It happens."

I mean, it had never happened to *me* before, but I tried to make it sound like I knew what I was talking about. Ezra kept his eyes fixed on the ceiling.

"Ash, I really like you," he said, "but I'd feel awful if I ruined our friendship. Or if I made things awkward between us. I'd never forgive myself if I messed it all up."

I didn't know what to say. I thought about touching him, reaching out, letting him know that I wasn't upset. But Ezra still refused to look at me.

"It's just that…" he paused. "I mean, I had a few friends back at school, but I never felt like anyone got me. They thought I was fun, someone to have a laugh with, but I couldn't *really* be myself with them. I think that's why I like spending time with *you* so much. You seem to like me being completely myself. God knows why."

I'd sensed before that Ezra wasn't as confident as he pretended to be, but this was the first time I'd heard him say as much out loud. I wondered if he knew that I felt exactly the same way about him, that I could be myself around him too.

"Seriously, Ezra, you've got nothing to apologise for. We're both gay, we're both single, and we're both exploring this new friendship. Besides, it *was* only a kiss. It doesn't have to mean anything. Maybe we were just…getting it out of our system?"

Ezra turned to me. "Do you mean it?"

"Mm-hm."

He sighed heavily, as if he'd been holding his breath for the last few minutes. "Okay," he said, nodding. "I won't bring it up it again. But I'm really glad that you understand."

"Hey, don't mention it," I said.

With that out of the way, he quickly returned to the Ezra I recognised. It was almost like he'd been waiting for me to forgive him. We recounted the events of the night that we could remember, piecing them together as best we could – which songs we'd danced to, how many snakebites we'd had, why we'd gone to sleep in Ezra's room – though mentions of the kiss were all carefully avoided. When I reminded Ezra about the Muppet singalong on the bus, he covered his face with both hands. "I want to die," he groaned, theatrically.

But there was something in the air between us now, some note of awkwardness I wasn't prepared for. It was as if we'd crossed a line, an invisible barrier, and now – having seen each other half-naked – neither of us were quite sure how to act.

My hangover was so bad I started wishing I was back in my room. I wanted to take a shower and eat Super

Noodles, and I wasn't in the mood to think about the changing dynamics of our friendship. I thanked him for a great night out, then stood up and got dressed, plucking my clothes from wherever I'd dropped them – the floor, the chair, the back of the radiator. Just as I was about to leave, Ezra sat up in bed, holding the duvet against his chest.

"I can't believe I was your first kiss," he said, gloating like a kid after winning a swimming badge. "Weird, right?"

"I know," I said. "Very weird."

"And with me, you lucky thing! Whatever will the neighbours say?"

I laughed under my breath, more to myself than to him, but I could already tell he was feeling insecure. It was like he was performing a scene from a play, pretending to be a version of himself that he thought I hoped or expected to see. I wondered if I should call him out on it. Instead I just turned and left the room, letting the door swing shut behind me.

I spent the rest of the day doing nothing, lounging around on my bed and eating Skittles, playing mindlessly with my phone. But it was my first weekend as a student and it felt good to be by myself. I could do exactly what I wanted. I felt as luxurious as a cat.

I called Mum on Sunday morning and told her about everything that had happened so far, about the party in

Queensway and the night out at the Union, but I spent most of the time talking about Ezra. When I'd finally finished, she was so quiet I thought she'd hung up.

"Mum? Mum, are you still there? I can't…"

"Sorry, Ashley," she said, her breath catching in her throat. "I'm just proud of you, that's all. I always knew you'd be okay, but I'm really glad –"

"Oh, stop it," I cut in. "I've only been here for a week."

"No, you sound like a different person. I barely recognise your voice!"

I laughed and shrugged her off, making light of what she'd said, but I guess I *did* feel like I'd changed. For months I'd had visions of uni being a disaster, of calling my mum in floods of tears, begging her to come and pick me up. But now here I was, having fun and making friends. Maybe I *was* a different person. I barely recognised myself.

My first lecture of the year was titled *Shakespeare's Tragedies 1591-1608* and, since it was a compulsory module for all English students, was to be held in the main lecture theatre on campus. I left early because I wasn't exactly sure where the room was, but I still managed to embarrass myself as I searched for it, holding my campus map out in front of me like a tourist in a foreign country. As I walked, a number of older students turned to look at me, but none of them spoke or offered to help. I was turning red, becoming flustered.

I luckily found it just in time, following a long line of students who'd been queuing up outside. As we went in, I had to force myself not to gasp. The room was enormous – big enough to fit three of four hundred people – with wood panelled walls and ceilings, and velvet curtains the colour of rust. I found a seat about halfway down, then occupied myself by foraging for my notebook, pens and pencil case, trying not to look too awkward. The room hummed with conversation as more and more students filed in, but how did everyone else seem to know each other? We hadn't even had a seminar yet, but most people were chatting and joking like old friends. I wondered, nervously, if I'd missed some kind of event.

The course booklet said that these lectures would be run by the head of the English department, a woman called Artemisia Benson-Dotoff. When I'd told Ezra her name, he'd snatched the booklet out of my hand, laughing in disbelief.

"Oh, that's totally a fake name. Maybe she's a spy!"

"What, and teaching English just for fun?"

"Well, she's obviously undercover. Who'd ever suspect her?" he'd said.

But when she appeared at the lectern, the idea of her being anything other than an English teacher was almost impossible to imagine. I guessed she was somewhere in her sixties, with a severe grey bob and a shapeless yellow cardigan. She was also wearing the biggest pair of glasses

I'd seen in my life. She looked like an owl in a children's picture book.

She introduced herself to the class, telling us about her role and her specialties as a professor. She seemed nervous at first, constantly playing with her necklace, clearing her throat before each sentence. But this disappeared when the lecture started. She talked about hamartia and peripeteia, about the nine conventions of tragedy, about quartos, texts and folios. I was suddenly worried I wasn't smart enough for this class, that surely everyone would see how underserving I was to be here. But then I thought about what Ezra would say, how he'd tell me to be more self-confident. I was just as good as anyone else.

The second half of the lecture – mercifully slower than the first – was focused on *Venus and Adonis*, one of Shakespeare's earliest narrative poems. I didn't even know that he'd written poems that weren't sonnets, and when I found it in the course book, I couldn't believe I had never heard of it. The synopsis at the top of the page said:

Venus, Goddess of Love, becomes enamoured with Adonis, a man renowned for his mortal beauty. She tries to make him fall in love with her, but Adonis cares only for hunting; he wishes to be left alone. Eventually he is killed by a boar, causing Venus to merge love with human suffering and pain. This is why love often ends in tragedy.

One line in particular stood out to me, a description of Venus after being refused by Adonis: "She's Love, she loves, and yet she is not loved." I had no idea why I liked the line so much but I copied it down anyway. Something told me it might be useful.

Artemisia seemed to like the poem as much as I did, and when she recited certain passages, she closed her eyes and smiled secretly, as rapt and exultant as a nun. I thought it was sweet, kind of endearing, but I noticed a few people were laughing, mocking the way she delivered the poem. She carried on without noticing, but as she recited the final stanzas, as she paced up and down with her eyes closed, she crashed loudly into the podium. A stack of papers went skittering across the floor and the hall erupted into laughter. I couldn't believe it! You would've thought we were all toddlers, not students in their first year of uni. As she bumbled about to clean up, I resisted the urge to go and help her. I was too scared to alienate myself from the other students, too afraid of what they'd think. I really hated myself for that.

But as I looked around the hall, I noticed there was another boy who wasn't laughing, visibly cringing with embarrassment. His skin was smooth and tanned, golden-brown as if freshly baked, and a slim silver ring had been attached through his left nostril. His hair was dark – roughly as long as mine – but where mine was flat and coarse, his was thick, glossy, curly, like he had spent all day at the beach. But it was his eyes I couldn't stop staring at. They were round and heavy-lidded, vaguely feline, grey as rain – strangely at odds with the gold of his skin. I'd never seen a more beautiful boy. I didn't know where to rest my eyes.

Then, without warning, he suddenly turned in my direction. His face softened and he smiled, gazing up at me flirtatiously. My heart started pounding. I could feel my cheeks turning red but I smiled back at him anyway, then glanced away to look down at my notes. When I looked back, he was still smiling, only now he was biting his lip. I felt naked, exposed, like a layer of skin had been peeled away. It was like he could see underneath my clothes.

When the class was over, I gathered my things and ran out of the hall as fast as I could. I told myself it was because I was too nervous to risk speaking to him, but the truth was that I was feeling something I hadn't experienced before. My whole body was warm but it felt empty somehow too. I was so hungry I thought I might faint.

But it wasn't exactly for something to eat.

Four

"Oh my god, you like him!" Ezra said to me as we ate dinner. "You're already in love!"

"What? No, I'm not!"

"Ash, please. It's perfectly fine that you like someone. We just need to know his name. If we knew that, then we could find out what halls he's staying in. Obviously he's in your classes on Monday, but maybe, if we found out which seminar group he's in…"

I was starting to regret telling Ezra about Nose Ring Boy. I mean, we'd only smiled at each other. It was hardly a big deal. Besides, I couldn't imagine a boy as cute as him ever liking someone like me. He could probably have anyone he wanted.

"Let's not get carried away," I said. "We don't even know if he's gay."

Ezra waved his hand. "Oh, a minor detail. Practically everyone's gay these days. It's not like we're living in the Dark Ages. Now, tell me again what he looked like."

I sighed and told him exactly what I'd told him before: that he had curly hair and a nose ring, and that – unlike the others – he hadn't laughed at Artemisia. I'd said that we'd smiled at each other too, but I'd downplayed how he'd made me feel. I'd thought about him ever since I'd ran out of the lecture theatre, picturing his eyes: cold and cat-like. But I was obsessing over nothing. I had to nip it in the bud, stop it before I got carried away.

"Let's not talk about it anymore," I said.

"Fine. I'll let it go. Just as soon as you admit you're in love with him."

"I am not!"

"Well, you obviously think he's hot."

"I didn't say that."

"You didn't have to. You've been drooling ever since we got here."

Ezra was getting louder and louder. I noticed that a few people on the table next to us were looking over, trying to hear what he was saying. I shook my head.

"Fine," I snapped. "You win. I think he's hot, okay?"

Ezra smacked the table loudly. "I knew it! I knew you liked him!"

I groaned and covered my face with my hands. This was what I deserved for telling Ezra anything. I should've known he would act like this.

"Can we please just change the subject?" I said.

"Oh, come on. I'm only messing around."

"I know, but it's not really funny, is it?"

"Ash, I —"

"No, I know you're only having a laugh, but why do you like embarrassing me so much? I mean, I don't treat *you* that way. I already asked you to change the subject."

Ezra said nothing. He had a funny look on his face, somewhere between pity and admiration. He reached across the table and put his hands on top of mine.

"Listen," he said, feelingly. "I never want to make you uncomfortable. That's not what I'm trying to do. It's just that…Look, I know you're a bit insecure when it comes to boys, and I just don't want you to feel like you're not good enough — for anyone."

He *did* have a point there.

"So, if I can help you in some way," he said, "then I'll do whatever I can. Even if you just want to talk about how hot this guy is. Okay?"

I suddenly felt bad about being annoyed with him. He was only trying to help, even if it *was* in a way that I hated. It was clearly *my* problem, not his.

He took his hands off mine and put them down in his lap. There was a rare moment of silence between us, and I stumbled for something to say. I knew if I waited long enough, he'd find some excuse to carry on talking. I didn't have to wait very long.

"Have you really never done *anything* with a guy?" he asked.

I shook my head.

"You must have thought about it though?"

I paused. "Well…yeah, sometimes."

"What about sex?"

"What about it?"

"Do you think about that too?"

I glanced around, making sure no one was looking over. "Sometimes."

"Do you think you're ready to lose your virginity then? Or do you think you'd want to wait until you have a long-term boyfriend?"

"Oh, I don't know," I said, squirming in my chair. I was barely comfortable admitting these things to myself, let alone in the dining hall where anyone could be listening. "I guess I just thought that…you know, when the time was right…"

"Trust me, it isn't a big deal," Ezra said. "Well, sex seems like a big, life-changing thing, but it's totally normal really. What you should do is just —"

"Jesus! Do we have to talk about this now?" My voice sounded angrier than I'd intended. "I told you it makes me embarrassed. And I haven't even kissed a boy before! Well, apart from *you*, but that obviously doesn't count."

Ezra blinked at me, then nodded.

"Okay, fine," he said. "Sorry for mentioning it."

I was grateful that he was finally dropping the subject,

but when I looked back at him, I could see that my words had struck a nerve. I asked if he was alright.

"Yeah, of course," he said, bluntly. "Why wouldn't I be?"

Before I knew it, it was already the end of October. I had survived the first four weeks of uni, and thanks to Ezra, I'd had a much better time than I'd ever thought possible. All of my lectures were really interesting; I was getting good grades on my assignments; and for the most part, I felt I'd settled into student life like a natural. I knew it sounded weird, but it was like my life before uni had never happened, or like it had happened to someone else. The boy who'd cried on his mum's shoulder suddenly seemed like a different person.

The guy from my Shakespeare lectures wasn't in any of my seminar groups, but I still saw him every Monday morning for our classes with Artemisia. We never spoke or moved any closer to one another, but each week – at the end of every lecture – he would look over at me and smile, only turning away once I'd smiled back. There was no way he didn't know that I fancied him, but if there was a casual, easy way of getting him to speak to me, neither Ezra or I had found it. I always hoped I'd bump into him in the English department, but I never saw him anywhere other than the main lecture theatre, sitting under a window that bathed him in a rich, honeyed light, like a figure in a religious painting.

Now that the days were getting shorter, I started going to the library on campus a few evenings a week. I hated making Ezra eat on his own back in Queensway, but I loved how quiet it was among the rows of books, and the green glass lamps on the tables made me feel like the hero of a classic novel. Ezra was my best friend, and I often told him how glad I was that we'd met, but I also knew that it wasn't healthy for us to spend all of our time together. He was quite an intense person, and I often found myself making excuses to be by myself, even if it was just for an hour or two. I felt guilty every time, but I knew Ezra didn't have the same need for solitude as I did. Sometimes all I wanted was a bit of quiet.

I'd decided to get ahead on my reading for one of my elective classes: *Nineteenth Century Children's Literature*, where we would spend the next week looking at *Alice's Adventures in Wonderland*. Alice had only just seen the white rabbit go tearing along the riverbank when Ezra appeared out of nowhere, shaking the rain from a lace umbrella.

"There you are!" he said, dropping his things with a loud crash and then collapsing in the chair across from me. "I was wondering where you'd gone."

I closed my book. I already knew I wouldn't get any more reading done.

"Sorry," I said. "I was just making a start on *Alice in Wonderland*. I meant to message you, but…I guess I forgot. Anyway, I *am* sorry. I just wanted –"

"I shan't hold it against you," he said, stopping me with a wave of his hand. "But listen, I have news." He pulled off his gloves and reached into the pocket of his coat, drew out a folded piece of paper. He slid it across the table, then sat back smugly in his chair.

I gave the flyer a cursory glance. At the top, in dripping letters, it said:

Freedom LGBTQIA+ Society cordially invites you to their Annual Halloween Party. Fancy dress required. Strictly invitation only.

I looked up at Ezra expectantly.

"I got us an invite!" he said. "Normally it's just for members but I pulled some strings and got us in. I said we'd consider joining, but first we'd want to go and check it out for ourselves. There's no way we're signing up if it's lame."

"You know these people?"

"The guy who runs it is on my course. We started talking and he asked us to join. They want more first years, I think. Anyway, I said we'd consider it."

I was flattered he always thought to include me. We were like a package deal, a two-for-one special, but I wondered if he just didn't want to go by himself.

"When is it?" I asked.

"Tomorrow night. It's at some bar on campus. Apparently it's right next to the Union."

My heart starting beating faster. Why was I so nervous? I wanted more time to think about it, to prepare myself. Tomorrow didn't seem far enough away.

"Well?" asked Ezra. "What do you think? Are you in?"

I paused. "I don't know."

"Don't know what?"

"Well, we won't know anyone there for a start. And we don't have any costumes. Wouldn't you rather just stay in tomorrow night? You could show me *The Evil Dead*?"

Ezra gave me a sad smile. I got the impression he thought I was clingy.

"Darling, you know I only want to be with you, but don't you think it's time we made some *more* friends? I mean, we'll only be in first year once, and we practically spend every minute together. We already act like a married couple!"

I was offended for half a second, but then I remembered that I'd only been coming to the library to get some time away from Ezra. Maybe he was right. We barely talked to anyone else in Queensway, and apart from him, I hadn't met or spoken to any gay people since I got here. I was starting to think we were the only ones.

"Do you think it'll be fun?" I asked.

"Well, I'll be there," he said, "so yes. And maybe there'll be some cute boys there too. We can be each other's wingman. Come on, please?"

I sighed, then started laughing at his unnecessary attempts to convince me. We both knew I was a soft touch. I'd always do whatever he wanted.

"Okay, fine," I said. "Let's do it."

Ezra clapped his hands. "Tremendous! You get the drinks for tomorrow and I'll find us something to wear. Oh, this is gonna be so much fun!"

He stood up and picked up his bag, started putting on his gloves. "And hey, maybe Nose Ring Boy will be there. Then we'll know for sure if he's actually gay or not."

I shook my head and laughed, but in my chest – somewhere deep beneath my shirt – my heart started beating faster, pounding with a ferocity which frightened me.

Five

A woman with white eyes, huge and milky, was standing in the middle of the room, blood oozing from her mouth. Her skin was a pinkish grey, the colour of rotting meat, and her face was webbed with veins like tiny cracks in a sheet of glass. She was clutching a broken pencil, and with a loud, violent shriek, she stabbed it into a woman's foot. She laughed, shrieked again, twisted the pencil through the flesh. The blood was so thick that it looked like treacle.

"This is gross," I said flatly, over the shouts of the people on screen. "It's pretty nasty for such an old film. I thought you said this was meant to be fun?"

Ezra had decided to show me *The Evil Dead* while we got ready. It was Halloween after all, and he'd been talking about it ever since the night we had first met. I was usually okay with horror films, but this one had so much blood that I kept wanting to turn away from the screen. Ezra was only half-watching, but he laughed every time I covered my eyes, almost as if *he* was the one who'd scared me. I was starting to wish that we'd watched something else.

As I was held captive, Ezra was busy doing my makeup. He'd taken it upon himself to get our costumes sorted for the party, though I still had no idea what I was going to be.

He insisted I face away from the mirror so I would get the big reveal when he was done, but he was surprisingly tight-lipped when it came to giving me clues. I told him that I didn't want to be anything too out there, too ridiculous. I trusted Ezra, but I also knew we had slightly different interpretations of what that meant. I was always scared he would go too far.

I kept thinking that the main guy in the film looked really familiar. His name was Ash so I already liked him, but I kept wondering where I knew him from. Suddenly it hit me.

"Oh my god, that's Bruce Campbell!"

Ezra kept working. "Yeah?"

"Yeah! He's in *Xena*!"

"Oh, cool."

I stared at him. "Don't you think that's weird? *My* favourite thing and *your* favourite thing have this massive connection. You don't find that a bit odd?"

"Not really. I always told you it was fate that brought us together. We were destined to be friends, my darling. Now, hold still, okay?"

As he carried on with my makeup, completely unfazed, I wondered if I was overreacting. It *was* a pretty strange coincidence. Then again, maybe I was looking for ways to show Ezra how meaningful our friendship was. We'd never been around other people, and I was secretly nervous that

I would lose him to all the glamorous gays we'd meet at the party. Maybe I was scared he would get bored of me, that he would exchange me for someone more interesting. I worried our friendship was merely one of convenience for him.

I carried on watching the film, trying not to focus on the way Ezra constantly poked me in the eye with a makeup brush, moving my face in all the various ways he kept instructing: "Head up. Eyes closed. Mouth open." I could feel him putting layers of makeup on and I kept asking for reassurance, even though I knew I could wash it off afterwards. Ezra wouldn't like it, but it *had* been his decision to put it on without showing me. I hadn't even wanted to dress up. I was only going as a favour to him. Obviously, seeing Nose Ring Boy would be an extra bonus, but that wasn't why I was going. I really *was* only there for Ezra.

Once he was finished, he made me stay turned away from the mirror and pulled a huge shirt over my head. He looped a series of gold chains around my neck, tying them off and adjusting them until I was practically weighted down. I had no idea what I was going to look like. From Ezra's laptop, a green faced zombie roared at me.

"Okay, you're done," he said, leading me over to the mirror. "Ta-da!"

I opened my eyes.

My face was pale, almost white, and my eyelids were painted a silvery-gold. He had dusted my hair with glitter and twisted leaves around one of my ears. I looked down nervously at my outfit. I was wearing one of Ezra's shirts: white with puffed sleeves, frills of lace as soft as shaving foam. It's not that I looked bad; I just didn't know what I was meant to be.

"Well?" said Ezra. "What do you think?"

"I love it! Only…Well, what am I?"

"You're Apollo, obviously! The Greek god of art and poetry."

I raised my eyebrows.

"Okay, okay, it's not great, but it's the best I could do on short notice."

I thanked him again, told him I loved it, and sat back down while he got himself dressed. I carried on watching *The Evil Dead*, and when I looked back twenty minutes later, he was all dressed up and ready to go, admiring his costume in the mirror. He was wearing a red poet blouse with laces all down the front, though his was translucent, almost sheer. He'd brushed pink powder around his cheekbones and into his hairline, and stamped a black heart underneath one eye. He looked beautiful but cold, a little haughty.

"And you are…?"

"I'm Venus, Goddess of Love, ready to stab men through the heart with my arrows."

I stood up and went over to him, looking at our reflections in the mirror. There was nothing mythological about the way we were dressed. We looked like pirates on their way to the French Revolution, but somehow the makeup worked.

"Aren't you worried no one will know who we are?" I asked.

"Who cares? The key is looking like you've made an effort without actually wearing a costume. Besides, have you seen how boys dress up for Halloween? They'll all be wearing ripped shirts and fake blood and telling us they're zombies. How original."

I laughed. Ezra took a swig of the wine I'd brought, wincing.

"So," he said, dabbing his mouth, "are we about ready to fall in love?"

"No, not yet. Let's take a photo."

I wondered if he could tell that I was stalling.

He grabbed his phone, held it up, then took about 700 photos. He showed me afterwards but I had no idea which ones were good. I thought they all looked exactly the same. But as we grabbed our coats and got ready to leave, I started feeling more and more nervous. What if Ezra met someone and I didn't? What if nobody there liked me?

As the film reached its conclusion, Ash began screaming uncontrollably.

*

There were three bars on campus, all with bland and meaningless names: Solutions, Tribe, and Remedy. The LGBT party was taking place in Solutions, a white, sterile room masquerading as a trendy cocktail bar. There were neon strip lights around the ceiling, exposed brick walls, a few fake houseplants, and a sign above the door that said *Let's Dance!* in bright pink letters. The music was inoffensive – the kind that you hear in high-street coffee shops – and the extent of the decorations were a few loose chains of paper ghosts.

Ezra and I were sitting on our own, far away from the other gays. We'd come in and introduced ourselves, but Ezra – from the moment we'd arrived – looked like he couldn't wait to be anywhere else. A guy in a Joker T-shirt had handed him a Sharpie and a nametag when we'd first walked in. "Yeah, get fucked," he'd said under his breath.

I kept looking over at the gay society. There were about twelve guys, all sitting together in a booth in the far corner. I was surprised at how…well, ordinary they were. I was expecting them to be more like the gays I'd seen on TV – sassy and fashionable; buff and topless; maybe even a drag queen or two. But they were like any other group. They weren't particularly cute, but then they weren't unattractive either. They were just painfully normal. Like me.

As Ezra had predicted, all of them were dressed as half-arsed zombies, torn T-shirts revealing as much

shaved flesh as humanly possible. I recognised one guy
from Queensway – I think his name was Theo – but there
was still no sign of Nose Ring Boy. I told myself he might
show up later but I knew he never would. He was far too
beautiful for this group.

I turned back to Ezra. "Are you upset?"

He took a sip of his snakebite, then slammed it down
loudly on the table.

"I'm not upset," he said. "I was just expecting
something a bit more…I don't know. Exciting? These guys
look like a bunch of Sixth Formers."

I knew what he meant. I didn't want to seem
disappointed, but when I looked over at the booth, I felt
my heart begin to sink. Was *this* who we had to be friends
with?

"Look, there's, like, ten of them," I said. "There are
7,000 students here. Statistically speaking, there are a lot
more gay people here than just these guys."

"Right, but they obviously don't go to the gay society.
It must only be the freaks and losers who join up. God,
what was I thinking?"

He looked sulkily out of the window, folding his arms
across his chest. I didn't think they were losers, just maybe
not the types of guys I could imagine us being friends with.

"We're not better than them," I said.

"Huh?"

"I said we're not better than them, Ez. I mean, we go on and on about wanting to make friends, and then we don't give anyone else a chance. They might be really nice guys for all *we* know. I think we should go back over there."

He looked at me coldly. "It's not that I think I'm better than them, but come on, you can't tell me you seriously want to hang out with those people."

"Don't be so judgemental. How can you just write them off?"

"I'm not! How is it any different to those girls you met on the first night, the ones who sat with you at dinner? You wrote them off because you thought you could do better. It's exactly the same thing."

Ouch.

He was right. I knew he was. I didn't have a leg to stand on.

"Okay, fine," I said. "Whatever."

We sat in silence for a while, trying to avoid each other's gaze. I was about to suggest we go back home when I noticed something happening by the door. I looked over and saw that the guy in the Joker T-shirt was pointing at us. He was talking to two guys who were looking over in our direction, and after giving him a quick nod, they started walking towards our table. Were we in trouble? I had no idea what to do. I pretended not to notice but I was too self-aware to try and act naturally. I attempted to drink and just ended up dribbling.

The guys coming over were holding hands. The taller one had long hair, much longer than mine, and it was tied back in a messy bun and stuck through with brass clips. His skin was a soft brown, the colour and texture of Golden Syrup, and there was a tattoo on his forearm: a shaded hare and a rising sun. The smaller one was more witchy. His shaved hair was bleached white, a gleaming silver like the moon, and he was wearing a black T-shirt that said *Slay* in pointed letters. He had rings on each finger too – blue and purple and blood-red.

They walked over to us and smiled.

"Hey," said the shorter one. "Do you mind if we sit with you guys?"

Ezra brightened immediately. "Not at all."

"Thanks! We didn't have an invite so we were told we couldn't sit over there. They said we should come and talk to you guys instead."

"Yeah, you have to be a member apparently. God knows why."

He laughed. "I'm Sam. This is my boyfriend Haz."

They sat down across from us, and after some quick introductions from Ezra and I, they started telling us a little more about themselves. Haz was half Iranian but had lived in the UK all his life. His cardigan was so big that it draped luxuriously off one shoulder, and there was another tattoo on his collarbone: a moth with green and golden wings.

Sam, who was from Hertfordshire, was the more outgoing of the two guys. Each of his movements were strong and deliberate, and he never once seemed to second-guess himself. A tattoo across his wrist depicted the phases of the moon. I saw it waxing, growing fat, waning away again under his sleeve. I was kind of obsessed with these boys already.

"How long have you guys been together?" asked Ezra.

"Oh, about a month now," said Sam. "We met on the first night, but we've literally spent all our time together since then. We don't really know anyone else yet. We thought we'd gate-crash the Halloween party but I didn't realise it was so exclusive."

Haz nodded. "Yeah, we were just saying that we're like a married couple already. I was telling Sam that we really need to try and make more gay friends."

Ezra shot me a quick glance. "That's so funny," he said. "Ash and I were saying the same thing yesterday!"

"No way. How long have *you* guys been together?"

"Oh, we're not together," he replied. "We're just friends."

The word *just* hung in the air between us. Why did that bother me so much?

"So, what halls are you guys in?" Ezra asked.

"We're in Pemberton," said Sam.

This was the big, modern, glass-fronted building on

campus. It was the newest build and everyone knew it was the nicest. Everybody wanted to be there, but since accommodation was drawn randomly, these two were obviously the lucky ones.

The conversation soon moved to our families. When Ezra mentioned his parents were artists, Haz was visibly excited. He was studying art and knew exactly who they were.

"Oh, we're not really close," said Ezra, finishing his snakebite. "They were never around much when I was growing up because they were so focused on their work. They were mortified when I came out as gay, which was weird since they're both artists and always go on about how liberal they are. Anyway, we don't really talk much anymore."

I was stunned. He'd never told me anything about his parents before, even when I'd asked him directly. I knew they weren't close, but other than telling me what they did for a living, he'd never said a word about them. I was going to bring it up, but I didn't want to start a fight in front of Haz and Sam. I told myself it was because I didn't want to hurt or embarrass Ezra, but really, I didn't want to reveal how little I knew about him.

As Ezra continued talking, I realised I hadn't spoken in fifteen minutes. Ezra obviously hadn't noticed. I asked if anyone wanted a drink.

"Yeah, I'll help you," Sam said, smiling.

We left Haz and Ezra and moved over to the bar, standing in silence as we waited to be served. I could feel Sam's eyes on me, curious. I tried to think of something to say.

"So, tell me about you," he said, smiling again. "You don't talk a lot, do you?"

"Oh, Ezra talks enough for both of us. He's better at meeting new people than me. I always say the wrong thing and end up making a bad impression."

"Don't sell yourself short," he said. "I have to tell Haz the same thing all the time. He's much more introverted than me. He'd never leave his room if he had *his* way."

"Really? He seems so confident."

"Oh, it's all an act. I always say that if you pretend to be confident, people will believe you're confident, and really, isn't that the same thing?"

"I don't know," I said. "I guess."

He was about to continue when the barman came over to serve him. As he ordered a round of drinks, I thought about everything he'd said. I knew that he must be right because I'd never doubted their self-confidence. I couldn't imagine either one of them feeling as nervous or anxious as *I* did. I looked back at Haz and Ezra. They were both talking with their hands and nodding, laughing at one another's jokes. Anyone who didn't know them would just assume that they were best friends. I started wondering where I would fit in.

This is the beginning of the end. This is where it all starts to go wrong.

*

Sam and I went back to the table with our drinks, and the four of us spent the whole night talking, telling each other about our families, our star signs, what we wanted to do after uni. Whenever I felt myself fading into the background, I would notice Sam looking at me encouragingly, and then I'd force myself to join in. It was honestly one of the best nights I'd had so far, and I was glad Ezra had persuaded me to come.

After hugging them goodbye, Ezra and I tipsily walked back home. I could hear leaves crunching in my ear, and I almost forgot we were both dressed up.

"Thanks," he said softly, under the yellow glare of a streetlight.

"What for?" I asked.

"For coming with me tonight! I had a really good time, and I wouldn't have done it without you. Those guys are exactly the kind of people I was hoping to meet."

"Yeah," I said, "me too."

We carried on walking, barely even feeling the cold. But I kept thinking about Ezra, about how open he'd been, how honest, how seemingly willing he was to confess.

"You never told me that thing about your parents," I said.

"What thing?"

"You know, about them not being around when you were a kid, or them not accepting you when you came out. You never told me."

"Yes, I did. Didn't I?"

I shook my head. "No. I *have* asked you about it though."

"Oh," he said. "Sorry."

I waited for more but nothing came. He seemed a bit colder with me now, as if he had used up all his warmth for one night – and not on me. We carried on in silence for a while.

"I hope they text us tomorrow," I said.

"Why wouldn't they?"

I didn't know what to say. I'd had a really good night – it was so much better than I was expecting – but now that we were alone, Ezra seemed like a different person. He'd been so chatty with Haz and Sam, so eager to please them, make them laugh, that I suddenly felt a bit replaceable, as if I'd since become less important. And Haz and Sam had loved him! They'd been sweet to me all night, but there was a voice inside my head that was saying I'd never be cute or cool enough, that I was disposable, in the way. They wanted Ezra and not me.

As I glanced over at Ezra's costume, I couldn't stop thinking about *Venus and Adonis*, about that line I'd copied down in my notebook. Only now it was being said to me by that voice inside my head: *You love but you're not loved, you love but you're not loved*.

Six

But Haz and Sam *did* text us. In fact, I woke up the next day to find I'd been added to a WhatsApp group called *The Art Poofs*. The picture was of a cherub in a crown of ivy leaves, round as a Christmas pudding, and drinking wine from an upturned bottle.

The first message was from Sam.

Union tonight?

Ezra said yes immediately and I decided to follow his lead. I obviously wanted to see them again, but I could still hear that voice in my head telling me I wasn't good enough, that they didn't *really* want me to come. No matter what I tried to tell myself, the thought was always there, persistent as a cough. Why would anyone want to be friends with me?

But I was determined not to let those feelings ruin things, and before I knew it, the four of us were at the Union, dancing together to the shitty music. While Ezra bounced around like a three-year-old at a birthday party, Haz danced like a bird – eyes closed and arms outstretched – smiling blissfully through each song. Sam, on the other hand, was the sexy one of the group, always grinding, swaying his hips, running his hands across his chest. But every now and then, he would throw his arms around our shoulders, pulling us closer in towards him.

"I fucking love this song!" he'd shout.

After an hour or so, we went out to the smoking garden so that Ezra could have a cigarette. Sam had his arm around Haz's waist now, and I noticed that he talked like he'd known us forever, like we'd always been a group of four.

"You guys are awesome," he said, moving upwind of Ezra's cigarette. "I can't believe we only met you last night. It feels way longer."

"I know!" Haz exclaimed. "You guys are so much fun! Like, I'm really glad I have Sam, but it's nice to have other people to hang out with as well."

Ezra nodded, blowing out a thin cloud of smoke. "Oh, please. We think *you* guys are great! You'll never get rid of us. We'll be inviting you out all the time!"

The conversation went on like this for a while, going round in a circle of vague compliments while I nodded or laughed awkwardly. I was trying to work out how I was feeling when we were approached by a girl with pink hair, bleach-dry and thin like candy floss. She asked if she could borrow Ezra's lighter, and as he fumbled around in his pockets, she looked at each of us in turn, assessing our clothes, the way we were stood.

"Are you guys in a band?" she asked.

"No!" said Sam, laughing.

"You should think about it. You guys look cool."

She lit her cigarette and disappeared into the crowd, leaving Sam still laughing behind her. "It's not the worst idea," he said. "I mean, we *do* look good together."

I laughed along with him, but I wasn't convinced the girl had meant to include me in her appraisal. I could hear the voice again in the back of my head, telling me they'd look better if I wasn't there, that they'd be happier without me. I tried my best to just ignore it.

I followed them back inside, but after coming through the double doors, I lost sight of them in the crowd. I started weaving my way to the dancefloor when someone shoved into me from behind. I thought it must be Ezra at first, but when I turned around, I came face to face with a bunch of guys that I didn't recognise. The one in front was a big, rugby-player type with furry arms and a square head. He grunted, "Watch where you're going, faggot."

I thought I'd misheard him. "Sorry?"

"Oh, are you deaf? I said watch where you're going, fag."

The guys behind him started laughing, cracking their knuckles. I was rooted to the spot. I wanted to hide, to turn and run, but it was so crowded I couldn't move.

"Listen," I said, trying to back away. "I'm not…"

But then Ezra appeared in front of me, forcing me backwards and taking my place. "Try picking on me instead, yeah? Well, come on then. Say that again."

The guy looked over at his friends, rolled his eyes. "Fucking batty boys," he said.

He looked like he was about to push past us, but before he could do anything, Ezra launched himself forwards, grabbing the guy's shirt and then dragging him down to the ground. Several things happened at once. The guy yelled out or screamed; Sam appeared out of nowhere and tried pulling them apart; a woman shouted for security. I could barely make out what was going on, but every now and then, the lights would flash on Ezra's face, turning him wild and unfamiliar, bright then dark then bright again.

I felt Haz come up behind me, felt him grab me around the shoulders.

"You're okay," he said. "Come on."

He steered me out of the Union, past the smoking garden and slightly up the hill, away from the music still throbbing behind us. I must've been in shock. I wanted to go back and make sure Ezra was okay, but before I knew it, Haz was hugging me, patting my head and shushing me like a baby. I wanted to cry, but only because I thought it would give the whole encounter a bit more meaning.

I didn't know what to say. I wanted to ask if I'd been a dickhead.

Sam and Ezra were both kicked out and joined us a couple of minutes later. Ezra's face was red and puffy from where he'd been hit. His hands were clenching and unclenching by his side, and he looked dizzy, a little dazed. He staggered like someone just learning to walk.

"I'm sorry," I said, staring down at my shoes.

"Don't you dare apologise," said Sam. "*I'm* sorry we lost you. I thought you knew those guys. It was only when Ezra said you didn't that we came back."

I looked over at Ezra who was watching me sheepishly.

"You okay?" he mouthed.

I nodded.

"God, I can't believe guys like that still exist," said Sam.

Haz nodded. "Did they get kicked out too?"

"Nope. They only saw us and thought *we* must've started it."

"Typical."

After being inside the Union, the quiet outside was making my ears ring. As we stood there, Haz and Sam fussed around me, making sure I was okay, forcing me to tell them if I was upset. But it was Ezra I was worried about. He'd been punched in the face for me, he'd stood up for me without thinking – and the others had flown in straight afterwards. The voice in my head, I realised, had been quiet the whole time. And somehow that was it. I stopped doubting that these boys cared about me. How much reassurance did I really need?

I turned back to Sam. "You guys should try and get back in," I said. "I don't want to ruin your night. Go back inside. Honestly, I'll be fine."

Sam looked at me like I was crazy. "No way!" he snapped. "It's all for one and one for all. Anyway, I've got a bottle of Vodka in my room. Why don't we take it down to the football field? Fuck the Union. We can have our own party, just the four of us."

Haz clapped his hands. "I'm in!"

Ezra glanced at me to see what I wanted to do. I smiled. "Let's go!" I said.

And we did.

Seven

The next day, Ezra's left eye was waxy and swollen, the blackish-purple of a plum. Naturally I was horrified. I hated the fact I was partly responsible, but Ezra seemed pleased with his fierce new image. He drew on a split lip with a red lipliner and spent most of the day taking selfies, trying on various expressions. First he was wounded, broken-hearted, then he was angry and ready to fight. When I looked at his Instagram later that day, I saw the result of his hard work: a sinister, black-and-white portrait with a caption from an old movie:

"The mightiest monster in all creation, ravaging a universe – for love!"

Haz and Sam, worried I was being a martyr, text me continuously throughout the day, just wanting to see if I was alright. They'd been so nice to me after the Union – pouring me drinks, letting me talk, trying to get me to open up – but I was telling the truth when I said I was fine. I'd only ever been scared for Ezra. But knowing they had my back had made me feel bigger somehow, bulletproof. Was this what it felt like to have friends?

I told Mum about them too, though I thought it was best not to mention the fight. I didn't want her to worry, to feel like I couldn't look after myself. And besides, I secretly liked the wholesome version of uni that she imagined I was living. To her, my life possessed all the attributes of a fun, screwball comedy. It might as well have been the Cub Scouts.

On Monday I was back in my Shakespeare class, learning about *Antony and Cleopatra*. Well, I was trying. Nose Ring Boy looked especially cute today. He'd taken off his sweatshirt to reveal thick, muscled arms, and his hair was tied back and twisted through with a rubber band. I couldn't focus on the play at all. How could anyone be expected to focus with a boy like *that* sitting in their class? How would I ever make it through the term?

Artemisia talked us through her slides on Shakespeare's Egypt, each bullet point filled with references to hot sand, red suns, murky rivers swamped with crocodiles. But every quote I read from the play only seemed to make sense in relation to *him*. "Eternity was in his lips and eyes! O happy chair to bear the weight of Nose Ring Boy!" Shakespeare would be rolling in his grave, but when I looked at his portrait in my book, I could practically hear his voice, low and insistent, saying: "Love is much greater than literature. Go thou forth and marry this boy whose nose drips silver!" *Maybe I'll leave it to the professionals*, I thought.

At the end of the lecture – after Antony and Cleopatra had both killed themselves – I looked over at him, waiting for him to smile at me. But he just pulled his sweatshirt over his head, packed away his laptop, and then left without a second thought. Had I done something wrong? As I crammed my stuff into my backpack, my mind raced through several possibilities. One, he had met someone else; two, he was only being polite in the first place; and three, he'd only smiled because he felt sorry for me, like I was someone he needed to pity. Normally I would have been embarrassed by this, but then I thought about the boys, about Sam telling me not to apologise. "Fuck you then," I said, but under my breath so that no one heard.

I had a one-hour gap between lectures, and since Ezra was in a seminar, I went to the café inside the English department. It was maybe the ugliest one on campus – with pinewood walls and plastic furniture – and it always smelled strangely chemical, like the back of a used plaster. But it was the closest one to the lecture hall, and since I'd been distracted all morning, I figured I should probably read up on the play. I had an assignment due next week.

I ordered a hot chocolate and sat at a table in the corner. I took out my book and started flicking through Act One, but just as I started to read, I noticed Charlotte from Queensway was standing nearby, looking around for a place to sit. She was wearing a pink coat with a white fur trim, and underneath, a T-shirt with a cartoon rabbit that said, *Some bunny loves you!*

My instinct was to pretend I hadn't seen her, but then I thought about what Ezra had said at Solutions, about how I'd treated her unfairly.

"Hey, Charlotte!" I said, waving. "There's a chair here if you want a seat."

She turned around, surprised. "Oh, um, great," she said. "Okay."

She sat down with her coffee and pulled a textbook out of her bag. It was called *Introduction to Astrophysics: The Stars and Us.* I really *had* underestimated her. I glanced at the book and saw pages and pages of diagrams, stars mapped out on complex grids, dotted lines and netted spheres. I realised, ashamed, that I'd never asked her what she studied.

"Thanks for the chair," she said. "I, um…I didn't think you liked me."

"No, I do!" I said, trying not to sound too enthusiastic. "It's just that…you and your friends were getting on so well at the party. I kinda felt like I was in the way."

"Really?"

"Yeah! You guys were all so nice. I just thought you'd be better off without me."

"Not at all!" she said, pulling off her coat. "Oh, I'll tell the girls you said that. We thought we'd offended you or something. We never saw you again after dinner."

Ezra was right. I thought I'd just been looking for people more like me, but I'd written them off without giving them a chance. I wanted to apologise, to explain, but how could I do that without looking guilty, without saying I knew I was in the wrong?

Instead I just changed the subject, asked her how everything was going.

"Oh, yeah, fine. Queensway wasn't my first choice of halls, but everyone's super nice. And now all my friends are there too, so I wouldn't want to be anywhere else."

"And the course?"

"All good," she said, cheerily. "It's a bit complicated, but…yeah."

I thought about how to respond. "Cool."

"And what about you?" she asked, taking a sip of her coffee. "I always see you around with the same guy, the one with the glitter and the statement lipstick."

"Yeah, that's Ezra."

"Are you guys dating then?"

"Oh, god, no," I laughed. "No, we're really just good friends."

She smiled like she didn't believe me, but I understood how it must've looked. Two gay guys spending all of their time together. I didn't blame her for wanting to ask.

We fell into a comfortable silence after that, both of us reading and making notes. But the café was getting busier. Since there was nowhere else to sit, lots of students were standing in the spaces between tables, leaning against walls or beside the bar. I was just about to turn back to my notes when someone in the doorway caught my eye, lit from above like a holy relic.

My heart jumped.

It was *him*.

I could hardly believe he was real. I'd never seen him anywhere other than the main lecture theatre, and seeing him in such a mundane place felt slightly wrong somehow, unnatural. Like a solar eclipse, he seemed to make everything else disappear.

He looked over and saw me. I quickly forced my eyes back to my notes. God, if I hadn't invited Charlotte to sit down, there would've been space for him at my table. *Serves me right for trying to be a good person*, I thought. I kept my eyes fixed on my notebook, trying to pretend that I hadn't noticed, but when I glanced back at the door, I saw he was coming towards me, smirking. What on earth was I going to do? Was he going to talk to me? Introduce himself?

I licked my lips, looked down at my hands. I felt him approaching us like a comet.

"Hey," he said casually, when he was standing beside our table. "You're in my Shakespeare class, right? *Antony and Cleopatra*?"

I nodded like an idiot. He was even more beautiful up close, the only person I'd ever seen look good in fluorescent lighting. His eyes were so grey they were almost silver, and his skin was perfectly tanned and smooth; there wasn't a line or a blemish anywhere.

I swallowed, tried to speak. I resisted the urge to reach out and touch him.

"I was just wondering if you wrote down the assignment," he said. "I must've forgot. I was kind of in a rush earlier. I can't find it in my notes."

"Oh, yeah, sure," I said, fumbling clumsily through all my papers. I could feel Charlotte's eyes on me, bemused. I tried to pretend that she wasn't there.

"Here you go," I said, handing him a page I'd ripped out of my notebook.

"Sick. Thanks, man. And when's it due?"

"Next Monday. In the seminars after the lecture."

He nodded. "Cool, cool."

He looked at the paper, trying to decipher my messy handwriting. If only I'd known he was going to see it! I didn't want him to think that I was sloppy, disorganised, that I couldn't keep my things in order. But he just pulled out his phone, took a photo, and then handed the paper back to me. Everything he did was graceful; it was like he'd practised, rehearsed each movement. I wondered if he knew how attractive he was.

"Listen," he said, "I'm really struggling with this play, and I don't know anyone else on the course. Would you maybe want to study together this week? I thought we could go to the library and help each other with the assignment."

I could feel my face turning red. "Um…yeah. Cool. Sounds good."

"Great! I'm Jonah by the way. Here, give me your phone. I'll type in my number."

I nodded dumbly and passed it to him, watching his thumbs dance across the screen. I realised he didn't know my name. I wondered if all beautiful people were as inattentive as him, if he'd even noticed he hadn't asked. He was so good-looking I just forgave him.

"Sweet," he said, handing my phone back to me. "Give me a text, yeah?"

He smiled blankly at Charlotte and shook out his hair as he walked away. I was in shock. It was like a bomb had just gone off, but everyone else was carrying on as if nothing important had just occurred. Another line of Shakespeare floated through my head: 'So great a thing should make a greater crack.' I looked at my phone and there was his name, Jonah, followed by an emoji of a lightning bolt. *Oh my god,* I thought. *He's real.*

I realised Charlotte had been speaking. "Um...sorry?"

"I *said* that was the hottest guy I've ever seen!"

"I know! Jesus, what am I gonna do?"

"Text him, obviously. He clearly wants you to. He literally just asked you on a date!"

"It wasn't a date. He just wants some help with his essay."

"Yeah, but he could've asked anyone."

"Maybe, but…"

"Urgh, you boys are clueless," she said, rolling her eyes. "I'm *telling* you he just asked you on a study date. Just the two of you. At night. Alone in the library."

My mouth was so dry I couldn't swallow, but Charlotte wouldn't look away.

Was she right? Was it a date? He'd been smiling at me for four weeks now, and he obviously knew I liked him. And he'd been taking notes for the whole hour. How could he not have written down the assignment? It was the most important part of the lecture.

"You *do* like him, right?" she asked.

"I guess? I mean, I don't really know him. I only see him once a week."

"Oh, please. You went bright red when you had to talk to him!"

I shrugged and started laughing, too nervous to think of a comeback. When I looked at her again, her eyes were shining, twinkling devilishly.

"You're gonna have *such* a good time," she said.

She turned back to her book on astrophysics – but it was me who was seeing stars.

Eight

Although my instinct had been to get as much advice as possible, I decided not to tell Ezra about my study date. It wasn't that I *wanted* to keep it a secret from him, but that I knew he would turn it into a big production. I was nervous enough already! Nobody had ever asked me out before – least of all someone as cute as Jonah – and I didn't have the faintest idea about what to expect. Everything I knew about first dates had come from movies I'd seen on TV. I was clueless, uninformed. I didn't have anything else to go on.

I decided to just forget about it, trying to delay my inevitable freak-out.

I finally text him on Wednesday morning.

Hey! It's Ash from Shakespeare class. Still want to study together?

It took nearly an hour for him to reply.

Sure. Library tonight @ 7? x

I text back immediately:

OK, see you then! x

Now I really *was* terrified. What on earth was I going to wear?

I didn't have any lectures on Wednesdays, so I spent the whole day in my room reading *Antony and Cleopatra*. I wanted to be prepared for anything Jonah might ask, hoping I could impress him with my knowledge of the play. I underlined some key quotes and made an outline for my essay, but I couldn't put it off forever. When the sun started to go down, I knew I needed to get ready. I sighed, opened my wardrobe. I tried to talk myself out of cancelling.

Ezra had given me a few of his old shirts, swearing they'd look better on me than they did on him, that it was a crime for me not to wear them. But purple snakeskin and paisley velvet didn't feel very much like me. I went for a shirt I hadn't worn yet – black with white crocodiles so small they looked like polka dots. I figured it would be good for studying *Antony and Cleopatra*, but not flamboyant enough to look like I'd made too much of an effort. I had to keep telling myself that it wasn't a date, that he probably *did* just want help with his essay. I reluctantly pulled on my coat. I saw it was nearly time to go.

Outside, puddles shone gold with the reflections of streetlights. It was incredibly dark, but by now, I had done the walk so many times I didn't really find it scary. It took me about twenty minutes to reach campus, but as I made my way to the library, I heard my name outside the humanities building. I turned around to see Haz skipping to catch up with me, books clutched against his chest, long hair billowing out behind him.

"Hey, Ash!" he said, waving as though I wouldn't recognise him.

"Hey! How's things?"

"Good, thanks! Where are you off to?"

"Oh, the library. I'm just…" I bit my lip. Surely I couldn't tell him. Nobody but Charlotte knew about Jonah, and I didn't want to embarrass myself if it really *did* turn out to be nothing. "I'm just going to the library," I said.

Haz raised an eyebrow. Obviously I wasn't convincing.

"Okay," I sighed. "I have a study date with a guy from my Shakespeare class."

"Not Nose Ring Boy!" he said, genuinely surprised.

I nodded. I must've mentioned him after the Union.

"Yeah, he asked if we could study together. But I don't know anything about him, Haz. I've only spoken to him once. I'm nervous!"

"Oh, don't be. He obviously likes you if he invited you, and that's the hard part over and done with. Just be yourself and you'll be fine."

"Yeah, but…" I paused, scared he would think I was fishing for compliments. "What if I say something embarrassing? What if he thinks I'm a massive twat?"

"Why would he?"

I stopped myself saying what I meant: that if he saw what I was really like, how boring I was, then there was no way he'd ever be interested. I already knew I was nothing special.

Haz cleared his throat, adjusting the bangle on his wrist: a copper fish. "Look," he said, "I used to be exactly the same as you. I always felt like I had to blend in, like I had to hide myself away. But if you keep doing that, then you don't give anyone else the chance to know the *real* you. And isn't that just a bit tragic?"

I didn't answer right away. Sam had told me that Haz wasn't as confident as he seemed, but I was surprised I had so much in common with him. I was trying to think of something to say, something to show that I understood, but Haz just snorted, started laughing.

"Jeez. Now *I* sound like a twat."

"You don't!" I said, laughing along with him. "I'm just being stupid. But thanks for talking to me. That actually really helps."

"No worries," he said, blushing.

We stopped walking outside the library. I'd never been alone with Haz before, and I didn't know how to say goodbye. But Haz didn't seem awkward at all.

"Good luck, okay? Text us and let us know how you get on. You'll be fine."

"Thanks for the advice," I said. "Say hi to Sam for me!"

"Will do!"

I watched him walk away, then opened the doors and headed inside.

I knew Haz was right, but I was starting to think that other people brought out the worst in me. I was never so anxious or unsure of myself when I was on my own. I was always obsessing about how people saw me: Ezra, Haz and Sam, even Jonah now too. I was so desperate to be liked, to be seen and understood. But then – wasn't everyone?

I took my usual spot on the second floor and messaged Jonah to say where I was. Then, to avoid falling into a pit of self-doubt, I pulled out my books and made a start on the assignment. I needed to keep my mind occupied and away from Jonah, away from whether this was or wasn't a date. But nothing seemed to work. I was so scared I wanted to puke.

He turned up around twenty past seven, cheeks flushed, red with cold. His hair was wild and voluminous, and his nails were painted a glossy blue.

"Sorry I'm late," he said, pulling off his coat and draping it over the back of the chair. He pulled his sweatshirt off too, revealing a T-shirt slashed in half that ended just above his navel. I had to force my eyes from his stomach – flat and firm, the colour of honey.

"No problem," I said, waiting for him to sit down and set up his laptop. I tried to keep my eyes on my notes. "So, shall we talk about the assignment? 'Compare and contrast the depictions of Rome and Egypt in Shakespeare's *Antony and Cleopatra*.'"

He stared at the screen for a few minutes, looking utterly confused. Then he pulled out an energy drink from his bag, neon green with claw-like writing. When he opened it, the can snapped and hissed like a snake. It made me think of Cleopatra.

"I just don't think I get the play," he said, taking a swig and wiping his mouth. "I mean, how does anyone understand the language?"

"Huh. You always look really into it in the lectures."

Silence.

I'd let out that I'd been watching him.

I felt like a stalker, but Jonah just looked at me and grinned. His teeth were white but slightly pointed, a little like those of a wild animal. For some reason I found it cute. Ezra, Haz, and Sam were all good-looking guys, but Jonah was the most beautiful boy I'd ever seen. I could hardly believe he was a real person. It was like sitting down with a celebrity.

"I guess I'm more into the modern stuff," he said. "I can't wait till we get onto all the twentieth century books. Shakespeare's never been my forte."

"Really? Like what?"

"Oh, you know. *Slaughterhouse-Five, The Great Gatsby, The Catcher in the Rye*. That kind of thing. I find that stuff way more interesting than Shakespeare."

I was too embarrassed to admit I hadn't read those books, and so to avoid an awkward silence, I started talking about the play. He made some notes and asked me questions, typing furiously away on his laptop. I wanted to try and move things along.

"So, where are you from?" I asked.

"Bournemouth."

"Near the sea?"

"Yeah, my family lives, like, five minutes from the beach. The town's not very exciting, but I used to go down to the seafront every day in summer. I kinda miss it."

I somehow knew he'd be the outdoorsy type. I couldn't imagine him spending joyless hours in some air-conditioned gym. Instead, I pictured him climbing rocks; catching fish with his bare hands; riding a horse through dappled forests. I wanted to keep asking him questions but he was still typing away on his laptop. Then he suddenly raised his head.

"Can I ask you something?"

"Mm-hm."

"It's kinda personal though."

I wasn't sure where this was going. "Sure, go ahead."

"Are you, um…Are you gay?"

"Uh, yeah," I said. "Why?"

"Oh, no reason. Only…I think I might be too? I mean, I'm not sure. I've never been with a guy before so I'm not positive, but I think about it a lot. I thought it might be good to talk to someone. I figured you might be gay as well."

I tried to hide my disappointment. He wasn't interested in me after all; he just wanted a free therapy session. I knew I shouldn't have listened to Charlotte.

"And also…" he paused, biting his lip. "Because I think you're really cute."

I stared at him in disbelief. "You do?"

He nodded.

I looked down into my lap, too embarrassed to meet his gaze.

"I think you're really cute too," I said.

Jonah was silent for so long I wondered if I'd actually spoken aloud. I looked up, but our eye contact felt different now – scary and meaningful. I felt like I was playing with something dangerous, putting my hand too close to a flame.

"Why do you think I'm doing so badly in this class?" he asked. "I only end up thinking about *you* all the time, wondering if you're looking at me, or whether I should look at you."

I shook my head. He'd caught me by surprise again. I didn't know where to look, what was appropriate to say. I knew I needed to keep him talking.

"Can I tell you a secret?" I asked.

Jonah nodded.

"I didn't know your name until the other day, so all my friends have been calling you Nose Ring Boy."

He let out a puff of air from his nose by way of laughter. He smiled again, flashed me his teeth, impossibly white. "You told your friends about me?"

"I mean, not seriously. I just said that there's this cute guy in my class and they've all been making fun of me about it."

"Aw, that's sweet."

I rolled my eyes and he laughed again.

"But maybe we should get back to the play," he said. "I'm far enough behind as it is, and you're not making it any easier."

"Okay, you're right," I said. "I'm sorry."

We carried on working for another couple of hours, but every time he looked down at his notes, I would catch myself staring, trying to commit each part to memory – his eyes, his teeth, the nose ring glinting like a star. No one had ever told me I was cute before, and now I felt like I'd jumped forward too fast, like I'd missed a step, like I'd been thrown in at the deep end. How I'd ever finish the assignment in time was anybody's guess. I'd been too busy thinking about Jonah. I'd barely started the introduction.

When it was time to leave, we gathered our things and left together, loitering outside the library doors. Was he going to kiss me? Hug me? Invite me back to his room? I felt completely unprepared. Maybe I *should* have talked to Ezra.

"So," he said, a touch of nervousness in his voice. "Would you maybe want to go on a *real* date with me sometime soon?"

I tried to play it cool. "I'm sure I could fit you in."

"Okay, good. There's a fireworks party on Saturday night if you want to go. You could maybe come to mine, have some drinks first?"

"Sounds good."

"Sick. I'll text you about it tomorrow." He leaned in, moved his face closer to mine. "Thanks for all your help tonight, Ash. I really appreciate it."

He put his arms around me and pulled me into a hug. He was so strong that I felt like a child against him: fragile, breakable, small. I put my hands on his back and felt his muscles, hard as rocks. He smelled like fizzy drinks and chewing gum.

"Good night then," he said, and with one last dazzling smile, he turned around and walked away. I suddenly felt exhausted. My emotions had been all over the place, bounding up and down all night – terror, relief, nausea, excitement. I felt like I was about to collapse. Maybe I hadn't eaten enough. I steadied myself against the doorframe.

I'm in love with him, I thought. *And I'm dying for it too.*

Nine

"I can't believe you didn't tell me," said Ezra, sitting on my bed.

"It's not like that. I was just…"

"Just what? How long were you gonna keep it a secret from me?"

I was leaning against the wall, arms crossed, fumbling desperately for excuses. I'd had every intention of telling him about Jonah, but before I'd had the chance, Haz had sent a message to the WhatsApp group, asking me how my date went. It wasn't *his* fault. I never said that I hadn't told Ezra, so it was only natural that he'd assume I'd spoken to him. But I wasn't expecting Ezra to be so upset about it. I'd never seen him so pissed off before.

"Come on, Ez," I said. "It wasn't a secret. The only reason I told Haz was because I bumped into him on campus – literally right before I met Jonah."

"But you still told him. Can't you trust me?"

"Of course I can, but I knew you'd turn it into a big deal. I was nervous, alright? I wasn't planning on telling anyone."

Ezra looked away, focusing on a spot on the wall above the radiator. He was shaking his head in disbelief, and his mouth was fixed in a thin, straight line.

"I'm just trying to understand why you'd keep something like that from me. I've only ever been supportive, haven't I? I've never kept anything from *you*."

"I mean, you told Haz and Sam about your parents before me, *and* you got pissy with me when I brought it up. I don't see how *that's* any different."

Ezra turned his face to me, unimpressed. "So that's what this is about?"

"It's not about anything!" I groaned. "I didn't want to tell anyone about Jonah until *after* the study date. I would've told you when I got back but you were already in bed. I would've told you tonight if Haz hadn't messaged first."

He took a deep breath, trying to calm himself down. I understood how he must've felt. Ezra talked about himself constantly, often sharing things about his life that other people would've kept secret. But I had never been like that. Being the centre of attention was something that scared me, made me nervous. I'd rather just keep things to myself.

It was so blowy outside that the window rattled. I could feel a cold current of air coming through a gap somewhere. Or was it just Ezra that left me cold?

I thought about how best to placate him.

"Look, I'm sorry, okay? I shouldn't have said anything to Haz. But come on, you know you're my best friend. I'd never do anything to upset you on purpose."

Ezra sighed. "Alright," he said. "I forgive you."

That was it. There was no apology for him overreacting, or for him misreading the situation. I was forgiven. I was almost more annoyed at him now than I had been before. I decided to let it go, but Ezra, I knew, would milk this for all it was worth.

"Okay," I said. "So, are we good then?"

He shrugged, turned away. "I suppose," he answered, frostily.

I tried not to think about Jonah at all, or the fact he hadn't text me like he said he would. I decided to get on with my essay instead, hoping that if I could just sit down and make a start, I would have it done by Saturday morning. If he *did* text me, it would mean that I'd have all my work finished before the fireworks party, and if he didn't…well, then I'd still be free to do whatever I wanted at the weekend. It seemed like a win-win.

He finally messaged on Friday morning. My stomach lurched when I saw his name.

Hey U. Still up for a cheeky date 2morrow night? Definitely! Let me know when and I'll be there!

Two blue ticks appeared next to my message. He'd clearly seen it, but a few seconds later, he was showing as offline again. God, he must've thought I was pathetic. Jonah was someone who obviously played it cool. I knew I'd have to do the same.

He finally replied two hours later.

Sick. Im in Dodge. Meet me there @ 8? x

I waited a full twenty minutes before I replied:

Great, see you then! x

I put my phone down and heard it buzz across the desk. When I picked it up, I saw that Jonah had sent an emoji: a winking face, a pink tongue hanging out of its mouth.

Now it's official, I thought, and shivered.

Ezra had thawed out with me since Thursday night and, for the most part, acted as if nothing had ever happened. I wasn't crazy about how reactive he was, but I was still jealous of his ability not to dwell on things. If I brought up the argument now, he'd barely know what I was talking about. He was the kind of person who lived completely in the present, moving from one moment to the next. It was fairly impractical, but I thought it must be fun not to obsess the way that I did. I'd have so much more time to get things done!

I finished my essay earlier than I expected, and spent most of Saturday pottering around my room – picking things up and putting them down again, changing my sheets, making notes for my next assignment. If I sat and thought too much about Jonah, about the two of us alone in Dodge, I'd find a reason not to go. I was an expert at self-sabotage.

At five o'clock, Sam, Haz and Ezra turned up at my room. They'd taken it upon themselves to come and prepare me for the date – one of the benefits, they said, of being friends with a bunch of gays. I didn't want them to make a fuss, but since they were going to the Union later on, I figured they'd have a few drinks and forget all about me. Unfortunately, that didn't happen. They sat on my bed drinking wine out of plastic cups, instructing me on how I should dress, how I should act, what I should say, think, do. I knew they meant well but I wasn't convinced it was really helping. It was only making me more insecure.

While Ezra scanned through my wardrobe, declaring how ugly everything was, Sam was talking about sex, about what to expect and how to prepare. Haz was the only one I appreciated. He'd brought his Switch and was sitting cross-legged on the floor, trying to catch insects on *Animal Crossing*. I eventually felt the need to say something.

"Guys, I know you're only trying to help, but you're making me more nervous. Why don't you put some music on and I'll ask you if I need anything?"

Ezra nodded sagely. "Point taken," he said.

He pulled out his phone and chose an album to play on Spotify. As they talked, a woman started wailing over a piano, banging the keys as hard as she could. It wasn't exactly what I'd meant but at least the focus was off of me. I slowly started to fade them out.

I settled on one of Ezra's shirts, a black burnout velvet with tiny mother-of-pearl buttons. I got changed in the bathroom, and when I came back in, Ezra gasped and clutched his chest. He looked like a parent on the first day of school.

"He's wearing the black devoré!" he said, proudly. "*I* gave him that shirt!"

"Huh?"

"Never mind, darling. It suits you."

I rolled my eyes. "Thanks, Ez."

As I carried on getting ready, Sam and Ezra reminisced about their own first date experiences: sticky fumblings in the back of a cinema, skittish boys with half-closed eyes. Haz just played his game in silence, occasionally bitching about one of his villagers. Honestly, I had no idea what they were talking about. I was too nervous to even concentrate.

Once I was ready to leave, I started to usher them out of my room. They hadn't helped at all really, but I was grateful they'd made an effort. They moved over to Ezra's room instead, but as Haz and Sam filed inside, Ezra grabbed me by the shoulders.

"Take care of yourself, okay? We'll only be at the Union, so text us if you need anything. And you can always join us afterwards. You know, if something goes wrong."

Why would anything go wrong?

I was suddenly reminded of my mum.

I knew his heart was in the right place, but I hated the way that he talked down to me, as if I couldn't look after myself. I was starting to feel he was trying to mother me.

Or smother me? I wondered.

Of all the halls on campus, Dodge was definitely the ugliest. It was tall and square like a tower block, with cracked windows, a leaky roof, and the odd pipe coughing up black smoke. It had been painted a garish yellow, but on nearly every side, there were pink-grey stains running down the brickwork, the colour of raw or half-cooked meat. I text Jonah to say I'd arrived.

He appeared at the entrance a few minutes later, flushed and damp from a recent shower. He was wearing a shirt embroidered with stars, and there was a chain around his neck attached to a tiny gold medallion. It seemed to wink as it caught the light.

"Hey, bro," he said, nodding.

Bro?

"Um, hey," I said. "You alright?"

"Yeah, all good thanks."

I was waiting for a hug but he just smirked, nodded again, held the door open for me instead. Once inside, he turned around without a word and started walking up the stairs. He'd hugged me a few days ago, so something must've changed since then. But what? Maybe I looked less cute tonight. I knew I shouldn't have worn Ezra's shirt.

I followed him up the stairs to his room on the third floor. It was small and square with blank, white walls, as if he'd only just moved in. All of his attention had been focused on the corkboard above his desk, which was covered in photos of him and his mates. The bin was full of empty cans, either flattened or bent in half, and they were all the same brand of energy drink that he'd brought with him to the library. But the whole room smelled like his aftershave: heady and musky, slightly floral. It made me think of a poisonous flower.

He didn't speak until after the door was closed.

"So, this is it," he said, shrugging.

"I like it. It looks much better on the inside."

"Thanks. I know it's not exactly the nicest hall on campus."

"No, it's okay. Although, it *does* look like the kind of place a murderer would live."

Jonah looked at me mischievously. "Who says they don't?"

I chuckled under my breath. "I mean, I *have* told my friends I'm coming here, so they'll know where to look if I go missing."

"Good thinking," he said, "but I'm pretty sure you're safe with me. Although, isn't that exactly what a murderer *would* say?"

"Stop it!" I laughed.

"I'm kidding! Right, let's have some drinks."

He crouched down and opened the cupboard built in to his desk. Inside, there were bottles of rum, vodka, gin, and tequila, as well as a lone bottle of Sourz that was an icy, unnatural blue. I sat down clumsily on his bed.

"Are you having a party?" I asked.

"Nah, the guys from the football society come here after practice and we always end up getting pissed. Half of this stuff isn't even mine."

"I didn't know you played football."

"Yeah, ever since I was a kid. I'm not very good though."

I imagined that was a lie. He seemed like the kind of person who excelled at everything they did, even with the least amount of effort. It was another thing I was jealous of.

He pulled out two mugs, filled them with vodka and Coke, then handed one of them to me. The Man U logo was on one side, a devil holding up a trident.

"So," I said, "are there no cute guys on your football team?"

Jonah sat down next to me, crossing his legs. "Cute, yes. Gay, no. Well, I mean, I don't know for sure, but they definitely don't *act* gay."

"Which means what exactly?"

"Oh, you know. They like football and talk about girls all the time."

"You mean, you don't all make out in the showers after practice?"

Jonah laughed and shook his head. I was trying to think of something to say when I felt his knee pressing up against mine. I was so scared I didn't move. I glanced over at him.

"Hi," he said, and grinned.

We regarded each other in silence, not quite sure what we should do next. Eventually I looked away, trying to pretend that I wasn't terrified. I stood up and went over to his corkboard. It was covered with photos of him and his friends – sitting on the edge of a pier, posing at a music festival, standing topless on a moonlit beach. They were all wearing football shirts and sunglasses, all impossibly toned and muscular. I was starting to feel insecure. My body was average, a little chubby. I felt myself sucking in my stomach.

I was about to turn around when I noticed a photo in the bottom corner. It was tinted brown and slightly faded, completely different to all the others. An older man and woman were sat smiling in a pub garden, drinking beers underneath an umbrella. The woman had curly hair and wore a gold medallion necklace – the same one Jonah was wearing now.

"Is this your parents?" I asked.

He appeared next to me. "Yeah, that's them."

"They look nice. Are you close?"

"Me and my mum are, I guess. My dad left when I was little. He's married with kids now, but I haven't talked to him in years."

"That sucks. Mine died when I was seven."

"Oh."

"Yeah, he was sick for a really long time. He had cancer. My mum's never even dated since then. I don't think she's ever gotten over him."

Jonah clicked his tongue. "Sorry, man."

"It's okay," I said. "Thanks though."

As much as I wanted to bond with him, the mood felt heavy now, oppressive. I thought we should probably try and get off the topic of our painful childhood traumas. But as we finished our first drinks and started pouring another, Jonah's phone began to ring. He picked it up and looked at it. The name Simon appeared on the screen.

"Just one of the guys from football," he said, putting his phone on silent.

"Oh, cool. Is he gonna be at this party tonight?"

"Maybe. Um, yeah. I don't know."

I nodded. Jonah's phone continued flashing.

"You can answer it if you want," I said. "I don't mind."

"No, it's cool. I don't feel like talking to him right now."

There was an awkward silence while he waited for it to stop ringing. It felt like something *else* had changed, but I didn't know what it was. Should I ask him about it?

His phone buzzed again only this time it was a text. He read it thoughtfully, chewing his lip. He was quiet for a long time, then said, "Hey, why don't we stay here and watch the fireworks from the roof? It'll just be the two of us. This party sounds kinda lame anyway."

"You don't want to go?"

"Nah, I think there'll be a lot of people there."

Was that a bad thing? I wasn't sure what he'd seen on his phone, but being alone with him sounded ideal. "Um, alright," I said. "Let's do it."

After three or four mugs of vodka, Jonah and I climbed the stairs and made our way out to the roof. There was a huge *No Entry* sign on the door, but the handle itself had been broken off. There was just a circular hole that you could reach through and pull open. Someone had managed to drag a set of patio furniture out there, and wherever you looked, there were fag ends, broken bottles, plastic bags full of empty cans. But it was strangely romantic too. From one side, you could see across the whole of the main campus, and from the other, the football fields stretched down to a patch of woods behind the tennis courts.

We sat down on the chairs and looked out across the fields. Below us, students were milling around in groups, drinking beer and smoking cigarettes. Two guys stood apart from the others, presumably setting up the fireworks.

I thought there would be some music playing, maybe even a DJ, but it was literally just students. It didn't seem to be very official.

"Are they allowed to do this here?" I asked.

Jonah shrugged. "Probably not, but who's gonna stop them?"

He'd filled a hipflask with straight vodka, and as we sat and watched, we passed it back and forth between us. It tasted awful – about as pleasant as a mug of drain cleaner – but the fact we were sharing made me feel important. Our lips had indirectly touched! We were nearly halfway to a kiss! *Christ,* I thought, *stop. You sound like a thirteen-year-old girl.*

Suddenly, the fireworks exploded into the air. People gasped and cheered below us, and we leaped to our feet, rushing towards the edge of the building. The booming above us was so loud it felt like we were on a battlefield, but the fireworks were beautiful, glittering out like shooting stars. And it wasn't just these ones either. From our vantage point on the roof, we could see all the way to London. Bursts of colour shot up silently, blooming like time-lapse footage of roses. We stood in reverential silence. We didn't have anything else to say.

At one point, as we stood watching, I felt a hand grabbing my bum.

I looked over at Jonah, raising an eyebrow.

"What?" he said, innocently. "I'm not doing anything."

There was something about the way he held his mouth, the way his lips turned up at the corners, that made him look permanently amused. It was like there was always something on his mind, something funny, entertaining. He looked like a person with a lot of secrets.

I let him feel me up for a few minutes, feeling his fingers in my back pockets, or running in circles across my jeans. I looked at him and bit my lip, and then – before I could stop myself – I leaned forward to give him a kiss. Our lips met; I felt his tongue pushing into my mouth, hot and wet, and I surrendered to it completely. He wrapped both arms around my shoulders and I put my hands onto his hips, feeling my way up under his shirt. One of us moaned but I couldn't tell who. In the distance, people cheered.

When we finally broke apart, Jonah smiled at me, impressed.

"You're amazing," he said, breathlessly.

We turned back to watch the fireworks.

Jonah still had one arm around me, and as we watched, I remembered something we did in primary school. You would take a candle and draw fireworks on a piece of paper, but you could only see them when you covered it in paint, the wax appearing as if by magic. It was how I felt about my life. It had been flat, dull and colourless, only now – it was filled with fire.

Ten

The next afternoon, Ezra was trying his best not to throw up. He was wearing a red jumper that came down to his knees, some loose-fitting pyjama bottoms, and a pair of glasses with purple lenses. Under the John Lennon frames, I could still make out the ghost of his black eye: a faint, yellow-green streak. His hair stuck out at crazy angles.

"It looks like you swallowed a hand grenade," I said, letting him into my room.

"I feel like it too," he groaned.

He collapsed onto my bed like a child, making grabbing motions with his hands until I brought him a glass of water. His night at the Union – from what I could understand – had been a good one, though he'd drunk so many snakebites he could barely remember a thing. I'd thought as much when I'd got a text from him at 3:12 am saying, "Got tsing lobe. Don't did shythin I fshghsi!" I'd wondered what he'd meant, but he had no memory of pressing send. I guess it would have to remain a mystery. Perhaps it was meant for someone else.

I'd agreed to call Sam and Haz to tell them about my night. I thought they'd be too hungover to stick to the plan, but they were both unexpectedly fresh; it was only

Ezra who was still suffering. I sat next to him on the bed and then called the group on WhatsApp. I put them on speakerphone so that Ezra could hear and filled them in on what had happened.

"So you didn't stay over?" asked Sam.

"No, but I think he wanted me to. He asked me to come back to his room after we watched the fireworks, but it was already half past one."

"I get it. Leave him wanting more. Good plan."

"Well, I wasn't thinking *that*."

Actually, I had been. I'd had a really good time with Jonah, and of course I had wanted to stay, but in the back of my mind, I knew I needed to make him wait. I couldn't give him everything upfront. I had to leave so he'd start to miss me.

"One thing I don't understand though," said Haz, "is why you didn't go to the party. Isn't that the whole reason you were going over there?

"Not the *whole* reason, but…yeah. I don't know."

"He didn't say anything? You didn't think it was a bit weird?"

I wasn't sure what to say. The thought had been bothering me too. Jonah had seemed keen until he'd received that text from Simon – whoever that was. Maybe he just didn't want me to meet his friends from the football society. I thought I'd better tell them.

"Wait, you mean he's not out?" asked Sam.

"Well, he's never been with a boy before. He doesn't even know if he's gay."

"Oh dear. That isn't good, Ash."

"Isn't it?"

"Not if he doesn't want to be seen with you in public. Come on, you don't want to be someone's dirty little secret. You're better than that."

I'm not entirely sure I was.

"But…I mean, he wears crop tops and nail polish. And he's not exactly *butch*. Surely his mates must know he's not straight."

"Nah, lots of guys do that," said Ezra, suddenly chiming in. "It's trendy for them to act queer now. I've heard it even helps them get girls. Seriously, straight boys are so gross. Like you can just paint your nails and not deal with any of the fallout. Get real."

"Yeah," agreed Sam. "I think this guy must be a twat."

"He isn't a twat," I said.

"Well, he sounds like one to me. He's probably just using you to experiment on, to see what he's into. Lots of guys are like that. Especially now that we're at uni."

That one stung. Mainly because it was what I'd been worried about all along, that Jonah was too attractive for someone like me. But was everyone else thinking that as well?

"What are you guys trying to say?" I asked. "That I shouldn't see him anymore?"

"Well, *I* wouldn't," said Sam.

"Why wouldn't you?"

"I mean, he's not exactly a saint, is he?"

"How would *you* know? You've never met him!"

There was quiet on the other end of the phone. I could hear Haz and Sam shifting about, but nobody said anything for a long time. Finally, Sam handed the phone to Haz.

"It's fine, it's just…Look, I've been in these situations before, and you need to be careful, okay? I've been jerked around in the past by guys who were in the closet. They're nice to you in private, but they can treat you like shit in front of their friends."

"But…Jonah isn't like that."

"How do you know?" asked Sam. "What do you *really* know about this guy?"

"What do *you*?"

Another silence.

"Look, it's fine," said Haz. "We just want you to be careful, Ash."

I took a breath. "Okay," I said. "Fair enough."

But was it? I wanted to argue with them, to make them see how unfair they were being now. None of them knew what Jonah was like, so why were they trying to turn me against him? I thought they'd be supportive, that they'd be glad I was putting myself out there. I'd been excited to tell them about my first date, my first kiss, about the fireworks we saw from the roof. Why were they trying to ruin it? They all knew how much it meant to me.

Sam started talking about the Union, but I could already feel myself shutting down. When I looked back at Ezra, he had taken off his glasses. He was looking at me with a mixture of regret and understanding, like someone finding an injured bird.

I started wishing that he would just leave.

In Shakespeare class on Monday, we moved on to *Romeo and Juliet*. Why couldn't we have done a course on the comedies instead? All I wanted was to enjoy whatever I had with Jonah, to hold on to the way he'd made me feel when we were up on the roof. But everywhere I looked, it was like there was something trying to warn me. Haz and Sam had been bad enough, but now even Shakespeare was doing it too. Did I actually *want* to fall in love?

But Jonah, if it were possible, looked even cuter than I remembered. He was wearing a backwards cap that he kept on for the entire lecture, and a shirt with a low V, exposing the ridges of his collarbones. When the lecture ended, he smiled and winked cheekily as he packed away his things. I chuckled in silence and put on my coat, but when I turned back, he was already racing out of the hall, trying to leave as fast as he could.

Jonah always rushed out of class so I wasn't exactly surprised, but this time I wanted to speak to him. We were friends now, people who'd spent time together, people who'd kissed and shared their secrets. And besides, I wanted to know when he'd like to hang out again. I was already thinking about the weekend.

I followed him out to the quad, rushing past the students who were slowest to leave.

"Hey! Hey, Jonah!" I called after him.

"Oh, hey," he said. "You okay?"

"Yeah. Um, can we talk for a minute?"

"I'm kind of in a rush right now. What's up?"

He spoke like I was just a person in his class, someone he'd only just met – not someone he'd spent hours kissing a couple of nights ago. Had I imagined the whole thing?

"Well, I wanted to say that I had a really good time the other night."

"Yeah, same."

"So, I was just wondering if you wanted to hang out again soon?"

"Um, sure. Look, I'll text you, okay? I can't really talk now."

I mumbled an apology and let him go, watching him walk to the edge of the quad. A group of his friends were stood waiting for him. I kept my eyes down as I walked past, trying to pretend I had places to be. If Jonah noticed, he didn't show it. He was too busy trying to fit in, trying to look cool in front of his mates. And I was just someone he barely knew.

"Who's *that*?" said one of his friends, looking me up and down in disgust.

"No one special," he replied, then they disappeared around the corner.

Eleven

After handing my Shakespeare essay in at the English department, just as I was walking back to Queensway, my phone vibrated in my trouser pocket. It was Jonah.

Hey u. Sorry about earlier.

I stopped on the pavement to read what he'd said, standing underneath a tree that had flat, heart-shaped leaves, as brown and crusty as a scab. My thumbs were hovering over the keypad but I didn't know what to say. I wasn't angry that he'd blown me off in front of his friends; I was upset that I was nothing to him, a nobody, 'no one special.' The kiss, I knew, was probably a bigger deal to me – it was my first *real* kiss after all – but I'd hoped it had cleared things up for him, given him a reason to want to come out. I at least thought he wouldn't mind being seen with me in public. I must've overestimated my effect on him.

I slid my phone back into my pocket and carried on walking, trying my best not to overthink. But when I got back to my room, I saw that he'd messaged me again.

Dont b angry. Im just not ready 2 come out 2 my m8s yet.

Then, a few minutes later:

Sorry if I pissed u off.

Jonah texted like a ten-year-old. You'd never guess he was an English student from the way he typed his messages. But there was something sweet about them too, something innocent, child-like. They made me feel like I was back at school.

I decided to text him back.

It's fine. I understand that you want to keep us a secret, but you could've just said we were friends or something. You didn't need to treat me like that.

He text back straight away this time.

I know. Im sorry. Its fucked up.

I wanted to drag the argument out to punish him, to make him feel bad. But relationships were a delicate thing. I knew he'd be turned off if he thought I was petty.

Don't worry. Let's just forget about it.

Thanks m8! Ur the best. x

There was the word I dreaded. *Mate.* I was no different from his football friends, the ones he thought he was nothing like. Apparently making out on his roof hadn't elevated me above them yet. I was still just a friend. No, worse; I was just a mate.

I put my phone down on the desk and tried to think of a way to reply. I had no reason to text him back, but I wanted to keep the conversation going for as long as I could. Though I barely knew him, talking to Jonah made me feel like I was walking through a series of rooms. Vast, open spaces would give way suddenly to locked doors, to places I wasn't able to access. There'd been less of these once we were up on the roof, but even then I'd known that any wrong turn would lock me out again, that he would go back to his default setting: blank and uncommunicative. Having a conversation with him was a bit like a maze, like a game where I had to keep him talking. I knew that, before long, he would inevitably withdraw.

I checked my phone. There was another text from Jonah.

Come to Dodge again on Friday night. Ill make it up 2 u. I promise. x

This time, the emoji he'd chosen was a purple devil, grinning darkly, mischievously. A hot shudder ran through my body. He actually *did* want to see me again.

I typed my reply as fast as I could.

I'll be there x

Later that night, Ezra and I had dinner together in the dining room. Although I knew it would piss him off, I decided not to tell him about what was going on with me and Jonah. We hadn't spoken about him since the phone call with Haz and Sam, and I was still a bit annoyed with the way they'd handled things. They didn't even know him! And worst of all was that they'd said he was too attractive for me, that he was using me, taking advantage. I thought it might be safer to just avoid the subject from now on, or to go to someone else if I needed advice. Maybe they didn't understand. Maybe they weren't the friends I thought they were.

Ezra, as usual, was oblivious to all this, and was talking instead about some horror film he'd just watched for his Media class. He was talking about a tribe of cannibals in the jungle who had eaten a bunch of filmmakers, about real animals being killed and people dying in horrible ways. He was talking excitedly as he ate, but watching his mouth tearing, biting, chewing was making me feel queasy, not myself. I eventually zoned him out, just saying "Mm-hm" or "Really?" every time he took a breath. He was far too self-absorbed to notice.

"So yeah, the cannibalism is a metaphor for colonialism," he said.

"Mm-hm?"

"Yeah, and the soundtrack is great as well. I really want to buy it on vinyl but my record player is still at home. I don't think I'd have room for it here."

"Really?"

"Yeah, and it's pressed on red vinyl too. I mean, how cool is *that*?"

"Very."

He shoved the fork back into his mouth; the metal scraped against his teeth. "Oh, you definitely need to see it," he said, chewing. "It has this beautiful music, but then you see the cannibals eating all the main characters. And it's really realistic too! So gross!"

"Mm-hm," I said again, trying to look anywhere other than his mouth. I was staring down at my plate, looking at a chicken curry which now – thanks to Ezra – resembled a pile of human organs. Why could he never take a hint? Surely he knew that I wasn't interested.

I looked up at him with distaste.

Please stop talking, I thought, angrily.

Please stop talking.

Please stop talking.

After dinner, we bought a drink from the bar and went and sat on the bench where we'd first met. It was cold and dark, and we hadn't thought to bring our jackets. I could see my breath making wet clouds, and I wanted to go back inside, to be alone again in my room. If Ezra had been less high maintenance, I could go back and get some reading done. Why could I never just do what I wanted? I always felt obligated to stay with him.

The sky above us was a starless black, matte as sugar paper, but the light from the bar cast long shadows out onto the grass. I looked down at our silhouettes, stretching away into the distance. They looked separate and remote, like two strangers on a park bench. I was sitting right next to him but I'd never felt further away. He shifted closer and I recoiled.

"You wanna come back to mine and watch a film?" he asked, lighting a cigarette. "I haven't got any lectures tomorrow, and it's been ages since we last watched something."

"Sorry, I'm not sitting through *Cannibal Holocaust* with you."

"Oh, we can watch whatever you want. It doesn't have to be a horror film. I know you're a delicate flower when it comes to movies."

I gritted my teeth. "It isn't that, but my idea of a good film isn't one where everyone gets hacked to pieces. I mean, it's not exactly high art, is it?"

Ezra, eyeing me narrowly, blew out a puff of purple smoke. "I didn't realise you were a member of the Academy of Motion Pictures," he said.

"I'm not. I just don't like watching shit films, okay?"

Ezra nodded coolly but I could tell that I'd struck a nerve. He was looking up at the sky, pretending to be deep in thought. Really he was just avoiding my gaze. I could always tell when he was pissed off because it was the only time he was ever quiet. He was as shallow as a puddle. He thought he was hard to read, but I could practically see right through him.

"Well," he said eventually, "why don't you show me another episode of *Xena* then. I don't mind if that's what *you'd* prefer to watch."

"I'm not really in the mood tonight. I was gonna go back to my room soon anyway."

"Okay. Fair enough."

I sat in silence for a while, listening to Ezra sucking away on his cigarette. Like everything else he did, Ezra made a lot of noise when he smoked, smacking his lips and pushing the air from his lungs out forcefully, like he was spitting out a swear word. I thought back to the night we'd met, when I'd watched him smoke for the very first time. I thought he was mysterious back then. Now I mostly just found him embarrassing.

"So," he said, after a long pause. "I was talking to Sam earlier."

"Mm-hm?"

"He said we should go to the Union on Friday night. You didn't get to come with us last time, and it wasn't the same without you. I said I thought it might be fun."

"Thanks, but I don't think I can."

Ezra looked over at me. "Oh?"

"Yeah, I've got to finish my Shakespeare essay on Friday."

"The one you handed in today, you mean?"

Trust Ezra to remember *that*. He barely paid attention to a word I said, but he'd clearly been listening all along. I felt for sure he wouldn't care about my coursework, about which essays I'd been writing. Why would he bother? They weren't about him.

"Okay," I admitted. "I have another date with Jonah on Friday."

"What, Nose Ring Boy?"

"Do you know anyone else I'm dating?"

"No. Not that you'd tell me if you were," he said.

I looked over at the tree outside reception. In the dark, I could just make out two birds in the topmost branches. I thought they were kissing at first, but they were really just wrestling dead worms from each other's beaks. I sighed more heavily than I'd meant to.

"Look," I said, "I wasn't gonna say anything because I know you don't approve."

"*I* never said that."

"Come on, Ez. You guys made your feelings pretty clear the other day."

"When?"

"On the phone! You were all going on about how I was making a big mistake."

"Only because we care about you. Dating can be confusing when you've never done it before. We just don't want to see anyone take advantage of you. That's all."

"Because no one could ever *really* like me, is that it?"

Ezra's voice became firm. "That's *your* shit, Ash, not mine. You'll have to carry that one yourself. It's not *my* job to have to deal with your insecurities."

"And why do you think I have so many? You guys said that he was using me!"

"Well, he might be," he said, blowing out another cloud of smoke. "But wouldn't you rather hear it from us? Anyway, you can hardly blame *me* for you being insecure. I'm always telling you how great you are. I don't see anyone else saying those things to you."

I didn't bother trying to argue with him. I hadn't meant to start a fight, but as he spoke, I could feel myself getting more and more annoyed. When I looked down, I noticed my hands were balled into fists. It almost looked like I was going to hit him.

"Oh, whatever," I said, standing up. "I'm going back to my room. I'll talk to you later."

Ezra leapt up suddenly, throwing his cigarette onto the grass in one quick, fluid motion. We faced each other in surprise, tense as cats.

"What the hell is going on with you?" he said.

"Me? It's you! *You're* fucked off that I want to spend time with someone else."

"I'm not! I'm just trying to understand why you don't give a shit about us all of a sudden. You've been on one date with this guy, Ash. One!"

"Yeah, so?"

"So you barely know him! You've literally met him twice, and you're already willing to drop all your friends to go and see him."

I rolled my eyes. "Oh, it was one time, Ez."

"Yeah, and this Friday makes two."

I shook my head and looked down at my feet. This was starting to get out of hand.

"You're making this into something it's not," I said. "We're fighting because *you* aren't being a supportive friend."

"I am! I only want you to be happy."

"Yeah? Well, leave me alone then," I spat, and before he could stop me, I stormed off towards my room. I could feel Ezra watching me as I went, but I didn't turn back around. He thrived on drama anyway, didn't he? He loved getting into arguments. I could practically imagine him grinning as he watched me go, laughing to himself, enjoying this.

Twelve

Ezra and I avoided each other for the rest of the week. I went to the dining hall at six thirty each night, knowing that he'd never want to eat so early. The hall was usually deserted then, and I would eat as quickly as I could before heading back to my room, praying that no one would intercept me. I wasn't even still angry with him. In fact, I was starting to feel like it was *me* who had been in the wrong. Either way, I knew I should've handled things differently. Ezra had only ever had my best interests at heart – he'd proven that on more than one occasion – though I did sometimes wish he was less overbearing. Isn't it the job of a friend to just be happy for you, to support you no matter what? That was all I really wanted. Still, I'd already decided that I wouldn't text him and apologise. He could stay angry with me for all I cared.

Sam and Haz must've known about the fight too. They'd been silent in the WhatsApp group all week, and for some reason, I was almost more annoyed with *them* than I was with Ezra. I didn't want them to pick sides – though I'm sure they would've taken his – but I was surprised that they hadn't reached out, that they hadn't asked me how I was. I could've thrown myself out the window for all *they* knew, and if I had, they wouldn't have done a damn thing to stop me. But why was I so angry with them anyway? They had nothing to do with the argument, and it wasn't *their* fault that we weren't talking. Besides, it's not like I'd tried reaching out to them either. I'd been just as quiet with them as they'd been with me.

On Friday night, as I was getting ready to head off on my date, I finally received a text message. I thought it would be Ezra, desperately begging for my forgiveness, but it was only a text from my network provider, telling me my phone bill was ready to view.

"You're not still mad at me, are you?"

"I don't know. I haven't decided yet."

"Come on, Ash. Are you really?"

I was sitting on Jonah's bed, drinking another mugful of vodka and Coke. Since I was last here, Jonah had hung up a string of fairy lights around his corkboard. The lights – all twinkling gently – were a bright, frosty blue, the colour of ice on a frozen lake. It made the room seem cold somehow, impersonal. I almost felt like we were underwater.

"Oh, it's fine," I said, trying to sound like I didn't care. "I mean, I get it, but I'd rather you didn't treat me like a knob whenever your friends are around."

"I know, I know. I'm sorry!"

He was sitting on the swivel chair by his desk, and having spun it round to face me, was leaning forwards, legs apart. He looked a bit like a police officer, like someone coaxing out a confession. I saw that our feet were almost touching.

"Let's just forget it," I said. "It's really not that big of a deal."

"Yeah, but I don't want you to think I'm a massive twat," he said, topping up his mug with a little more vodka. "It's just that…well, I'm really scared to come out to them."

"I'm sure they'd be fine with it."

"You don't know them," he said. "You should hear the jokes they make in the changing rooms. I don't think any of them have even *met* a gay person before."

I wrinkled my nose. "But they're at university. And *this* university too. I mean, it specialises in the arts. There are tons of gay guys here."

"Oh, *they* know that, but it is kind of scary for them. It's so far out of their comfort zones that they don't know how to act around gay people. They're not bad guys really. They just think it's all a bit weird, you know?"

"Sorry if I'm not exactly heartbroken."

Jonah laughed. I knew they were his friends, but I didn't know why he was trying so hard to defend them. It was *their* fault that he was struggling to come out, that he didn't feel like he could be himself. I wondered what they'd say if they knew about *me*.

While we were both quiet, Jonah poured me another drink. It tasted strong, twice as strong as the last one he'd made. I'd have to pace myself and not try to keep up with him. He was obviously a much bigger drinker than I was.

"So, what about you?" he asked, stretching out and poking me with his foot. "Where are *your* friends tonight?"

"They're at the Union," I said.

"And you didn't want to go with them?"

"Nah, not really. I wasn't in the mood."

"Why not?"

I didn't know what to say. I couldn't exactly tell him that I'd blown them off to come here. I didn't want to seem like the kind of guy who would willingly ditch his friends, who would throw them out for a pretty face. Or maybe I just didn't want him to know how much I liked him, that I would've dropped everything for him.

"Actually, we're not really speaking at the moment," I said, taking another sip from Jonah's mug. "We're in the middle of a fight right now."

"How come?"

"Um…to be honest, it's because they don't really like *you* very much."

Jonah's expression didn't change.

"I mean, they don't know you," I continued, "but they think you might be messing me around. Or that because you're in the closet, you might be, like, using me

119

to experiment on. I don't know. It's complicated. I don't really know *what* they think."

Jonah nodded thoughtfully. His eyes seemed to be searching mine for something, though I couldn't tell what it was. Then he peered down into his mug.

"Well, if you ask me," he said, "I think your friends all sound like dicks."

"Oh, *you* can talk. Nothing says *I'm a great friend* like a little casual homophobia."

We stared at each other for a long moment, then we both burst out laughing. Jonah shook his head and sighed, then finished the rest of his drink in one.

"Oh, man. I can't argue with you there. Maybe we *both* need to make new friends."

But was it really as simple as that? Ezra, Haz and Sam weren't dicks, even if I *was* still a bit annoyed with them. I knew they cared about me deep down – at least more than Jonah's friends cared about him – but I couldn't help feeling as though our friendship had run its course. Maybe Jonah was right after all. Maybe I *did* need to make new friends.

"It's not that they're bad people," I said, looking down at my feet. "It's just…there's this guy called Ezra. He can be kinda selfish, I guess. He loves the sound of his own voice. And Haz and Sam, well, they're nice too. Except they know everything about everything. It sometimes feels like they're talking down to me."

"Oh, yeah?"

"Yeah. Like, I just kinda wish they would leave me alone, you know? I get that they care about me, but – god! Don't they have better things to do?"

I didn't know where all of this was coming from. I hadn't even thought I was still angry, so why was I raking up the past? And why was it starting to feel so good?

After a while, Jonah said, "Don't fall out with them over me."

"Oh, it's not just you. They've been annoying me for weeks. I just don't think that they understand me. I mean, we *are* all very different."

Jonah frowned, huffed, shifted his weight like he was tired.

He asked, "Do you mind if I put some music on?"

I shook my head, and while he fiddled around with a pair of Bluetooth speakers, I moved over to the window. It was so dark I couldn't see much more than the path that led down to the Union, a lurid yellow in the glare of the streetlights. But it was already swarmed with people. Girls in dresses and spiked heels were unsteadily tottering down the hill; bearded students were all trying to look cool in front of their girlfriends; a group of freshers were handing round a bottle, taking a swig before passing it on. I had no idea why, but I started wanting to go out. I wished we were going to the Union together, but I knew Jonah would say no if I asked him. He still needed to keep us a secret – at least for now.

The room was suddenly filled with Joni Mitchell singing about valentines and tapestries, about finding someone you could love. I thought it was a strange album for him to choose, but in the back of my mind, I wondered how conscious he was of these decisions. Was it a loaded action designed to tell me something he wasn't able to express, or had he simply picked an album at random, an album he didn't even know? Wanting to seem casual and mysterious, I decided to just ignore it, sitting on the bed like I hadn't noticed.

"This is my mum's favourite," he said, landing on his chair with a grinding creak. "I used to hate it when I was a kid, but I like it more now I'm not at home. It's always easier to like something when you don't have to hear it every day in the car."

"Joni Mitchell, right? Yeah, my mum loves this too."

"Sick."

I nodded, trying to think of something to say. The blue glow of the fairy lights seemed to counteract the gold of his skin, making him look pale, a little unwell. His skin was the colour of sea water, of the sky on a misty morning. He was still attractive in this light, but now he looked faint and barely-there. I felt I could put my hands right through him.

"It's a shame there are no fireworks tonight," he said, topping up his mug with even more vodka. "We could've gone up to the roof again."

"Yeah, that's true. I wish we had fireworks all year round."

Jonah chuckled quietly to himself. I got the feeling I had missed a hint.

"You know, I had a really good time with you the other night," he said. "I wasn't expecting you to be such a good kisser."

I laughed. "What's *that* supposed to mean?"

"Oh, I don't know. Just that you always seem so nervous around me! I was half expecting you to tell me to get lost when I started touching your arse."

I smiled and bit my lip.

"And it's a nice arse too," he said, seductively.

I had that feeling again of moving towards something dangerous. The air between us felt loaded, heavy with meaning. It was like the moment in a film before someone bursts into the room with a gun – but there was only me and Jonah, looking at each other in silence, both of us waiting for something to happen.

"You can stay here tonight," he said. "I mean, if you want to. I don't have football until the afternoon so we can have a lie-in together."

"Oh, right," I said.

God, I sounded pitiful.

To be honest, this was exactly what I'd been afraid of. I wanted to stay so badly, but I was scared enough just sitting in his room. How could I go to bed with him? I had no idea what to expect, what to say or how to act. Was it normal to sleep with someone after only the second date? I suddenly wished I was still friends with Ezra. This was *his* territory, not mine.

"Um…I want to, it's just that…Look, I'd rather take things slow if it's alright with you? I've never been with a guy before either, and I…"

"Oh god, say no more. It's cool, I understand."

"Are you sure?"

"Of course! I'm probably just as nervous as you are."

I somehow doubted that this was the case.

"I don't want you to think I'm a prude or anything."

"I don't," he said. "I promise."

He flashed me a smile. There were those teeth again, as white as snow, as white as stars. I took another sip of my drink, mainly to stop myself from staring. *Who needs friends at all,* I wondered, *now I have somebody like Jonah?* Ezra had been a good friend, and we'd helped each other get settled, but Jonah was the best person I'd ever met. I only had to look into his eyes – grey like stones but shot with silver – to know this was real, what I'd always wanted. I'd do anything for him now. I'd give up my friends if it made him love me.

Joni Mitchell started singing about not knowing where she stood.

"Have you ever slept with a girl before?" I asked. I wasn't sure where the question had come from. I hadn't expected myself to ask him that.

Jonah nodded, almost guiltily. "Once or twice," he said.

"When you were younger?"

"Back in Sixth Form, yeah."

"With girls from your school?"

"Yeah, and a couple of times at parties."

"And how was it?" I asked.

He was silent for a moment, gazing out of the single window. The night outside turned his face a cool, glassy white, making his expression hard to read. With the moon on one side of him and the blue lights on the other, he looked a little like a corpse, like a body pulled out from a lake. He was still beautiful now, but sinister.

"It'll be better with you," he said, and winked.

Thirteen

I left Jonah's room in the morning. I snuck out while he was still asleep, making as little noise as I could. I wanted him to wake up missing me, calling out for me, trying to work out where I'd gone. He didn't need to know that I was only going home to do some reading. For all *he* knew, I was on my way to another date. I wanted to keep him on his toes.

On the bus, I kept thinking about the night before, turning the events over in my head like they were rocks I'd picked up on a beach, feeling their weight, inspecting their colour. I hadn't planned on staying the night, but after the conversation about taking things slow, I felt pretty sure he'd respect my boundaries. He had done too, for the most part. We'd stripped down to our pants – his body was even more perfect than I'd imagined – and spent the night spooning up against the wall, our bodies curved into the shape of a question mark. His hands strayed south once or twice, but he stopped when I smacked them away, whispering apologies into my ear. But I had to remind myself to take things slowly. I was already having visions of us moving in together, shopping for groceries in the big Tesco, holding hands as we walked around campus. But these were just silly fantasies. We still barely knew each other, and though

I was starting to understand him, there was still so much that I didn't know.

I wanted to see every part of him. I wanted him to see all of me too.

Back in Queensway, I took a shower and settled into my room to get some reading done. Even after brushing my teeth, I could still taste Jonah on my breath, as hot and sweet as a homemade biscuit. I thought I'd find it gross but it was magical, unfamiliar – the secret smell of someone else. It was like our bodies had merged together, like I was becoming a different person. My whole biology had changed. My skin smelled more like him than me.

Around midday, as I was reading my copy of *Pinocchio* for my Children's Literature course, I heard someone knocking on the door. I closed the book, folding down the page so I wouldn't lose my place, and then went over to see who it was.

Ezra was standing in the hallway. He was dressed more demurely than usual, wearing a plain brown shirt and jeans. His nails were unpainted, and since he hadn't brushed his hair, it looked like he'd just rolled out of bed. I guessed he was trying to seem repentant.

"Hey," he said. "Can I come in?"

I nodded. I shut the door and saw that he was holding a card behind his back. The envelope was a silvery-grey, the exact colour of Jonah's eyes. He handed it to me nervously.

"This is for you," he said.

I opened it. On the front was a cartoon teddy bear shyly holding a purple heart. At the bottom, in an ugly cartoon font, it said, *I'm Beary Sorry!*

I made a little humming noise to suggest laughter. Ezra looked embarrassed.

"It's a stupid card, I know."

"Well, it's a pretty terrible pun. Like, what does it even mean? Is it supposed to be *I'm very sorry* or *I'm barely sorry*?"

Ezra sighed. "Just read it, Ash."

I flipped it open, running my eyes across his handwriting, wonky and child-like.

Ash, you can't stay mad at the most awesome person you know. I'm sorry for what I said the other day. Maybe you were right. I WAS a bit jealous that you were choosing someone over me. You know I'm as needy as a kitten really. I guess I was scared that you wouldn't want to be friends anymore, or that you'd forget about me once you got a boyfriend. I was just being overly sensitive. You're the best friend I've ever had! Anyway, let's go out drinking tonight and rekindle our friendship. Do say yes. Love, Ezra xx

I closed the card and drew him into a hug.

"Thanks, Ez," I said. "I'm sorry too."

"It's okay," he said, pulling away from me. "I hate not being able to talk to you. Last week was really shit. Can we just pretend that it didn't happen?"

I nodded. "I don't even remember what we were fighting about."

He looked at me strangely, trying to see if I was being genuine. I could already tell he wanted to ask me about Jonah. He opened his mouth but then closed it again, scared to remind me about why we'd been fighting. He was more nervous now, more awkward, and I wasn't exactly sure what he wanted. I decided to ask him about his night.

He sat down on my bed and gave me a quick sketch of what had happened. Apparently the Union was lame, so him and the boys hadn't stayed out late.

"What time did you get back?" I asked.

"Like, midnight? I came and knocked for you to see if you were still up, but you must have been asleep. Unless you stayed at Jonah's last night..?"

"No, I was here. I was already in bed by then. I passed out around eleven."

I didn't know where *that* had come from. I was surprised Ezra had broached the topic of Jonah so early on, but even more shocking was just how quickly the lie had come to me. I hadn't even hesitated. And worse – I didn't feel bad about it.

"So," he said, looking up at me, "did you not have a good time last night?"

"No, I did. It was really fun. I don't think it's anything serious though. We had a few drinks, talked for a while, and then I got the bus home. So, yeah, it was fine."

"That's good. I think it's wise not to take things *too* seriously. I mean, you don't really know each other, do you? You don't want to get too involved too quickly."

"Exactly," I said, turning away to neaten the bookcase.

"Anyway, Haz and Sam want us to go to Remedy later since you missed the last couple of nights out with us. Wanna come? I know they'd love to see you."

My instinct was to say no, to find some excuse to stay in by myself. I was still a bit annoyed that Haz and Sam hadn't text me all week, and I felt sure Ezra had told them about the argument. But I didn't want them to think I was holding a grudge. We hadn't been together as a group in ages – not since Ezra had been punched at the Union.

"Okay, I'm in," I said, reluctantly.

"Great," he replied, jumping to his feet. "The old gang back together!"

I laughed and told him I'd see him later on, but as I led him out of my room, he turned back to me, suspicious, as if he'd just had a sudden thought.

"Are you sure there's nothing you want to tell me?"

I feigned ignorance. "Like what?"

"I don't know. It feels like there's something you want to say. You can tell me if you're still upset with me. I'd rather we just hashed everything out now."

"It's fine, Ez. We're all good."

"And you're *sure* there's nothing you want to say about Jonah?"

I told him everything was fine, that we should just forget it and move on. He seemed pleased enough with this, but as he left, I felt myself getting annoyed with him again. Why was he always badgering me, poking holes, trying his best to provoke a reaction? He couldn't ever just let things go. Sometimes I wished he would mind his own business.

That afternoon, as I napped, I dreamt that Jonah and I were dancing in a huge, ruined house. He was standing behind me, running his hands along my hips, across the base of my spine, but when I turned around to face him, it had been Ezra all along, pale and featureless as a statue. He reached up and grabbed my shoulders, pulling me closer. "Our friendship's like this house," he said. I smiled at him or laughed, but even in my dream, I felt the pang of what he meant. This was a house falling into ruin, precarious and dark, getting ready to collapse.

Remedy was only a little way from Dodge but I had never been inside before. It was more like a traditional pub than Solutions was, with heavy wooden furniture, exposed brick walls, and chairs upholstered with red moquette. The four of us were sitting in a booth beside the door, tucked away from the larger tables. There was no music playing – or if there was, it was too quiet to hear – and I was scared I'd have nowhere to hide if there was still some undercurrent of tension. I'd been fretting about seeing Haz and Sam ever since the fight with Ezra, but we fell straight back into the dynamic I remembered: Sam and Ezra leading the charge while Haz and I were more reserved. But I'd forgotten how easy their company was, how much fun we always had, how undemanding the conversation. I hadn't realised I'd missed being around them all so much. I must've missed them without even noticing.

"No, you're definitely a Hufflepuff," Sam said to Haz. "100 per cent."

"Urgh, but I want to be a Gryffindor!"

"Tough shit. You're the biggest Hufflepuff I've ever met. Ezra and I would be in Slytherin, and Ash, you'd be in Ravenclaw."

I jumped at my name. "What?"

"I said you'd be in Ravenclaw."

"That's the nerdy one, right? Sorry, I was never really a *Harry Potter* fan."

Haz choked on his beer. "Excuse me?"

"Don't mind him," said Sam, grabbing a handful of napkins and passing them to Haz. "It was his whole life growing up. He's clearly never gotten over it."

Ezra sipped his snakebite and wiped his mouth with the back of his hand. It left a long, red smear like an open wound. "Can I be a Death Eater instead?"

"You can't just *be* a Death Eater!" said Haz.

"Why not?"

"Because it doesn't work that way!"

Sam rolled his eyes. "Guys, it isn't real. Chill out, yeah?"

I had no idea what they were talking about but I enjoyed listening to them anyway, watching them fight with each other like children. I loved spending time alone, but being on my own all week had made me realise how much I liked them. Even Ezra was more bearable when it wasn't just the two of us. I had a feeling we worked better in groups.

"Okay, what about *Game of Thrones* then?" asked Haz. "That one should be easy. I'd be in House Tyrell, and you two would definitely be Lannisters. Ash?"

"Sorry, I didn't watch that show either."

"Oh, don't pretend you aren't a massive nerd," said Ezra, turning to me. "If you don't have your nose in a book, you're watching *Xena: Warrior Princess*."

Haz's eyes lit up. "You like *Xena*? I haven't watched that since I was a kid!"

I nodded. "Yeah, me and my mum used to watch it together, but I still have all the DVDs. I know it's kinda silly, but…I just really like it."

"That's cool. We'll have to watch it together some time."

Sam shook his head. "I'm surrounded by nerds," he said, despairingly.

As I looked across the room, half-listening to Haz and Sam, I suddenly saw Jonah. He was leaning against the bar with a group of guys I didn't know, all slicked down and wet with hair gel. *So this is where he comes,* I thought. He must have finished football practice and gone out with a few of his mates. I'd wondered why he hadn't text me.

But Jonah held himself differently around his friends. He was more manly and aggressive, sticking his chest out, rarely smiling. He looked more dangerous like this, and for a second, I was startled. I'd grown accustomed to seeing him as someone gentle, kind, sweet-tempered. He looked so different I barely recognised him.

Ezra saw me looking. "Isn't that the guy you're dating?"

Haz and Sam glanced over. I realised all four of us were staring.

"Christ, you could at least make it look subtle!" I said.

"Hm, he's cute," said Sam, nodding approvingly.

I wanted to die.

"You're still seeing him?" asked Haz.

"Um…yeah. Like, not seriously, but…I guess…"

I was hoping someone would come to my rescue, but they all just sat there in silence, waiting to hear what I had to say. I risked a glance and looked over at the bar. Jonah had noticed I was there. He looked at me coldly, almost like he could see right through me, then he turned back to his friends, laughing at some joke that I couldn't hear.

Jonah and I had an agreement. I knew he couldn't risk his friends finding out about us, about him questioning his sexuality. So why was it still so painful?

Ezra leaned forwards. "Aren't you going to say hi?"

"Nah, I only saw him last night. It's not a big deal."

Haz and Sam exchanged glances.

"What?" I said, shrugging. "He's with his mates now."

"You could at least say hello," said Ezra. "He *is* your friend after all."

Was he testing me? It was like he wanted proof that I actually knew him. I sighed. I knew if I told the truth – that Jonah didn't want to be seen with me in public – that they'd think he was an arsehole, that I was an idiot for getting involved. I couldn't face it. I thought I'd already solved the problem by telling Ezra it wasn't serious.

"Look," I said, taking a deep breath, "we talked about it last night and we agreed not to see each other anymore. He's a nice guy and we had fun, but we're really wrong for each other. And like you said, he's still in the closet. It would never work out between us."

Ezra looked puzzled. "You never told me that."

"Didn't I?"

"No. You just said it wasn't serious."

"Well, it only happened last night. I guess I was still a bit upset."

Haz and Sam seemed to take this as fact, saying how they thought it was for the best, that I'd been smart to break things off. I turned to Ezra and saw that he was watching me intensely, looking for any signs I was being dishonest. I met his gaze until he looked away.

They went back to discussing *Game of Thrones* and I turned back to my drink, trying not to look over at Jonah. I was hoping that was the end of the conversation, that we wouldn't ever have to discuss it again. But secretly, I was weirdly proud of myself for tricking them into believing me. I hadn't meant to deceive anyone, but I knew they'd never approve of what I was doing now. And besides, they didn't *need* to know how I felt about every tiny, little thing.

If I've already told one lie today, I thought, *well, why not make it two?*

Fourteen

On Wednesday night, after having dinner in the dining hall, I was so tired that I decided to go to bed early to watch *Xena*. After everything that had been going on with Jonah and Ezra, I was starting to crave some light entertainment. I really just wanted to switch off.

I picked an episode at random – 'Maternal Instincts,' one of my favourites from season three. It's an episode where Xena and Gabrielle – having been lying to each other all season – finally break apart as friends, mainly because of a demonic baby and the death of both their children. Okay, so it wasn't exactly a fun one, but I hadn't seen it in a few years and I was looking forward to re-watching it. I placed my laptop on my chest, skipped through the menus and hit play. I knew the entire script by heart. I mouthed the words along with the characters.

I'd seen it so many times that my mind kept wandering back to Ezra, about the night with the boys in Remedy. The irony that the episode was all about lies wasn't lost on me, and I tried to remember exactly what I'd said, what I'd told them about me and Jonah. I couldn't afford to slip up and contradict myself. I'd have to be careful not to get caught out.

Towards the end of the episode, as Xena and Gabrielle were standing in front of their children's funeral pyres, my phone buzzed against the pillow, making the bedframe jump, vibrate. I rolled onto my side and saw Jonah's name flash across the screen.

What u doing ;)

There he goes again, I thought. *Texting like a ten-year-old.*

Hey! Nothing much. I typed. **Just getting into bed.**

Nice. What u wearing?

Just my pants.

Mmmmm ;)

I rolled my eyes. He could at least *pretend* he wasn't only interested in my underwear. We hadn't spoken since the night in his room, and he hadn't even text about seeing me in Remedy. I'd been starting to think he was angry with me. Then again, what did it matter? He was texting me now, and he obviously still fancied me. That was the only thing I wanted.

I was trying to think of how to reply when he text me again.

Im naked lol.

I shook my head. **I bet you are!**

Wanna see? x

My heart started racing. I'd seen him in his pants – and I'd obviously thought about seeing the rest – but is this how I wanted to do it?

Another text.

Ill show u if you show me.

My pants?? I replied.

Yeh. And whats inside them.

No!

Was that too harsh? I didn't want him to think I was some innocent little virgin, someone offended at the thought of sexting. I quickly added:

Haha

Jonah replied immediately.

Come on dont b a prude.

I'm not, but wouldn't you rather see my pants in real life? I asked.

Yeh but I wanna see them now as well

I looked at my phone for a long time, trying to decide what to do next. I'd be lying if I said I wasn't a bit turned on, but – couldn't he wait? I'd already asked him to take things slow.

Another message, a photo. I opened it without thinking.

Jonah was standing in front of a mirror, and though his face was out of frame, he was completely, indecently naked. He looked like a Greek statue in the British Museum, all sculpted lines and sloping curves, flesh as hard and smooth as marble. His body was hairless – presumably to show off his muscles – and his skin, firm and flawless, was the pinkish-gold of an autumn sunset. The pose could've used some work though. He was flexing his free arm like a body builder: the international symbol of a dickhead. If I didn't know him, I would've laughed, but I just stared at him instead. I should be grateful he'd sent me anything.

Only 4 u, he typed underneath.

Wow. You look amazing!

Now u

No! haha!

Uve seen me. Come on. It's only fair.

No!

Three flashing dots appeared, then disappeared again straight afterwards. I had to send him something before he lost interest. I mean, it *was* only fair, right? I didn't want to text him *anything*, but it wouldn't be right to just leave him hanging. We were dating after all, and he *had* seen most of me in his bedroom. I didn't want him to think I was frigid.

*Xen*a had already finished, so I got out of bed and turned on the light above the sink. I pulled my pants down and took a quick photo of myself, obscuring my face in the cracks in the mirror. It looked more artful than I'd intended, my face shattered into pieces, cracked and splintered with silvery lines. It was almost like something you'd find at a crime scene.

I deleted it as soon as it was sent. I knew that Jonah could still see it, but I wanted to forget I'd ever taken it. What was my problem? We were dating! It was something other people did all the time, so why did I feel so weird about it? I felt like I'd done something wrong, and before I knew what I was doing, I started rinsing my mouth out with Listerine.

I gargled, spat blue, then pulled up my pants and checked my phone.

He'd sent an emoji: a thumbs up. Then he had disappeared offline.

Was that it? I'd never sent a nude before but I at least thought it would keep the conversation going. Maybe that was all he wanted. Maybe that was all he'd *ever* wanted.

I moved my laptop, got into bed and tried my best to go to sleep, but something kept playing on my mind. I looked at Jonah's photo again. I realised suddenly that he wasn't standing in Dodge; he'd taken it in his bedroom back at home. I could see the décor in the mirror behind him – dirty white walls, a Man U bedspread, faded stickers above the headboard. He'd said the photo was only for me but he must've taken it before uni.

Apparently, it seemed, I wasn't the only person lying.

Fifteen

Jonah had been invited to a party on Friday night, so I knew I wouldn't see him again until our Shakespeare class on Monday morning. I wondered if Ezra might want to do something with me instead. It had been a while since we'd hung out alone together, and since I wasn't going to see Jonah, I figured Ezra was the next best thing. I mean, what else was I supposed to do? While he was smoking his after-dinner cigarette, I asked if he wanted to go to the cinema. "I thought you said all my films were shit," he purred, batting his eyelashes at me.

God, I wanted to smack him sometimes.

"Well, we haven't spent much time together recently," I said. "Why don't we get the bus and go into town, just the two of us?"

Ezra shrugged. "Okay, sure. There's a cinema that plays old movies if you fancy it? I can look on the website and see if there's something we might both wanna see."

"Great," I said. "You choose. Honestly, I don't really care."

"I'll remind you of that," he said, dropping his cigarette and stamping on it with his boot, "when you tell me how terrible my taste is. Alright then, Friday it is."

*

Ezra's choice ended up being a black-and-white movie called *Brief Encounter*. It was a sad film about this couple that fall in love at a train station, only they can't be together because they're both married. Ezra really enjoyed it but it left me feeling weirdly hollow, as if all my insides had been scooped out. I couldn't stop thinking about the man and the woman in the film, about how all of their scenes together seemed so ominous. We all knew how it was going to end. We could only prepare ourselves for the inevitable.

When it was finished, we caught the bus from outside the cinema. Ezra insisted we sit downstairs even though it was almost empty. Falling down the stairs on a moving bus, he said, was definitely *not* how he wanted to die. We settled on a row towards the front, and I let Ezra take the window. Whenever he moved, his leather jacket creaked like a closing door.

"Did you like the film then?" he asked.

"I did. It was pretty sad though."

"Mm, I love a cheeky romance. They make me happy for some reason."

"They do?"

Ezra nodded. I thought about the night we'd met, about how pissed off he'd been that guys only ever wanted him for sex. I reminded him about it.

"Oh, that doesn't mean I actually think love exists," he said. "Well, I do, but I don't think it ever works out. At least, it never has for me."

That was the thing about Ezra. He was so self-absorbed that he thought *his* experience was the only one, or that his was more important than other people's. I was about to ask about his parents' relationship, about how long they'd been together, when I stopped myself at the last second. I got the sense it was a bad example. He'd basically said as much before.

"Hey," he said, suddenly. "When's your birthday again?"

"March the fifteenth. Why?"

"Oh, no reason."

Weird.

The question came out of nowhere so I decided to ignore it. We were still getting over last week's argument, and I figured he was probably just trying to make conversation, trying to smooth things over between us. But as we sat in silence, I started thinking about Jonah. I guess I was still feeling a bit funny about sending him that photo of me – especially since I hadn't really wanted to. I knew he hadn't forced me into anything, but I couldn't help feeling as though I'd betrayed myself. I was pretty sure *that* wasn't normal.

"Have you ever sent a nude?" I asked, trying to sound flippant.

"Yeah, loads. Why?"

"Oh, I was just wondering."

He looked over at me. His eyebrows were furrowed but his lips were turned up at the corners. "Who are you sending nudes to?" he asked, playfully.

"No one!"

"You *so* are!"

"I'm not!"

"Well, why mention it then?"

I rolled my eyes. "I was only asking. Jesus! Forget I said anything."

We relapsed into silence. I could feel him looking at me but I kept my eyes forward, attempting to keep my expression neutral. *Maybe I should just tell him,* I thought. I took a deep breath and let it out as a sigh. "Okay," I said, "I sent a nude to Jonah."

"I thought you weren't seeing him anymore?" he snapped, suddenly angry.

"I'm not! This was a few weeks ago."

"When?"

"I don't know. It's just been playing on my mind."

Ezra stared at me doubtfully. He looked like he was about to make fun of me, but then his features started to soften. "It's okay, Ash."

"Is it? I feel kinda funny about it."

"Well, you shouldn't. It's normal. As long as you're both consenting adults, then you've got nothing to worry about. It's only a bit of fun, isn't it?"

"I guess so."

I wondered if I should admit that I hadn't wanted to send it to him. The words were already in my mouth but I managed to hold them back, managed to choke them down like tears. It was done now, wasn't it? What was the point of feeling guilty?

"Hey," said Ezra, turning back to me. "It's still early. Let's go back to yours and have some drinks. We can watch *Xena* if you like."

"Thanks, but I know it's not really your thing."

"Come on, I chose *Brief Encounter*. It's only fair we watch something of yours now."

This was a tactic Ezra often used when he didn't want to go home alone. He was always asking to come back to mine, or to go for drinks, or to do anything that meant he wouldn't have to be by himself again. But Jonah wasn't around. I didn't have anything else to do.

"Okay," I said, smiling at him. "Sounds good."

I figured, if nothing else, it would give us something to talk about. I appreciated how chatty he was, but it was when we had nothing to say to each other that we started to argue. Besides, I *wanted* to rekindle our friendship. Maybe sharing would be a good thing.

As the bus bounced and jerked through the late afternoon dark, Ezra and I received a text at the same time. We both pulled out our phones. It was *The Art Poofs* group chat. Sam and Haz were asking if we wanted to go out for drinks.

Ezra looked at me expectantly.

"You go," I said. "I'm not really in the mood. Say hi to them for me though."

"No way! I promised to spend the whole evening with you. *And* I want to watch *Xena*! Although…," he paused. "Why don't we just invite them back to Queensway?"

I scoffed. "Haz and Sam won't want to watch *Xena* with us."

"Of course they will! They're always up for hanging out."

I didn't know why I was so hesitant. I loved Haz and Sam, and we always had a good time together. So why was I putting off texting them?

"Okay, sure," I said. "Why not?"

It was the only thing I could think to say.

A couple of hours later, the four of us were packed into my room, passing round cans of lukewarm beer. The laptop was open on my desk and we were huddled together on my bed, ready to start watching an episode of *Xena*. But I was already having my doubts.

"Maybe we should watch something else," I said. "I'm not convinced this is really your thing. And, you know, it's kinda personal, and…"

Sam shook his head. "No way! Let's do it."

"Yeah," agreed Ezra. "Come on, Ash. Whack it on."

I looked to Haz for reinforcement. He was playing with my action figure.

"I mean, I liked it a lot when I was a kid," he said, sliding the sword into Xena's scabbard. "I'd really like to watch it again now."

Traitor.

"Great," said Sam. "Now pick an episode that'll make us love it."

Jeez, I thought. *No pressure then.* Honestly I had no idea which one to show them. They'd be more inclined to enjoy one of the comedies, but they weren't always my favourites, and I didn't want them to think that it was only ever camp and silly. But the dramatic episodes might not make sense out of context, and they wouldn't be invested in the character's journeys. I scratched my head, turning the DVDs over in my hand.

"Let's just watch whatever's already in your laptop," said Sam. "The one after the last episode you watched. Which one's that?"

"Oh, I can't. The next episode's the musical, and…"

The three of them gasped audibly.

"There's a musical?!" they yelled at once.

Oh god. Now I didn't have a choice. It wasn't that I didn't like the musical – it was one of my all-time favourites – but I was fairly sure it was the very *worst* place for them to start. It was so different from the other episodes! It was hardly reflective of the show as a whole.

"Alright," I said, "but I need to give you some background first."

They all looked at me.

"You know, some context and stuff. You won't understand it otherwise."

I could see they were starting to regret their decision. Ezra and Sam took long swigs from their beers, visibly grimacing at the aftertaste. They didn't want to go into this sober.

"Okay," I said, clearing my throat. "So, at the start of season three, Gabrielle gets attacked by a demon and gives birth to an evil baby called Hope. Xena tells her to kill it but Gabrielle can't, but she tells Xena she did anyway. Then Xena goes to China to kill this guy called Ming T'ien, but Gabrielle betrays her. Well, sort of. Then Hope comes back and kills Xena's son Solon. Gabrielle kills Hope, and that's where we are now. Make sense?"

The three of them blinked at me.

"Um…" said Haz.

"Oh, we'll pick it up as we go," said Sam. "Just play it already!"

I pressed play and then settled in next to Ezra. As the episode went on, I kept telling myself not to shush them. I wanted them to have fun, but there was also a part of me that wanted them to listen to the dialogue, to feel engaged with what was going on. *It's only Xena*, I thought. It *isn't that important*. But it *was* important to me. I wanted them all to take it seriously.

After the teaser, Xena and Gabrielle enter Illusia, a magical world where they have to sing to express their feelings. It *was* a pretty weird episode. All the costumes were based on Tarot cards, and the imagery was bright and dream-like, more *Alice in Wonderland* than a normal episode. But watching it through *their* eyes made me feel embarrassed, made me cringe. I was becoming more and more critical as I tried to guess what they were all thinking.

"I mean, it *is* pretty silly," said Sam, right after my favourite part. "It's so low budget! It must've cost, like, ten pounds per episode."

"It was the 90s!" I said, pointing to the screen. "This was before everyone just relied on CGI. Look at the sets, the costumes!"

Ezra patted me on the shoulder. "Yeah, you tell him," he said. "You're allowed to like whatever shit you want."

I bristled. Was he getting back at me for what I'd said about *Cannibal Holocaust*? Or was he just showing off? He wouldn't have said that if we were alone.

I ignored him and carried on watching. Xena, in a red skeleton dress, danced a tango with the God of War.

Gabrielle, wearing a diadem of stars, danced through a nightmarish version of her hometown. But the whole forty-five minutes was, to be frank, excruciating. I kept standing up for *Xena*, this show I loved more than anything, but the boys just laughed the whole way through. I thought they'd at least take an interest for *my* sake. This was something I loved! I didn't expect them to run out and buy the boxset, but they knew how much it meant to me. Every time they laughed, it was like they were attacking me as a person. *"Look at how stupid Ash is! Can you believe he watches this shit? What an absolute knob!"*

Once it was finished I got up and turned the sound off. I was preparing myself for a massacre, but they just started talking about something else, as if they hadn't even watched it. It was like they didn't even care enough to make it part of the conversation.

I opened another beer and then sat down by the window, listening to them talk about some new song they liked, some random singer I'd never heard of. I wished I could've gone to see Jonah instead. I knew he wasn't perfect, but at least he didn't make fun of me, or make me feel stupid for the things I liked. I wondered if *he'd* take an episode seriously.

Maybe I've outgrown my friends, I thought. *We had lots of fun, and we were there when we all needed it, but we don't have anything in common. Maybe there's nowhere left to go.*

As they talked, Ezra stood up and came over to me. He glanced down at my laptop.

"Are we finished?" he asked.

I looked up at him, looked away.

"Yeah," I said, nodding. "I think we are."

Sixteen

I spent the weekend by myself. I wasn't still angry that the boys had made fun of *Xena* – what was I expecting? – but it *had* made it obvious that we didn't really have much in common. I suppose I could've confronted them about it, but they'd just tell me I was being too sensitive, that I obviously couldn't take a joke. Instead, I decided to phase them out, to start making excuses, to stop replying to their texts. Ezra would be harder to ditch, but I figured we could still eat dinner and hang out from time to time without him knowing that I was pissed off. It wasn't *his* fault that we'd outgrown each other. I didn't want to cause a fight.

But on Sunday evening, Ezra came knocking at my door.

"You'll never guess what *I* just heard," he said, pushing past me and throwing himself down on the bed. "It's 80s night at the Union on Friday."

Was that it? Was I supposed to be impressed? "Um...so?"

"So we have to go!"

"We do?"

He shook his head like I'd said something stupid. "Of course we do! Apparently it's the best night of the year. Everyone dresses up and everything. And, well…"

I waited for him to finish. He was smiling innocently, looking up at the ceiling as if to appear heavenly, cherubic. I could see that he needed prompting.

"Well…what?"

"Oh, it's fine," he said, getting up and swanning over to the door. "Just that it's a very *special* night. *Magical.* A night that comes but once a year."

"At the Union? But there's a theme night, like, twice a month."

"Yeah, but this time's different, Ash. It's important to *me*."

"Why? What's so great about this one?"

"Take a guess," he said.

Honestly, I had no idea. I wasn't in the mood to play games with him, to figure out what he was trying to say. I just wanted to be left alone.

"Look, I don't know what you're going on about, but I'm tired, and I…"

Ezra rolled his eyes. "Forget it. Just say you'll come, yeah?"

I took a breath. This was exactly what I'd hoped to avoid. I wanted our friendship to be more casual, laid-back, the kind that didn't make any demands. I couldn't think of anything worse than going to the Union with him now. Couldn't he see that?

"Okay, fine," I said. "I'll come, but I still don't get why it's such a big deal."

Ezra grinned at me mischievously. "You just wait," he said, wiggling his eyebrows.

I didn't have a clue what he was making a fuss about, but I was already regretting the fact I'd said yes. I would have to make something up, find a way to get out of it later.

Another lie, I thought, remotely.

Although I'd been aware that the year was coming to an end, Christmas seemed to explode on campus without warning, springing up almost overnight. When I went to my Shakespeare class on Monday, there was an enormous Christmas tree outside the front gates, decorated with red and silver baubles. There were fairy lights in all the windows of the main buildings, and tinsel had been wrapped around the bannisters, green and furry as a growth of mould. It wasn't *ugly* exactly, just too early, premature. It wasn't December for another few days, and we still had four weeks left of term. I was too pissed off to feel merry and bright.

This wasn't helped by the fact that we were finally moving on to *Macbeth*. It definitely hadn't put me in the Christmas spirit, even though it was one of my favourites. I thought Jonah might prefer this play too, but for some reason, he never turned up to the lecture that morning. I had lunch in the English department afterwards, but I didn't run into him there either. I wasn't going to text him but I wondered if he was alright. He'd never missed a lecture before so I fired off a quick message, hoping I didn't sound too desperate.

Hey, Jonah. You doing OK? You weren't in the Macbeth lecture.

Hey yeh just didn't feel like it today, he said.

Oh, cool. Just wanted to check!

There was a long pause, then he wrote:

I miss u. cum 2 dodge on friday?

I wasn't sure what to say. We hadn't spoken since the night we'd been sexting each other, and I was still feeling a bit dirty – not just because I hadn't wanted to do it, but because I knew he'd lied about his photo. Still, if I wanted to see the boys less, I'd have to make more of an effort with Jonah. He was the only person I really cared about.

I text him back, said I'd be there.

I didn't say anything to Ezra about not going to the Union. I thought it made more sense to cancel at the last minute, a time when any excuse would seem more urgent, unavoidable. If I told him *too* early, he would hound me until I gave in. Haz and Sam were going anyway so it wasn't like I was abandoning him. I had no reason for feeling guilty.

I text him right before dinner on Friday. I said that I had a headache and – knowing he would come to my room to check on me – that I was going to the library to get some work done. I said to send my love to Haz and Sam, and that I hoped they all had a good time.

I knew he was upset when he didn't text back. I didn't want him to be annoyed with me, but 80s night really wasn't my thing. Anyway, we were always doing what *he* wanted to do. He still had friends to go with, and once he'd had a drink, he'd barely notice I wasn't there.

He'd forgive me in a few days.

At least, he always had before.

The fairy lights around Jonah's corkboard made the room look like an aquarium. They were cycling through different colours now – purple, blue, orange, pink – and though they were all pretty, they made everything look false. The room was so cheerful it felt like a trap.

I'd been excited all week about seeing Jonah again, but now that I was here, I was starting to wish I was somewhere else. He was playing ambient waterfall sounds through his speakers – water dripping, running, trickling over wet stones – and though it was relaxing enough, it made me feel like I couldn't breathe. It was like I was in a giant fish tank, everything bright and artificial. It felt like I was trapped and I couldn't get out.

I stood up and went over to the window. I played it off like I was checking my hair, but I really just wanted to see outside. Jonah cleared his throat behind me.

"What's up with you tonight?"

"Oh, nothing much," I said, feeling the warmth of the radiator against my shins. I could see a few latecomers heading to the Union. There were guys in flannel shirts and leather jackets, girls with massive, backcombed hair. I was kind of jealous I wasn't going.

"How come *we* never go out anywhere?" I asked, turning to face him.

Jonah looked confused. "I told you I wasn't ready to come out yet. My friends would know something was up if they saw us together. I'm not ready for that."

"Couldn't we just pretend to be friends or something?"

"Is that what you want?"

"I mean, it'd be nice to feel like we could actually do *some* stuff together."

It sounded like I was sulking. I needed to backtrack before he started to see me as a child, like someone moody, off-putting. But Jonah didn't seem to notice.

"Why do you care anyway? I thought you hated the Union?"

"I never said that. It's just –"

"Yeah, you did. You said it wasn't your scene."

"I didn't. I just said my friends were going and I wasn't in the mood then."

"Whatever. Why are you making it into a *thing*?"

I didn't know what to tell him. Why *did* I want to go out with him so badly? Obviously I hated feeling like a secret, like I was someone to be embarrassed of, but there was a part of me that wanted to show *him* off as well. I knew Jonah was out of my league. I wanted people to see us together, to see *me* with him. Was that so wrong?

"Okay, never mind," I said, sitting back down. "Forget I mentioned it."

Jonah looked at me for a long time, then turned away and finished his drink. There was something in the air between us tonight that felt hostile, a little aggressive. I'd assumed it was coming from him, but I wondered, like mud, if I'd actually dragged it in with me. I hadn't spoken to anyone all day, and cancelling on Ezra had put me in something of a funny mood – although I couldn't have said why. I watched Jonah refill his glass. I hadn't intended on confronting him about the nude he'd sent me, but it felt there was something unspoken between us. I knew I wouldn't be able to enjoy myself until I got it out of the way.

"Actually, I wanted to ask you something."

"Shoot," he said, checking his phone.

"It's about the photos we sent each other."

Jonah laughed but didn't look at me. "Yeah, that was so hot."

I didn't know why his voice made me sceptical. I knew my picture was nothing special really, so I still didn't believe him when he said things like this. Maybe I just couldn't imagine him being that sexually attracted to me. His body – smooth, firm, and perfectly formed – made me feel like the ugliest person alive. How could he fancy someone like me?

I cleared my throat. "Have you sent lots of nudes before?"

Jonah seemed to sense a trick. He put his phone down, looked at me assessingly, then seemed to regain his composure. "Yeah, a few. Why?"

"Oh, no reason. It's just that…" I paused, had another sip of my drink. "You said it was just for me, but you obviously took it before uni."

"Yeah, so?"

"So, it obviously wasn't just for me then."

I thought he'd get annoyed, but Jonah just smiled at me knowingly. "I meant it's for you *now*. I've taken loads of photos like that. Some are just for me, and some are for other people. That was the one I had on my phone. I didn't mean to make you jealous."

"I'm not!"

"It's cool, you can admit it."

"I'm really not! I was just wondering, that's all."

"Have you not sent one before then?"

I shook my head.

"Aw, I'm flattered," he said, leaning over and refilling my mug. "It was hot."

"Well, you didn't say anything after I sent it."

Jonah shrugged. "I was horny. I definitely enjoyed it though."

"Yeah?"

"*Definitely*," he said.

He screwed the lid on the vodka and put it back in the desk cupboard. I was trying to think of something to say, looking for a reason to keep him talking, when my phone started going off. It was Sam. I switched it to silent.

"Sorry," I said.

It stopped ringing and started up again. This time it was Haz. *They're obviously drunk,* I thought. I wasn't in the mood to hear them pleading with me to come out tonight. I wasn't even in the mood to speak to them. I put my phone face-down on his nightstand.

"Everything okay?" Jonah asked.

"Oh, it's just my friends. They're at the Union tonight and they wanted me to come. They're probably just wasted already."

"You should have gone with them."

"What, instead of hanging out with you?"

He shrugged again. "I mean, if that's what you wanted."

There was another long pause. It seemed neither of us knew what to say to each other now. I didn't know why he was acting so cold with me, like he didn't care that I was here, but when I glanced at him again, his face was nervous, almost hopeful.

"Do you want to stay here tonight?" he asked. "I know you said you wanted to take it slow, but after the other night, I thought maybe you…"

"Okay," I said.

"Yeah? You don't have to if you don't want to."

"No, I do. I *really* do."

I'm not sure why I said it. I wasn't sure I even trusted Jonah that much, but he was cute and he seemed to like me. Maybe it was because I was drifting apart from my friends, but I found myself wanting validation from him. I wanted to please him, make him happy.

"We don't have to do anything," he said, "but I've got some condoms, and…"

"Okay."

We looked at each other in silence. My heart was thundering in my chest and I felt like I might throw up, but why on earth was I holding back? I wanted to kiss him again, to sleep next to him, to feel his weight on top of mine. But also, in the back of my head, I knew he'd eventually lose interest, that this was my one chance to make him love me. What if I never met a boy as attractive as him again? I remembered what I'd been telling myself all term – to waste no time, to say yes to each opportunity. I didn't want to say no and regret it later.

"Let's do it," I said.

Jonah shot me a devilish smile – naughty, slightly carnivorous; it almost looked like he wanted to eat me. He stood up silently, and without another word, he pulled his sweatshirt over his head. He stepped closer, pushing my legs apart and standing in between them.

In the corner of the room, my phone flashed red like a sudden warning.

Seventeen

That night I dreamt I was in the wreckage of a car. I was slumped against the window of the passenger's side, my hair thickly matted with drying blood. Lights outside were flashing blue and red, blue and red, but I couldn't move or open the door; something heavy was blocking the way. I tried looking up. I was being pressed down by a huge tree that had landed on top of us, practically cutting the car in half. But I wanted to see who'd been driving. I could see a body in the driver's seat, slouched like a ragdoll over the steering wheel. I tried peering around the tree trunk but I still couldn't see who it was. The car was so mangled I couldn't move.

I woke up in Jonah's bed. His left arm was stretched across me, pressing me down into the mattress. I groaned and rolled onto my side, pushing his arm back over towards him. Jonah slowly opened his eyes. He looked confused for half a second, like he didn't know where he was or what I was doing in his bed. Then he smiled. "Morning, sexy."

"Morning," I replied.

I snuggled into his shoulder, breathing in deeply, smelling his skin. He smelled like the beach in the middle of summer – salty, musky, animalistic. I wondered if I'd ever been so close to another person. He put his arm around my shoulders, letting me nestle against his chest. Then, with his free hand, he grabbed his phone, scrolled through his messages.

"I should get up," he moaned. "I've got football in a few hours."

"Oh. Okay."

"Yeah, it's a big game today so I should probably start getting ready."

"What time's the game?"

"Soon," he said coolly, then started texting someone else.

But why did things feel so awkward between us? Now we'd actually had sex, I was hoping he'd be more affectionate, that he'd want to show me how much he liked me. But nothing had changed; he was just the same as he was before. Maybe I wanted too much from him. I mean, we'd literally just had sex! How could that *still* not be enough?

I rolled away from him and climbed out of bed. I quickly grabbed my underwear and started getting dressed, picking my clothes up from where I'd left them. I didn't know why I was so embarrassed to be naked in front of him. He'd literally seen every part of me, but I felt more exposed now than before. I buttoned my jacket all the way to the throat.

"Okay, I'm off then," I said, attempting to sound cheerful.

"Hang on," he said, voice cracking. "Come here first. Say bye properly."

He pulled me into a hug, kissing me wetly on the mouth. His skin, where he hadn't shaved, was as rough and scratchy as a tree. It was coarse enough to leave a mark.

"Thanks for coming over," he said.

"Thanks for having me. I had a really great time with you last night."

"Me too. It was fun, wasn't it?"

Fun? I thought. *Is that how you'd describe it?*

"Uh, yeah," I said, weakly. "Really fun."

I pulled away, stood up and started searching for my keys. The fairy lights around his corkboard – having been left on all night – gave only a faint, phantom glow, making the whole room look transparent. They flashed blue and red like the glare of an ambulance.

"Can we do this again soon?" I asked. "Next week maybe?"

"Mm-hm. I'll let you know when I'm free."

I nodded. "Okay, great. Well, I best head off then."

"Cool. See you," he said, then turned to the wall to check his phone.

*

I left Dodge and started making my way back home. It was just after eight o'clock. The sky was the colour of an apricot – orange and peach, a creamy white – and was dusted with clouds like powdered sugar. It looked as fake as a photo on Instagram. But the sky seemed closer too, as though I had grown a few feet overnight. *Has the world changed,* I wondered, *or have I?*

As I walked, I pulled my headphones out of my pocket. I was thinking of listening to my favourite *Xena* podcast, but as I started untangling the cord, I remembered that Haz and Sam had been trying to ring me. I pulled out my phone. I had eight missed calls from Sam and eleven from Haz. *Jesus!* I knew they'd wanted me to come, but I didn't think anyone cared *that* much. Maybe they knew I was phasing them out. Maybe they'd wanted to change my mind.

I typed a message into the WhatsApp group.

I'm guessing you lot had fun. I've got a billion missed calls from you guys!

My phone started ringing immediately. It was Sam. It wasn't even five seconds since I'd finished typing. I smiled and shook my head. These guys were ridiculous.

"Hey, Sam," I said. "How's it –"

"Where were you?"

Something in his voice made me stop walking. It was pointed, cold, nothing at all like the Sam I remembered. He sounded furious for some reason.

"Sorry? What's going on?"

"I said where the fuck were you last night?"

I swallowed hard. I couldn't understand why he sounded so angry. What had *I* done? He couldn't be pissed off that I hadn't come to the Union. Could he?

"Listen, I don't –"

"Of course you don't," he spat. "You haven't got a clue."

"What are you talking about? Why are you so upset with me?"

"Because Ezra got beaten up last night."

I felt my breath catch in my throat. It made a tiny, audible gasp.

"He got beaten up so badly we had to call an ambulance. He was asking for you, but you'd fucked off somewhere, hadn't you?"

"I was…I had a headache. I was in the library, and I –"

"Oh, come off it. Haz went to find you and said you weren't there."

I took a deep breath. "Is Ezra okay?"

"Yeah, he's alright. No thanks to you."

"And…where is he now?"

"He's back in his room. We went to hospital with him last night, but they let him out a few hours ago. His face is fucked-up though. He needed stitches all over one eye."

"Oh my god."

Sam's voice softened a little. "Yeah, it was bad, Ash. *Really* bad. And on his birthday too. Poor guy. I mean, nobody deserves that."

His birthday?

Suddenly it all made sense. Now I understood why he'd been going on and on about the Union, why he'd been asking me when my birthday was. He'd been dropping hints for weeks, but I'd been so dismissive I hadn't noticed. Why hadn't he just told me?

I sighed, took another breath. "Are *you* guys okay?"

"Yeah, we're both fine. Listen, I'd get over here as soon as you can if I were you. Ezra isn't very happy."

"With me?"

There was a long silence on the phone. I almost thought I'd lost signal, but then he chuckled in disbelief. "Do you *ever* think about anyone else?"

I struggled to respond. "I don't…I, um…"

But Sam had already hung up.

I stared at the screen, only half-understanding him, then – before I knew it – I was striding back towards Queensway, eyes stinging against the cold. But things couldn't be *that* bad if they'd discharged him already. And why was Sam so annoyed at me anyway? Obviously I felt bad for Ezra, but it's not like *I* was responsible. It probably would've happened whether I was there or not, so why was he so pissed off? I could hear my heartbeat in my ears, but even that couldn't block out Sam's words. *"Do you ever think about anyone else?"*

I broke into a jog outside campus, but as I went, I suddenly realised how wrong I'd been. I'd missed Ezra's birthday, I'd lied to him, and I'd ignored Haz and Sam when they needed me most. I was so concerned with having sex, with getting what I wanted, that I'd completely written them off, pushed them aside for a better offer. And it wasn't just that. I'd been annoyed with them for even ringing me! No one had ever called me selfish before, but now I could see how self-centred I was. I felt like the worst friend on the planet.

I was nearly back at Queensway when I heard someone calling my name. Charlotte, Emily, and Sarah – all bundled up in coats and scarves – were walking a few metres ahead.

"Ash! Hey, Ash!" one of them shouted.

God, not now, I thought. *Not now.*

I nodded but stuck to my pace, hoping they'd see I was in a rush. But the girls were completely oblivious. They skipped merrily towards me.

"Where are you off to?" asked Charlotte, our paths finally intersecting.

"Just back to Queensway."

"Yeah?"

"Yeah. Sorry, I'm in a bit of a hurry."

"Oh my god!" Emily squealed. "You're doing the walk of shame! I *thought* you looked hungover! You have to tell us everything. Which boy did you –"

"I didn't! I mean, I'm not..."

"But you're gay! You guys are always hooking up, right?"

I was about to tell her, politely, to go fuck herself, but she immediately started telling us about some one-night stand she'd had once, about some guy that she'd met in a taxi. I had no idea what she was talking about. I pictured Ezra lying in a hospital bed, tubes stuck in both arms and blood leaking from his mouth. *I have to get out of here,* I thought.

"Look, I need to go," I said, interrupting Emily's story. "I really can't talk now."

Charlotte put up her hands. "Oh, we only wanted to say..."

I dodged past her and started jogging towards the halls, trying to put them out of my mind. I was back in Queensway in three or four minutes. I scanned my key card outside the main doors and then flew around to Ezra's room, running down the hallways as fast as I could. The door was open when I got there. Haz and Sam were inside, creased and sad in last night's clothes. I thought they'd been crying, but it was just makeup they hadn't removed yet, crumbling to dust underneath their eyes. I looked over at the bed. Ezra was on top of the duvet, his head propped up on a stack of pillows. He was so washed-out he looked like a ghost.

"Oh fuck," I said.

It sounded weak, inadequate. But what was I supposed to say?

I heard Sam make a little sound of irritation behind me. I turned my head but he was pretending to be occupied, tidying something on Ezra's desk. Haz gave me a thin smile, but he looked like he didn't know what to do. I crouched on the floor beside the bed.

One of Ezra's eyes was glued shut, completely black as if covered in paint. The other had a huge lump underneath, the blueish-purple of an aubergine. There were nine stitches in his left eyebrow, and it looked so clumsily sewn together that it puckered all of the skin around it. His lips were pale and cracked and dry. I could see the blood in the corners, crusted.

I knelt down beside him and held his hand. He opened one eye. It was watery, shot with blood; I could see the whites and the pinkish roots.

"Hey, Ez," I said.

"Where were you then?" said Sam, still not looking at me.

Ezra shushed him. "It doesn't matter. He's here now."

His voice was lower than normal, croakier. I could see how much pain he was in already, how much it hurt for him to speak. I stood up and turned to Haz.

"What happened last night?"

"Let's go outside."

"Fucking hell," said Ezra, faintly. "I'm not an idiot. You *can* tell him."

Haz seemed hesitant, a bit unsure of himself, but after a while he gave a nod. "Okay," he said, and sighed. "Well, we ran into those guys from the Union again, the ones that Ezra got in a fight with. They obviously remembered us, and I guess they wanted to get him back. We were just queuing up to get in and they...well, you know."

"Yeah," said Sam. "Those guys that made fun of *you*. He'd been defending you then, and look where it's got him. I mean, he shouldn't have bothered, should he?"

"I know," I said. "I'm sorry."

"Sorry? What good's that to anyone now?"

Haz gently touched his arm. "Sam?"

This seemed to do the trick. He took a breath and let it out again slowly. His cheeks were still red, but now he looked more like the Sam I knew.

"Alright," he said. "Alright. I'm think I'm gonna go out for a walk."

He grabbed his phone and then stormed out of the room, still without ever meeting my gaze. I watched him go, abashed. Haz gave me the kindest smile he could manage.

"Don't worry about him," he said. "He's just tired."

"No, it's okay. I mean, he *is* right. I should've been there."

Haz opened his mouth. I could tell he wanted to ask me about where I'd been, but he seemed to think better of it. He nodded instead. "I better go and see if Sam's okay."

He left me alone with Ezra. I crouched down beside him again.

"God, I'm so sorry, Ez. This shouldn't have happened."

"It's alright."

"No, it isn't. I should've been there. And I shouldn't have lied about where I was. But I wish…I mean, I can't believe that I…"

"What?"

"That I missed your birthday," I said, sighing. "You've been dropping hints for weeks. I can't believe I just ignored them. I must be really fucking stupid."

Ezra shrugged. He tried to shift upwards but was wracked with a fit of coughing. It sounded heavy, full of phlegm. I was scared he'd start coughing up gobs of blood.

Sam was right, I thought. *This is my fault.*

It was *my* fault that Ezra had got in that fight after Halloween, and it was *my* fault it had happened again. I'd been getting more and more annoyed with Ezra for weeks, and he didn't deserve that at all. It was *me* who was in the wrong. I wondered if I'd taken him for granted. He was always talking about what great friends we were, how important we were to each other. Maybe I'd assumed that he'd always be there – no matter how badly I treated him. I'd gone from having no friends before uni to being the worst friend in the world.

"So, what happens now?" I asked. "Do you need to go back to the hospital?"

"Only to have my stitches out. I'm gonna look rough as guts for weeks though."

"Does it hurt?"

"Let's just say it's a miracle I'm alive," he said, swallowing.

Well, at least he's kept his sense of humour. I knew Ezra could take care of himself, but I kept picturing those guys attacking him, sneaking up on him, an ambush. I imagined Ezra in high spirits, minding his own business at the Union. I imagined their fists falling on his face, him calling out for help. I looked down and saw him watching me.

"Does it look bad?" he asked. "I haven't seen it yet."

"Oh, um…It's not *that* bad, it's just –"

"Don't lie," he said. "There's a mirror in my makeup bag. Can you show me?"

I felt like I should ask Haz and Sam first. "Is that a good idea?"

"Come on, it can't be worse than I'm imagining. Please?"

I sighed, walked over, grabbed the bag next to the sink. It was made of the same clear vinyl as a pencil case, and while I'd always found it ugly, now it just made me want to cry. His makeup looked so pathetic, so sadly hopeful inside of it – his lipsticks, his powders, his little pots of coloured glitter. I fished around for his mirror and brought it to him.

"Are you sure about this?" I asked.

He nodded. I held up the mirror so he could see and watched his face for a reaction. His expression didn't change. I wasn't sure if it was the swelling or if he really *had* been expecting worse. After a while, he started laughing.

"Oh well," he said. "It's done now."

"Come on, Ez. Don't be a martyr. Does it *really* hurt?"

"Not too much. Although I wish I hadn't posted that photo on Instagram now, the one where I drew on that busted lip. No one's gonna believe that this is real."

"Trust *you* to think about that," I said.

He smiled and looked away, staring up at the ceiling. His face took on a dreamy quality, like he was thinking about something else. "That was a joke," he added, wistfully.

"Oh, I know it was! I'm only teasing."

God, I couldn't even get *this* part right!

I couldn't think of anything to say, so I took the mirror back to his makeup bag. There were bloody tissues in the sink, brown and crispy as dead leaves, and I felt I should probably clean them up. I didn't want the boys to think I was useless, that I couldn't do anything for myself. When I turned back around, Ezra was watching, smiling sadly.

"Don't listen to Sam," he said. "You're a good friend, Ash. I mean it."

I smiled at him and nodded, then turned away to hide my face. But as I did, I caught sight of the photo of us on the wall, the one he had taken the night we'd met.

We were so happy then, I thought. *Why aren't we happy anymore?*

Eighteen

After Haz and Sam left, I stayed with Ezra for the rest of the day. He seemed to hate the room being silent, so I dragged a chair over to his bed and tried my best to keep him distracted. I talked about whatever topic sprang to mind – the people on my course, the books I'd just finished, my favourite episodes of *Xena* – anything to stop him dwelling too much on what had happened the night before. We talked and joked like we had when we'd first met, excitedly, teasingly, as if none of our fights had ever happened. But I still felt really guilty. If I had just said something whenever he annoyed me, those tensions never would've built up. It was no wonder I'd been so pissed off with him. I never told him how I was feeling.

But despite acting as though our friendship had turned a corner, we didn't talk about the Union, and I told him nothing about Jonah. I think we wanted to keep it light, to not have to talk about things too deeply. I kept trying to tell him that I'd had sex, that I wasn't a virgin anymore, but I couldn't find a way to work it in. It always felt like I was bragging. Then again, it was keeping things from Ezra that had caused these problems in the first place. It was like I was walking on a tightrope, teetering. I told myself I would tell him later.

When it started to get dark, I could see that Ezra was getting tired. I put his laptop onto his nightstand so he could watch a film, and told him to text me if he needed me. But once I was back in my room, I was pretty much ready to fall asleep. It had been an eventful twenty four hours, and all I wanted to do was stick on an episode of *Xena,* to just switch off for forty-five minutes. I picked an episode from the first season called 'Dreamworker.' Here, Xena has to enter her own nightmares – a realm known as the Dreamscape – in order to defeat her inner demons. It was a total classic. I climbed into bed and hit play, but I found I couldn't really concentrate. I was still thinking about Ezra. I couldn't stop picturing his face.

Towards the end of the episode, my phone flashed, started ringing. I glanced down and saw Sam's name. *Oh shit,* I thought. *I'm in trouble.*

I picked it up. "Hey, Sam!" Even to me, my voice sounded pathetic. It was like I was trying to act innocent, like there was nothing I had to feel sorry for. "Um…are you okay?"

"Yeah, fine," he said. "Listen, I think I owe you an apology."

"Oh, god, you don't have to say –"

"No, I do. It wasn't fair of me to take it out on you, or to blame you for not being there. I was just tired. It was a long night. I guess I was still a bit on edge."

"I mean, it's totally understandable."

"Yeah. Anyway, that's all I wanted to say."

My eyes wandered to the screen. Xena was fighting an evil version of herself.

"Well, thank you," I said, "but you really don't have to apologise. I'm sorry I wasn't there. And that you and Haz had to sort it out by yourselves."

"No problem," he said.

There was a long, awkward silence.

"Are you and Haz okay?" I asked.

"Yeah, it's just…"

Just what?

I could hear his rings clattering against the back of his phone. It sounded like he wanted to say something, but he was hesitant, shy, like he was worried he might upset me. Was he going to ask about Jonah? Or about where I was last night? I braced myself for the worst.

After a while he said, "Let's just forget it, yeah?"

I nodded, smiled, then remembered he couldn't see me.

"Okay, yeah," I said. "Sounds good."

"Cool. Well, I guess…um…have a good night then."

"You too. Will I see you guys again soon?"

"Oh, probably," he said, then hung up before I could even reply.

*

I spent Sunday with Ezra too. I took my notebook and a copy of *Macbeth* with me so I could make a start on my next assignment. The essay wasn't due until the end of term, but it was 5000 words long, and I wanted to get it out of the way. I'd already chosen my essay question: "To what extent are Macbeth and Lady Macbeth sympathetic characters? Who exactly is to blame for the play's events?" But now I'd committed to the question, I couldn't say *who* was the most responsible. Macbeth had been the one to kill the king, but it had been Lady Macbeth's idea. And what about the witches? I'd assumed the play was a straightforward one, but the more I thought about the characters, the less I felt I understood them. Every story had heroes and villains, but I found it hard to tell which was which. What did *that* say about me?

Ezra was sitting on his bed, watching a DVD on his laptop. He'd chosen an old horror film from the 70s called *Black Christmas*, and was laughing as the sorority girls were being picked off one by one. He tutted and scoffed at various points of the film, demolishing a family pack of Skittles which he was fisting with one hand. Surely *that* was a good sign.

"You alright over there?" I asked, not turning away from his desk.

"Yes, thanks, Dad," he said, sarcastically.

I rolled my eyes and shook my head, but then I thought about his parents. Where had *they* been through all of this? My mum would have driven to hospital, bribed the nurses to be admitted. She'd never let me hear the end of it. His hadn't even sent a text.

"How are your mum and dad?" I asked.

"Huh?"

"You've told them everything, right?"

Ezra made a little noise, half angry, half puzzled. I turned around. I thought he was crying, but it was just his eyes, sticky with pus. He wiped his lashes on his sleeve.

"Hey, I'm sorry. I didn't mean to upset you."

"No, it's cool," he said, clearing his throat. "I, um…I haven't told them. I mean, why bother, right? They'd only say it was all my fault."

"Really?"

"Yeah, they'd say I provoked them, or that it was because of the way I dress. They think I draw too much attention to myself. They'd tell me I deserved it."

"Come on, Ez. They wouldn't think that."

"You don't know them," he said. "They kicked me out of the house when I told them I was gay. I had to go and live with my nan for a year."

"Jeez, you never told me that. How old were you?"

"Fifteen? They said they didn't want a faggot for a son." He chuckled thoughtfully. "Tough shit, I guess. The only reason I came back was because my nan died. There was nowhere else for me to go. I'd still be living there now – you know, if she was alive."

"God, I'm so sorry, Ez."

He shrugged. "Whatever. It's done now."

I tried to remember what he'd said about his parents. He'd told us they were shocked when he came out and that they didn't approve of his lifestyle. He'd also said that they didn't talk much anymore, but I had no idea things had been that bad for him. No wonder he was so needy! Everyone just treated him like an inconvenience, like someone they wanted out of the way. And *I'd* done exactly the same thing. I was even more selfish than I knew.

I left Ezra to his film and turned back to my *Macbeth* essay. I'd been working for an hour and my notebook was still empty. I'd only written down one quote: "False face must hide what the false heart doth know," though I couldn't remember exactly why.

How would I ever get this essay done? I had no idea what I was even saying.

I looked down at my phone and saw I had a new text from Jonah.

Hey u

He'd been in the back of my mind ever since yesterday morning. Ezra had taken up most of my thoughts but Jonah was there in the background, hovering behind them like a song. I had a sudden memory of the other night: my chest pressed up against his; his taste on my lips; various combinations of hands, mouths, and fingers. I shifted around on Ezra's chair.

Hey, I typed. **You OK?**

Just thinking about the other night ;)

Oh yeah?

A pause, then:

Want another go on Friday? I haven't finished with u yet.

I shivered. How on earth had this happened? A few weeks ago, Jonah was still Nose Ring Boy – the cute guy in my Shakespeare class – and now we were…a thing? Was he my boyfriend? Were we official? Was this something I needed to bring up?

I'd love to! I replied.

But what did he even want from me? We'd been on three dates already, and now we'd also gone *all the way*. I knew he still didn't want to come out, but we could at least be exclusive, even if we *were* still a secret. And who knows? Maybe he'd be more inclined to tell people he was gay now that he actually had a boyfriend. The thought made me excited. *Ash and Jonah. Jonah and Ash.* We sounded strong and important. Biblical.

Behind me, I heard Ezra's phone go off, the little drumming sound from Grindr. I turned around and saw him reading his message, dabbing his eyes again with his sleeve, careful not to press too hard on his bruises. I suddenly felt like I couldn't leave him. I couldn't just ditch him on a Friday night again, not without telling him where I was going.

Can I let you know? I wrote, turning back around. **I want to see you again soon, but I might have plans with my friends on Friday. I'll text you, OK?**

Oh. Yeh that's fine.

Are you sure? x

I didn't want to cancel on him, but this was all part of the game, right? You had to play hard to get to keep people interested. At least, that's what I'd seen in films.

I watched my phone, waiting for his reply, but Jonah had disappeared. I turned back, with reluctance, to my essay. I started making some notes, underlining some of the words in Macbeth's soliloquy, but something in the room felt weirdly different, a tension I wasn't able to place. It seemed too quiet, too still. It felt like the calm before a storm.

On Ezra's laptop, I heard the film come to an end, heard it cycle back to the menu. But Ezra didn't move. He was still typing away on his phone, engrossed in whatever was happening on Grindr. I wanted to ask who he was talking to but it was really none of my business. He hadn't asked who *I* was texting. I thought I should probably leave him to it.

"So," I said, spinning the chair around. "How was *Black Christmas*? There was a lot of screaming towards the end there. Did they ever find the killer?"

Ezra looked up like he hadn't heard me. There was a strange look on his face, one I'd never seen on him before: a little cold, almost angry. His mouth turned up at the corners like he had just been told a secret. For a second, I was scared of him.

"Oh," he said, "yeah. Turns out he was inside the house all along."

Nineteen

Now it was December, everyone on campus seemed to be fully in the Christmas spirit. Students in scarves and festive jumpers drank chai lattes in the cafés, and posters everywhere announced a whole host of themed events, from carol services in the chapel to fancy dress nights at the Union. They had even installed a fake snow machine outside the main building, creating an artificial blizzard each day, which – when it finally settled on the pavement – soon turned brown and smelled like cat food. But nobody complained. Everyone was in such a good mood that they just pretended not to notice. Gradually it turned into a thick, greyish sludge.

Jonah was in the Shakespeare lecture that week, and though I kept looking over, I could never seem to catch his eye. What was his problem? I hadn't expected him to suddenly come out to the whole campus, but I thought having sex with me might've meant something, that we would've moved a step forward, that it might've cleared a few things up for him. Maybe he was nervous around me now – especially since I'd told him that I was busy on Friday night. I didn't want him to think I regretted it. I couldn't wait to do it again.

Ezra's bruises slowly started to fade, turning from a blackened purple to a dull, yellowish green. I asked if he wanted me to go with him to have his stitches out, but he said he'd rather go alone. I think he wanted the whole thing over and done with, but I was surprised at how quiet he was, how reticent, untalkative. I'd taken him to be the kind of person to make a song and dance over everything – but this time it was different. Now he wanted to draw as little attention to himself as possible, emailing his teachers for the lecture notes so he wouldn't have to be seen on campus. He'd been beaten up in the past and he'd revelled in it then, taking selfies, showing off. So why wouldn't he tell me what had changed?

On Thursday evening, I was getting ready to bring Ezra's dinner to his room when my phone started ringing. It was my mum. I couldn't remember the last time I'd called her.

"Hey, Mum! How's it going?"

"Oh, thank god you're alive," she said, letting out a sigh. "Do you know what I thought when I hadn't heard from you? I thought you were dead."

I rolled my eyes. "I mean, you could always call *me*."

"You're right," she said, drily. "What a neglectful mother I am."

"Oh, stop it. How *are* you?"

"I'm good! But how are things? I've been worried about you."

"You have?"

"Of course! I'm always worrying."

There was an awkward pause, about two or three seconds too long.

Then she said, "So, anyway, what's new?"

I hesitated. I hadn't told her about Ezra getting beaten up, or the fight we'd had, or that I was basically in a relationship. The last time she'd called, I'd told her only the bare-bones. It hadn't felt dishonest at the time, but now I could see I had been unfair.

"Sorry for not calling," I said. "It's just that…Ezra got beaten up at the weekend."

Mum gasped.

"Yeah, he got attacked by some guy at the Union. He had to go to hospital and everything. He's fine now, but I've been looking after him all week."

"Oh my god. What did his parents say?"

Trust her to think of them first, I thought.

"He hasn't told them yet," I said. "I don't think they're very close. They don't approve of him being gay. Ezra doesn't really tell them anything."

There was another moment of silence. If there was one thing Mum hated, it was parents who didn't support their kids. I thought she might launch into one of her speeches again, but she was quiet for a long time. Eventually she said, "That must be really hard."

"I know. He's okay though. His bruises are going down already."

"And are *you* alright? Nobody's been trying to beat *you* up, have they?"

I groaned. Why did she *always* make me feel like a five-year-old? It didn't matter how long I'd been away, or that I was legally an adult. Three minutes with her on the phone and I had regressed back to being a child. "No, Mum. No one's trying to beat me up."

"Oh, good."

We both waited for the other to speak. I could sense I was being funny with her because I was holding so much back, and then, before I could stop myself, I was telling her everything that had happened – about Jonah, my friends, how I'd missed out on Ezra's birthday. I told her about my nights at Dodge, about my first kiss up on the roof, and how I had changed in the last few months. The only thing I skipped over – out of deference to her – was the part where I'd actually had sex. She probably didn't need to know that.

When I was done, she breathed out heavily.

"Well, say *something*," I said, nervous.

"Just…I think…" She paused, sighed again. "Just remember to put your friends first. Boys come and go, but your friends will be there when things don't work out."

Why wouldn't things work out with Jonah? I thought that she'd take my side, that she'd tell me everything would be alright, but I just didn't have the strength to argue.

"Okay," I said. "Thanks, Mum."

"No problem. But I was just thinking, why don't you invite Ezra to ours for Christmas? It'll just be the two of us, and if he won't have fun with *his* parents…"

I caught sight of my reflection in the mirror, looking anxious, a little wary. I'd never brought anyone home for Christmas with me before. I'd never *had* anyone to bring home. I suddenly realised she was right; I was lucky Ezra and I were still friends. A week ago I was trying to phase him out of my life for good. *Now* look at where we were.

"Okay," I said. "Yeah, I'll ask him."

"Great. And darling, if you're going to have sex, please wear a condom."

Mortified, I hung up.

The next night, I assumed Ezra and I would spend the evening in his room, hanging out and watching films. But Ezra, when I got there, was already putting on his makeup. He'd covered the green patch under his eye and accentuated the bruises with purple powder, making them look intentional, dark, dramatic. He said he'd been stuck in his room long enough and that he wanted to go out.

He'd already text the boys and Haz had invited us back to Pemberton. We could drink and watch films there. He asked me what I thought of his Friday night plan.

"I don't know," I said. "I think I'd rather stay here."

"Why? We've been inside all week."

"I know, it's just…"

I'd carefully avoided talking about Sam and Haz to him. I obviously felt better after Sam had called me, but I wasn't exactly excited to see them. I didn't know where we stood, or what the dynamics were anymore. I wasn't convinced that they even liked me.

Ezra zipped up his makeup bag. "I know you feel funny about Sam," he said, "but it's fine. He's not angry with you. And the longer you leave it, the more awkward it's going to be. Better do it quick, like ripping off a bandage."

I had a sudden vision of Ezra's face covered in bruises, of the bloody tissues in the sink. I shook the image from my mind. "Alright, fine," I said. "I'll come."

Ezra smiled in a way that projected no happiness, no warmth. What was going on with him tonight? I sensed there was something on his mind.

"Good boy," he said coldly, then turned away to assess his makeup.

Pemberton was an S-shaped building, newly-built, and fronted with panels of thick green glass. Haz's room was on the first floor. I hadn't been able to imagine his room at all, but now I was here, I couldn't see it any other way. Beside his bed, he'd laid out a Persian rug patterned with red and orange diamonds, and hung a tapestry on the wall of a flowered tree in an ornate garden. His desk was covered in art materials – sketchbooks, tubes of watercolours, jam jars crusted with stripes of paint – and there were bolts of fabric stood up in the corner, all tied together with lengths of string. He gave Ezra a hug as we came inside.

"I love your room!" said Ezra, stealing my thunder.

"Aw, thanks," he replied, pulling away and hugging me. "Sam's always making fun of me for putting so much effort in, but it's home, right? I want it to feel cosy."

Sam was standing by the window, looking as awkward as I felt. I had the impression he didn't like talking about his feelings much, but there was still something unresolved between us. What else was there to say though? We'd both apologised already.

Ezra hugged him and then stepped aside to let me through.

Sam looked at me blankly. "Don't I get a hug?"

I smiled and grabbed him. The two of us started laughing, holding each other around the shoulders. Maybe we'd said all we needed to say. Maybe this was enough, this closeness, this physical contact between friends. We pulled away from each other, still laughing, but I noticed Ezra was watching narrowly, his face a picture of disgust.

"You guys are weird," he said, repulsed, but I couldn't tell if he was joking.

Haz disappeared and reappeared a moment later, carrying in a huge tray of champagne saucers. He put it down on the desk, filled each glass with prosecco, and then started to hand them out. I took mine nervously, not wanting to spill anything on the rug.

"I didn't realise we were being so fancy tonight," I said.

Haz laughed and shushed me. "They're not mine. I found the glasses in the kitchen. I don't think anyone's used them yet, so…"

"No, no, it's great. I feel very grown up."

Sam asked Ezra how he was doing. He told them about having his stitches out, about how much better he was feeling now, but he still wasn't acting like himself. There was something in his voice, some note of cheerfulness that didn't ring true. I wondered if I should change the subject, take the heat off him a bit. I reached up and ran my fingers across the tapestry, playing with the fringe, a tawny floss.

"Is this from Iran?" I asked.

Haz nodded. "Mm-hm. I've never been but my grandparents are always sending me stuff like this. It's cute though, right?"

"Would you want to go?"

"Sure, some day. It's not exactly great for the gays though. I'd have to pretend to be straight the whole time I was there."

"Well, you could *try*," said Sam.

Haz put his middle finger up. Sam grabbed it and pulled it to his mouth, gave it a quick, sloppy kiss. Ezra and I laughed but I found myself thinking about Jonah. I couldn't imagine ever being out in the open with him like this: going to parties, meeting friends, introducing him as my boyfriend. I wanted to – god, I wanted to – but I was scared he would never come out, that he didn't like *me* enough to go public. *Text him before it's too late,* I thought.

As the others caught up on their respective weeks, I asked if I could look at Haz's sketchbooks. I knew that he studied art, but for some reason, I'd assumed he had meant the theory side, or history; I hadn't realised that he was an artist. He handed a couple of them to me. They were filled with intricate pencil sketches – dark and crosshatched – that reminded me of art from the nineteenth century. On one page, two boys sat atop a giant, horse-sized swan. On another, three witches emerged from behind a cloud of putrid smoke. When I told him they were amazing, he tried his best to take them off me, but he looked the happiest I'd ever seen him. It was nice getting to know him better. I still didn't know him as well as I wanted to.

Once we were onto the second bottle of prosecco, we started watching *The Muppet Christmas Carol*. It was Ezra's choice, but since we were starting to feel the effects of the drink, nobody put up too much of a fight. In fact, *I* was the only one who'd been reluctant. Sam and Haz pretended to be cool, but three seconds in and they were drunkenly singing along, imitating mice, then cockney cabbages. And they thought *Xena* had been weird!

I obviously knew the story, but I'd never watched the Muppet version before. It was surprisingly touching. I'm pretty sure I saw Haz dabbing his eyes once or twice, and when the Ghost of Christmas Present arrived, Sam was grinning at him like an idiot.

"Bloody masterpiece," he said.

But Ezra didn't seem to be enjoying it. I knew he'd seen it loads of times before, but he seemed bored and disinterested; he was on his phone for two thirds of the film. It looked like he was texting someone, but since Haz and Sam were sat between us, I couldn't quite tell what he was doing. Whenever I glanced over, he was always smiling down at his phone, but it was the smile he'd given me earlier. It was beginning to creep me out.

While Scrooge was being shown his future, I got out my phone and opened Instagram. I wasn't following Jonah, but I'd seen his profile before and had started checking it now and again. I was expecting to see the same old pictures, but he'd uploaded a new one tonight. It was a photo of him at the Union, holding a balloon in the shape of a heart. There was no caption underneath, only a series of emojis: a shooting star, a rainbow flag, two stickmen holding hands. I scrolled down, scanned through the comments.

"Proud of you mate!"

"Congratulations!"

"Yass kween!"

"OMG!"

So that was it. He had finally come out. But why do it now? What had changed? Why did he suddenly feel ready? He'd asked me to stay over again so I knew I shouldn't feel threatened, but in my heart, I was also scared that things would be different between us now, that his future might not include me. I suddenly realised the film was over.

"Is something wrong?" asked Haz, refilling my glass.

The others were all staring. I locked my phone, quickly put it away.

"Not at all," I said, blushing, but I could see no one believed me.

Twenty

I text Jonah the next day.

Hey! I saw your Instagram post. Congratulations!

Two ticks appeared next to my message, but I didn't get a reply. I tried again.

Maybe we can hang out next Friday?

His reply to *that* was immediate.

Sorry I cant. It's a friends bday

Was it an excuse? It sounded like one. Normally I had to wait ages for him to text me back, but this was like something he'd had prepared.

No worries! Maybe the week after then?

Yeh cool. Ill let u know

Maybe he really *did* want to keep things casual between us. I hadn't seen him in a while so I knew I hadn't done anything wrong, but why was he being so hard to pin down? I told myself not to reply, that I should leave him wanting more, but that was easier said than done.

I typed my next message without even thinking.

Are you annoyed with me or something?

I read it back and winced. I already knew it was a mistake. I was about to send something else, but Jonah typed back right away.

Of course not! Definitely want 2 c u soon! xx

I breathed a sigh of relief.

Nothing had changed. Me and him were still perfectly fine.

But then I thought, *well, for how long?*

Before I knew it, the autumn term was almost over. Jonah and I hadn't managed to hang out again since the night that we'd had sex, mainly because one of us was always too busy. But a few days before the Christmas break, he text me to say he was coming back to campus on the 27th, a full two weeks before term started. Since most people would be gone until the 10th of January, he thought we could spend some time alone together, just the two of us in Dodge. It sounded too good to be true. For the last few weeks of term, something was always in the way – a deadline, a football match, an unnamed flatmate's birthday – so it would be nice to have him all to myself. I told him I'd text my mum, that I would see what I could do.

Ezra was also coming back early. I'd invited him home with me for the holidays, and though I could see he wanted to, he said there was no way he'd be allowed. Christmas was the one time of the year his parents wouldn't negotiate on. They hardly even talked, but they still wouldn't let him come to ours. "How would that seem to the neighbours?" they'd said. "How do you think that'd make us look?" Ezra had put them on speakerphone, letting me hear their conversation. Whenever they spoke, he looked at me with a half-smile, almost talking to me telepathically. *Here. Didn't I tell you? This is the shit that I have to put up with.*

So, he was seeing them for Christmas and coming back again on Boxing Day. I'd planned on staying with my mum at least until the new year, but with Jonah and Ezra around, I figured I might have to change my plans. I didn't have any reason not to.

But Ezra hadn't been himself around me since the night after he'd been punched. I was starting to think he might have PTSD, that it might have affected him more than I thought. I'd even suggested he speak to one of the counsellors on campus. He shrugged me off, told me he'd think about it, said he was sorting things out on his own. But once or twice a week he spent his evenings somewhere else. Maybe he'd managed to find someone to talk to.

On the last day of term, we met Haz and Sam in the café next to the English department. Since none of us had much money, we'd decided to do Secret Santa. I'd been given Haz and I had bought him a new sketchbook. The cover – a soft brown suede – was patterned with tigers, ferns and flowers, all of them twisted up together. It had reminded me of Haz's room, of the woven tapestry pinned to the wall. I watched his face nervously as he unwrapped it.

"I love it!" he said, turning it over in his hands. "Do I have to guess who it's from?"

"Not yet," said Sam. "Not until everyone's opened their gift."

"Okay, my turn," said Ezra, tearing into a present wrapped in gold foil. It was an antique cigarette holder, not long and feminine like I imagined them to be, but short and thick, around four inches long. The tip, made of sterling silver, was carved with an intricate floral design. I knew that it must've been expensive. It made my present for Haz look lame.

"Thank you," he said, sounding not even remotely grateful. "It's lovely."

Sam tried to smile. "Okay, Ash. Your turn."

I had a feeling I knew who my Secret Santa was already. My present was wrapped in black paper, glossy to the touch and covered in huge, crimson roses. It looked like Victorian wallpaper, like something torn from a gothic novel. Surely it had to be from Ezra.

I opened the present. Inside was a black T-shirt folded neatly into a square. I turned it over and gasped. On the front was a photo of Xena, proudly emerging from a wall of flames. I knew that it had to be vintage too. I'd never seen anything so perfect.

"Oh my gosh," I said, staring at the image.

I glanced over at Ezra. He was looking down at his hands, picking off flakes of his week-old nail polish, but I knew it had to be from him. No one else would've bought me that.

"Thank you," I said to the table, trying not to make it too obvious.

"Amazing," said Sam. "Now me."

Inside a tiny square box, Sam pulled out a moonstone ring. It looked silvery-white from a distance, but up close, it was full of colours – blues and greens and frosty purples. He slid it onto his middle finger and held it up to catch the light. "Bangin'," he said, happily.

All in all, I was impressed with how well we had done. Everyone but Ezra seemed really pleased, and even that was understandable. He was less open than he used to be, less comfortable expressing his feelings. I think we all felt really bad for him.

"When are you guys coming back to campus?" I asked.

Sam took a sip of his coffee. "Just after New Year's, I think. I don't want to spend too much time away from this one," he said, nudging Haz.

"I guess this'll be the longest you've been apart."

Haz shrugged. "*I'm* looking forward to it," he said, and smiled.

We spent the rest of the time talking about our Christmas traditions – when we watched the Queen's speech, what time we opened all our presents. Haz and Sam seemed excited to be going home, but Ezra mostly just sat and listened. He hadn't spoken to his parents properly since before the start of term, and I knew the thought of spending time with them was making him anxious, slightly on edge. I really wished he was coming with me. I could imagine how well he'd get on with my mum. I could already picture the two of them in the kitchen, dancing around to the radio while I pretended to be embarrassed. I wondered if I'd done enough to persuade him. I hope he knew how much I wanted him there.

Once we'd finished our drinks, we all said our goodbyes. The last few weeks of term had erased all of the tension between us; now we were just four best friends, complaining about how much we were going to miss each other. And I *would* miss them too. I didn't know how I would've survived the term without them, even if we did have our ups and downs. But what friendship group didn't? I was lucky to have them in my life, and ever since Ezra had gone to the hospital, I'd never taken them for granted. I swore I never would again.

After saying goodbye to the boys, Ezra and I left the campus and started heading back towards Queensway. My mum was picking me up in a few hours and I still hadn't packed away my things. As I held onto my new T-shirt, I looked over at Ezra, touched.

"Thanks for my present, Ez. I love it. Honestly, it's the best gift I've ever received."

"Oh, it's fine," he said. His voice was flat, unmelodious. "I bought it ages ago. I forgot I even had it. But I'm glad you like it. You can wear it and think of me."

"Of course I will. Seriously though, thank you."

"You're welcome. Thanks for being such a good friend."

He said it like he didn't mean it, like the opposite was true. There was that pang of guilt again, hot and sudden, sharp as a stabbing. I didn't know why I still felt guilty about him calling me that. We *were* friends again – maybe even better than before – and if I'd made some mistakes, I felt I was starting to make up for them. So why did it still bother me?

"Are you sure you don't want to come to mine for Christmas?" I asked. "Mum and I would love to have you. She could even talk to your parents if you…"

"No, it's cool. Thanks though."

"Okay, no worries. What are friends for, right?"

He shot me a funny look, like he was trying to work out what I meant. I wanted to tell him about my plans to come back early, but I thought I'd keep it a surprise. I figured he'd be more excited if I just turned up randomly, if I walked into Queensway when he wasn't expecting it. Especially after spending Christmas Day alone with his parents. I couldn't think of anything more depressing. And I hadn't even met them!

Poor Ez, I thought, sadly. *Nothing ever seems to work out for him.*

As we walked down the road, he tried smoking a cigarette, but it was too windy for him to light one. He coughed into his hand. I watched the sparks blow away on the wind.

Twenty one

I was hoping Mum would get to meet Ezra when she came to collect me, but she ended up stuck in traffic and Ezra was gone before she arrived. I was scared she didn't believe that he was a real person, that I'd made him up or that I'd lied about having friends. But I was so glad to see her when she pulled in – waving like I was a kid coming home from school – that I didn't give Ezra a second thought. I was so excited I wanted to shout, but I tried my best to look unfazed. I wanted her to see me as an adult, self-sufficient, as someone who didn't need looking after. I was a different person now. I was a better version of myself.

After a long hug, I led her through reception, down the hall and into my room. She looked around at my things, pretending not to be checking for dust.

"You've done a good job keeping it clean. I almost brought the hoover with me!"

"Thanks for the vote of confidence," I said.

"Have you been hanging up your wet towels?"

"Yeah. Of course I have."

I sounded defensive.

"And how's the food? You're not just eating Pot Noodles, are you?"

"Jesus! No, I'm fine, Mum."

I didn't mean to be impatient, but why did she always make me feel like I needed coddling, like I couldn't be trusted to live on my own? I thought we had both moved past that.

"Alright," she said. "It was only a joke."

It wasn't but I let it slide.

"And you're sure you've got everything?" she asked.

I nodded.

"Okay. Let's get this show on the road then."

We loaded my stuff into the car and started making our way back home. Mum asked me about my friends, my course, which lecturers were my favourites, but though I could tell that she wanted to ask, she did her best not to mention Jonah. In the past she'd often warned me about safe sex and STIs, but since I'd never been with a boy before, everything she'd said had been hypothetical. Now that it was real, she didn't want to know the specifics. And that was fine with me. I didn't want her to know about Jonah. It was private, secret, something I didn't want to share. Or, perhaps more likely, I was afraid that she wouldn't approve.

Mum had taken the week off work and we spent a lot of time catching up, talking about what we'd missed, and just hanging out around the house. We cooked dinner together like we had before uni, and we watched *Xena* every evening too, choosing random episodes here and there. She'd even waited for me to come back so we could put up the decorations. We pulled out the plastic tree that we kept up in the loft, dressing it in tinsel, lights, ribbons – anything we could find in the box marked *Xmas*. It was pretty ugly when we were finished, but we'd had so much fun putting it up that I think she actually quite liked it. She had a tiny photo of Dad, framed in a square of sequined plastic, that she hung underneath the angel.

"Now it's perfect," she said, and hugged me.

I spent the rest of the time reading my books for the spring term. I'd chosen a new elective – the complete works of the Brontë sisters – but when I flicked through the books on the course, the writing was tiny, hardly legible. Still, I'd be ahead as long as I finished a couple of them before term started, and once I was back on campus, I wouldn't have anything else to do. I figured I could read all day and then hang out with friends in the evening – Ezra one night, Jonah the next. I'd have to let know Ezra know where I was going, but I felt I was ready to tell him the truth. I didn't want to keep any more secrets.

Since being home, I'd text him a few times and got back short, one-word answers. I wondered if he was annoyed with me. I knew he was probably busy with his parents, but given how little they talked, I'd assumed he'd be happy to be distracted. Jonah was the same, although *his* texts were less surprising. When he replied, it was often only in emojis – a thumbs up, a smiley face, once or twice a purple devil. It was like he'd run out of things to say to me, like writing a message was too much effort. But what had I expected? I mean, we weren't exactly close friends. He'd be more responsive when I saw him in person.

At least, that's what I was telling myself anyway.

Christmas Day was lovely. Mum and I gave each other our gifts in the morning, sitting around the tree like we did when I was little. Mum had bought me some new clothes – a pair of jeans, some socks and underwear, a couple of shirts she had found in Primark. But even though I was having a great time, it didn't really feel like Christmas. I wanted it to be special, unforgettable, but the whole day felt routine. Was that how it felt to become an adult?

After dinner, we sat in front of the TV, trying to find something to watch. There was no *It's a Wonderful Life*, no *Gone with the Wind* on this year. It was all just Christmas editions of game shows. It was starting to feel like a boring Sunday.

"Have you spoken to your friends today?" she asked.

I'd got generic 'Merry Christmas!' texts from the boys, but that was all I'd heard from them so far. No one had told me what they were doing, or what they'd received, or how they were getting on with their families. I was a little disappointed. I knew they were busy, and I *was* having a great time, but it would've been nice to feel like they cared about me, that they wanted to see if I was okay. It felt a bit like they'd forgotten me.

"Not really," I said. "They text me this morning, but they're probably too busy now. Haz and Sam both have big families."

"And Ezra?"

"I don't know. He's been quiet for a few days. I hope he's alright."

She nodded, hummed, carried on flicking through the channels.

"And what about your boyfriend?" she asked, still not looking at me.

"Jonah? He's not my boyfriend."

"No?"

"Not really. Um...It's kind of complicated."

"Oh?"

I was starting to regret telling her about him. "Yeah, I guess we're kind of seeing each other, but it's not official or anything. He only came out a few weeks ago."

"Has he been with boys before?"

"Not before me, no."

"And you trust him? He's not messing you around?"

"Jesus, why does everyone keep saying that?"

Mum turned to me sharply. "Who's saying that?"

I swallowed, feeling caught out. Why hadn't I just kept quiet?

"The boys," I said. It sounded like a confession. "They were worried I'd end up getting hurt by him not wanting to commit, but they're only looking out for me. They don't even know him, Mum. He's a nice guy. Really he is. I think you'd like him."

She looked at me nervously, almost sadly, as if she was thinking of something to say. "Just…" she paused, turned back to the TV. "Just be careful, alright?"

But I *was* being careful, wasn't I? Jonah was keeping me at arm's length anyway, and I'd always been realistic about our relationship, even if I *did* feel like I was in love with him. I couldn't see Jonah doing anything to hurt me intentionally. Why would he?

"Okay," I said. "I will."

But I don't think either of us were convinced.

I felt bad about going back early, especially after having had such a nice time at home. I decided to go back on the 28th – mainly because it was the only day that Mum was free to drive me. I was worried about Ezra being stuck there on his own, and now that Jonah was back too, I had no reason to stay away. But it was Jonah I was most excited about. Seeing him one-on-one would make him remember why he liked me, why he was drawn to me in the first place. I told myself it was all we needed. I could already picture us alone in his room, his skin transformed in the glow of his fairy lights, blue and pink and fiery red. Maybe he'd take me back up to the roof. Maybe he'd kiss me, tell me he loved me, say he was lucky to be my boyfriend. It was the only thing I wanted. I needed to show him how good things could be.

After driving for an hour, Mum dropped me off in the Queensway carpark.

"Do you want me to come and help you unpack?" she asked, pulling my bags from the boot of the car. "I can do some cleaning too if you want. I don't mind."

"No, thanks. You've done enough for me already."

"Are you sure?"

"I'll be fine, Mum. I can manage." I put the bags down on the tarmac and then pulled her into a hug. "Thanks for a great Christmas. I had a really good time."

"It *was* nice, wasn't it?" she said, giving me a squeeze. "But don't be a stranger, Ashley. I know you're busy, but call your mother from time to time, alright?"

"I will, Mum. I promise."

I waved her off and started dragging my bags inside. I'd only been gone for six days, but my room was dark and smelled of mould. Had it always smelled like that? I opened the window and began to rummage through my bags, looking for chocolates to give to Ezra. Mum had bought them really, but I'd eaten more than enough for one year. Besides, Ezra would never buy chocolates for himself. He never thought about food at all.

I carried the chocolates to Ezra's room and knocked on the door. There was no answer. *Huh.* The bar and the dining hall were both closed, and I'd walked past the common room on my way in. I checked everywhere I could think of – the computer centre, the laundry room, the benches outside the dining hall – but I couldn't find Ezra anywhere. Where was he?

I went back to my room a little deflated. Haz and Sam still weren't back yet so he couldn't be with them. I realised he must be on campus somewhere; it was the only place I hadn't checked. He was either (a) in one of the cafés, or (b) in the library. He sometimes went there to watch films in the downstairs screening room. I figured it was my best shot.

I sent him a text as I started walking.

Hey, Ez! What are you up? Hope Queensway isn't too lonely!

I slid my phone back into my pocket. I'd always thought the week between Christmas and New Year was a depressing one, but it was a nice day, fairly mild, and though the sky was blank and grey, the sun seemed to glint like a silver coin.

I reached the library and checked my phone. Ezra had already replied.

Hey! Queensway is fine, thanks! Just watching some films in my room. As usual!

I must have missed him. Maybe he'd popped out for something and I'd just swung by at the wrong time. How annoying! Oh well, I supposed it didn't matter. I could grab my books from the library and still be back in less than an hour. I was about to open the door when I was struck by a sudden thought. Why not go and see Jonah instead? He'd come back yesterday, and none of his flatmates were there all week. I could at least see if he was in. If he was busy, I would just say hello and leave him to it. That seemed innocent enough.

I walked over to Dodge, thinking as I went about what to say. I only wanted to catch up with him, to find out about his Christmas. And to remind him that I existed. I was starting to think that we had *never* been more than friends, but then I remembered the taste of his mouth, the breathy sounds he had made in bed. There was no way that he could've forgotten.

Once I was outside, I realised I'd have to text him to be let in. I pulled out my phone and started typing him a message, asking if he was still at home. I was just about to press send when the alarm starting going off; the door flew open and a cleaner walked out, pushing a trolley full of mops and brooms. She appeared to be in her fifties, with hair scraped back into a messy bun. She looked up at me impatiently. "Going in then?"

"Oh, yes. Sorry!" I said and breezed past her, thanking her for holding the door open. I took the stairs two at a time, listening to her tutting behind me. It had been weeks since I'd been with Jonah and I couldn't wait to see him again now. I straightened my clothes, flattened my hair with the palm of my hand, and then knocked twice on his bedroom door.

I heard voices, a soft giggle.

Oh shit, I thought. *He's got company.*

What on earth was I doing here anyway? He'd be pissed off if he had a friend over and had to explain to them how he knew me. This was exactly what he'd wanted to avoid, why he'd wanted to keep things separate. Should I run? Hide? I had no idea what I should do.

"Just a minute!" I heard him shout.

There was another giggle, a loud creak, the sound of somebody crashing about.

Oh god, oh god, oh god.

The lock was drawn back and the door suddenly swung open. Jonah was in his boxers, red-faced and panting, out of breath, as surprised to see me there as I was.

My eye travelled over to his bed.

I knew who it was before I looked, before the door had even opened.

My heart sank.

It was Ezra.

Twenty Two

"Ash? What are you doing here?"

I could feel Jonah staring at me. He was standing in the doorway, leaning impatiently against the frame and trying to block Ezra from view. But it was already too late. There was a weird expression on Ezra's face now, the one I'd grown more and more accustomed to. He smiled at me, amused. It almost looked like he was gloating.

"I think you should go," said Jonah, oblivious to what was happening between us. "I'll talk to you later, okay? This isn't really a good time."

"Yeah," said Ezra, mockingly. "We're a bit tied up at the moment."

I wanted to hit him; I wanted to push past Jonah and wring his neck, make him cry. I would've done anything to avoid just standing there, gaping dumbly at him like an idiot.

Then somehow I was running away from them, running down the hall, through the door to the stairwell. My heart was pounding and my thoughts were coming too fast. *What the fuck is going on? What's Ezra doing with Jonah? And why did he look so smug? He knew I liked him and he fucked him anyway. What kind of a friend does that? How could he?*

At the bottom of the stairs, I threw open the main door. It hit the wall outside with a metallic clang, like a bell ringing far away. I needed to get back to my room. I needed to be alone, to have some time by myself to think. There was only one thought in my head now, looping incessantly, loud as a drum. *Don't cry, don't cry, don't cry.*

I hurried on, making my way towards the main gates. I wanted to get as far away from them as possible, to put as much distance between us as I could – but I found it hard to catch my breath. I could barely walk in a straight line. My heartbeat was throbbing in my ears.

Ezra's voice was loud behind me.

"Ash, hang on!" he yelled. "Wait up!"

Ezra had followed me out of Dodge. His clothes were a mess – he'd obviously just thrown them on again – but I noticed he was wearing Jonah's shirt now, black with yellow stars, the one he had worn on our very first date. He was obviously marking his territory, showing me how close he was to Jonah. I waited for him to catch up, having no idea what I was going to say. His cheeks were flushed and red, but I couldn't tell if it was from the cold or from whatever he'd been doing in Jonah's room. God, I wanted to be sick.

I turned and started walking away. "I don't have anything to say to you."

"Oh, no. You don't get off that easy."

He grabbed my arm and pulled it sharply, spinning me right back around to face him. I could still see his black eye, but since the bruises had almost healed, it made him look dangerous, unfamiliar. I barely knew who this person was. I couldn't see Ezra in him at all.

"What the fuck are you doing?" I said, wrenching my arm away.

"Me? Nothing. What have *you* been doing?"

"Come off it, Ez. You know what I'm talking about."

Ezra frowned, lit a cigarette. "You mean me shagging Jonah?"

I already knew what they'd been doing, but hearing him say it out loud was like a slap, like a punch in the stomach. Could he not see how much it hurt me?

"You told me it wasn't serious," he said casually, plucking a hair off Jonah's shirt. "You said you weren't even seeing him anymore. Imagine my surprise when he actually messaged me. He told me all about what you'd been up to."

I stared at him. "He…he messaged you?"

"Mm-hm. On Grindr. He said he was looking for something more serious. I knew who he was but I thought you hadn't seen him in months. I asked him about you and he told me everything. Everything you weren't brave enough to tell me yourself."

I shook my head. My mouth was so dry I could hear my voice cracking. "This isn't about me. It's about you! You knew I liked him and you fucked him anyway."

"But I *didn't* know that. You told me you wanted to keep things causal, that you'd already broken up. *And* that you hadn't been with him in ages."

"It isn't like that. What I said was –"

"And my birthday, Ash." His face suddenly looked sad. "You weren't even honest with me about that, even after I'd been to the hospital. You had plenty of time to tell the truth. I mean, I would've understood. You couldn't even tell me where you'd been."

I needed to get the focus off of me. I was the victim here! Okay, so I'd lied to my friends, but sleeping with Jonah was unforgivable. He was *clearly* the one in the wrong.

"How long has this been going on?" I asked.

"Since the week after my birthday. It's kinda funny really. You were in my room when he first messaged me. I was watching *Black Christmas*. Remember?"

I couldn't believe it. That was almost a month ago. A whole month where I hadn't suspected him, where I thought nothing had been wrong. And worse was that I'd actually felt sorry for him! I thought he was traumatised from being punched, that it had changed him, made him timid. Really he'd been going behind my back the entire time.

I shook my head again. "And you did it to punish me, is that it?"

"Yes! To hurt *you* the way that you hurt *me*!"

A cloud passed in front of the sun, turning everything dark grey. It made him look pale, dead, devoid of colour. He stared thoughtfully at his cigarette.

"You know, it's no wonder you call yourself Ash," he said. "You're never really there. You're always slipping through someone's fingers. You're even cold like ash too."

I rolled my eyes. "Oh, don't you play a scene with me. You can try and justify it however you want, but *you're* the villain here. God, I can't even believe that you –"

"And I won't ever believe you again," he snapped. "I trusted you. I thought you were my best friend, but you were lying to me the whole time."

"Yeah, and *you* went behind my back!"

Ezra smirked, took a drag of his cigarette. How on earth was he being so calm?

"I mean, you did too," he said. "Jonah told me you were always bitching about us, saying what bad friends we were, how we could never understand you. I couldn't figure it out at first. Because – what? We didn't like *Xena*? We were better friends to you than that."

"Oh, because you look like such a great friend now."

"You want to talk to *me* about being a good friend?"

"You fucked the guy I liked, Ez! What kind of a friend does that?"

He cleared his throat, looked unresponsive. "Well, what difference does it make now? Jonah likes me, not you. He told me how much you text him, always sniffing around him like a puppy. I'd think it was cute if it wasn't so pathetic."

"Oh, you don't know what you're talking about."

"But I do," he said, throwing his cigarette on the floor and stamping it out. I noticed he was wearing Jonah's trainers too. "He told me everything you did – how often you met, what you talked about, what you were good at." He smirked.

"Fuck you," I said.

"No, fuck *you*. You pretend to be all innocent all the time. Poor Ash with no friends, with no one who likes him. You think you're such a good person, but you haven't been honest with me once. Me! *I* was the best friend you ever had. I included you in everything. I tried to make you feel better about yourself, to make you feel like you weren't such a loser. And I shared everything with you! You wouldn't even have met Haz and Sam if it weren't for me."

I didn't have to listen to this.

"Get fucked," I said.

"Well, one of us will," he said, bragging.

We regarded each other in silence, like coiled snakes about to strike. Then he turned around and marched away, back towards Dodge, towards his boyfriend. I wanted to run after him. I wanted to say the things I hadn't had the courage to say before, but I knew that Ezra had already won. And not just the argument either. He had Jonah now, had stolen him, and I'd lost both of them at once. And how would I ever survive without them?

"No, fuck *you*," I said under my breath.

Even to me it sounded pathetic.

I turned and walked back across campus, slowly, taking my time; I felt like a soldier returning from war. I pictured Jonah telling Ezra about me, laughing at all the private things I'd said to him, what I'd done with him in bed. I wanted to vanish, disappear.

How did we ever wind up like this? How did we mess things up so badly?

As I walked, I suddenly realised I was wearing my *Xena* shirt, the one Ezra had given me for Christmas. Now I really *did* feel pathetic. I'd thought he'd given me the nicest gift I had ever received, but it was a lie, a bad joke. He'd always known what he was doing. "You can wear it and think of me," he'd said. I couldn't believe I had been so stupid.

At the main gates, the snow machine had been switched off for the holidays, but there was still a mass of grey-brown sludge where the fake snow had been left to dry. It was disgusting. The smell of it – thick and rotten, slowly congealing away to nothing – made me think of my friendship with Ezra: of the promise of something beautiful, of a reality like slime.

Twenty Three

My room still smelled like mould. I closed the window and saw three seagulls outside on the grass, pulling worms out from under their feet. I'd heard once that seagulls fly inland when there's a storm coming, but I didn't know if that was true or not; I thought it was probably just a myth. *The storm's already happened,* I thought. *It's already been and gone.*

I didn't know what to do with myself now that I was alone. I ended up wandering around my room, running my hand along dusty surfaces, looking for jobs that didn't really need doing. And all I could think about was Ezra. There he was again, lying in Jonah's bed, wrapped in the sheets like a fox in a snowdrift. The worst part was how good he'd looked, how attractive they were together. I couldn't stand how much I hated them.

Since I was the only person on my corridor, I decided to take a long shower, standing under the water for forty-five minutes. I tried not to think about Ezra and Jonah. I didn't want to keep imagining them together, wondering what they were doing, what they were whispering to each other. But no matter how much I tried, the image was too hard to shake off. I kept replaying the argument on a loop, trying to get everything in order. The day was like a shuffled park of cards; I could only piece together random images – Jonah's shirt covered in stars; a cigarette trampled underfoot; Ezra's face, proud and haughty. But again and again I could hear his voice, low and derisive, as slippery as an eel: *"You're cold like ash too."*

Once I'd dried my hair and changed my clothes, I decided to call my mum. I didn't want her to worry about me, but she gave the best advice and always seemed to know what to do. But I also wanted validation. I needed to hear that I wasn't the bad guy, that there was still somebody on my team. The phone seemed to ring for a really long time.

"Ashley?"

"Oh, hi, Mum. I just –"

"Sorry, hang on a sec."

I could hear her talking to someone in the background. I suddenly remembered that she'd gone straight to work after dropping me off. Since Mum was a receptionist in a hospital, she often worked long, unsociable hours. Why was I always such a nuisance?

I heard her sighing, heard a door closing. When she spoke, she sounded tired.

"Okay, I'm here now. What's wrong?"

"Oh, nothing much. It can wait. I forgot you were working tonight."

"Has something happened?"

"No, not really," I said. "Seriously, don't worry."

"Ashley?"

"It's fine, Mum. I'll call you tomorrow, alright?"

"Oh, okay." She sounded uncertain. "Well, I better get back to work then. Call me in the morning. Or text me later if you need me. I should be out around eleven."

It took all of my energy to sound upbeat. "Will do!"

I immediately regretted calling. I knew she'd worry about me now, and she had enough to deal with at work without me causing her any more problems. And what if she got in trouble for answering her phone while she was on shift? God, I couldn't get anything right.

I laid on my bed and stared up at the ceiling, making patterns in the Artex. As my eyes began to relax, I could make out abstract but definite shapes – a silhouette of Ezra's face; a spent firework; Jonah's forearm, thick and muscled. They were both everywhere I looked. It was like I was trapped, had no way out. Even my eyes were conspiring against me.

I wondered if Ezra was back in his room yet, if we were separated by a few corridors or the miles between here and Dodge. He might as well have been on another planet for how close I felt to him now. He already seemed like a stranger, like someone I'd never really known. I wondered if we'd ever actually liked each other, or just said that we had out loud.

Laying on my bed, it suddenly occurred to me that – since no one was around for two more weeks – I could die in my room without anyone knowing. It could be a whole month before somebody found me. I thought the idea sounded oddly comforting.

The next day, I tried to make a start on *Wuthering Heights*. I still needed to finish a couple of books before term started, but no matter how hard I tried, I couldn't focus on what was happening. Although I was scared of running into Ezra, I didn't want to stay holed up in my room for the rest of my life. Why should I? I wasn't going to hide away like a prisoner just to avoid him, and besides, I needed to concentrate. There were too many reminders of him here.

I put on my coat and left the room, looking for signs of Ezra's presence. When I found nothing, I bought a Diet Coke from the vending machine and went to the benches outside the bar. I thought a bit of fresh air might help me focus my thoughts, but even after finishing three chapters of *Wuthering Heights*, I still had no idea who Mr Lockwood was, or what Heathcliff was doing, or how any of the characters were even related. The only part that made sense to me was Catherine's ghost outside the window, scratching and sobbing against the glass, begging for someone to let her back in. She was lost and alone, completely forgotten.

You and me both, I thought, and sighed.

But as I started chapter four, I suddenly thought about Haz and Sam. They were my friends too, and though I didn't want them to take sides, they both knew more about boys than I did. Maybe one of them could give me advice. I decided to call Haz. He was the more sympathetic of the two, the one more likely to understand me. Or maybe it was because I was way too spineless to ever call Sam. I was secretly scared he would side with Ezra.

Haz picked up after two rings.

"Hey, Ash!"

"Hey! How are you?"

"I'm good, thanks! You?"

It sounded like he was outside. I could hear traffic in the distance and wind crackling as he walked. A hum of conversation, low and steady, made me think that he was in a crowd.

"I'm alright, thanks. Where *are* you?"

"We're in London. Me and Sam had some time between family stuff so we thought we'd meet up halfway. Sam wants to spend all of his Christmas money already."

"Oh," I said. "That's cool."

It was a bad time, a bad idea. I should've text first to make sure he was free.

"So, what about you?" he asked, breezily. "How was *your* Christmas?"

"Yeah, it was…"

It suddenly occurred to me that I had no idea how to bring up the argument. I'd hoped there would be a natural way of working it in, but I didn't really know where to start.

"Um, yeah, it was okay," I said.

There was a pause on the other end of the line. "Are you alright?"

My nose started stinging. I willed myself not to cry.

"Um…not really," I said.

Another pause. He let go of a small, tired breath. "I've already spoken to Ezra."

"You…you have?"

"Mm-hm. He called me last night, but I told him I wouldn't get involved. I mean, I don't really understand all the details, but he told me you walked in on them. And that you had a massive fight. I can't imagine how awful that must've been for you."

"It wasn't great," I said.

"I'm sorry, love. Are you doing okay?"

He sounded consoling, concerned, but there was something else behind it too, something that seemed a bit dismissive. I hadn't expected that from Haz.

"Did you know about him and Jonah?" I asked.

"Yeah."

"You knew they were sleeping together? Since when?"

"Oh, the last week of term maybe? I would've told you, but you *did* say that you weren't seeing him. I thought he was just some guy you'd dated a couple of times."

"And you didn't think to tell me? You knew I'd been with him at least."

"Yeah, but you told us you weren't into him. And I thought Ezra would've said something anyway. You know what he's like. He can't keep his mouth shut."

I didn't know what I'd been expecting when I'd called Haz, but it definitely wasn't this. It had been stupid of me to tell them that I wasn't into Jonah, but I still couldn't believe they hadn't mentioned it, or tried to warn me about what was happening. It felt like everyone had turned against me, like they were laughing behind my back.

"So, you thought you'd just let me find out for myself then?"

"I would've told you if I thought it was a problem," he said, "but I honestly thought you knew. We all believed you when you said you didn't like him."

"Oh, so it's my fault?"

"I didn't say that."

"No?"

"No! Ash, I don't know what you want me to do."

There was another long silence between us. Why was this conversation going so badly? All I wanted was for Haz to give me some sympathy, to tell me that I wasn't the one in the wrong. I knew I'd made mistakes, but why wasn't anyone treating me like a friend? I thought Haz and Sam would've come to my rescue, the way they had when we'd gone to the Union. They were like superheroes back then. What were they now?

I heard Haz sigh, clear his throat. "The thing is," he said, "Ezra never should've started sleeping with him. I can see that now. He's definitely not faultless, but –"

"Faultless? I was in love with him, Haz! Fine, I shouldn't have lied to him, but I only did it because you lot were judging me!"

"What?"

"Why do you think I felt the need to lie in the first place? When I called you after Fireworks Night, *you* were the one who told me that Jonah was messing me around."

"Hang on," said Haz. "That's not fair."

"Isn't it? When I told you I had feelings for him, you jumped down my throat telling me how unhealthy it was, how it was all a big mistake. God, you're so judgemental!"

I heard the phone being snatched out of his hand. Sam's voice, deep and angry, was suddenly shouting in my ear. "What are you upsetting Haz for?"

"I'm not! I was just trying to say that I'm –"

"You and Ezra are as bad as each other. Just leave us out of it, yeah?"

"No, wait! I –"

I tried to explain, to get my point across, but the line was already dead.

This is it, I thought. *It's over. I don't have anyone left on my side.*

I stared at my phone, wondering if I should bother to send Haz a text. No, it was too late to apologise; I should give him some time to calm down. I shakily opened my book, making a start on chapter four. I was trying to take my mind off things, but the words were blurred, bleeding outwards, expanding slowly across the page. I realised I was crying – but for what? For Jonah? Ezra? The fact that Haz and Sam hated me too? Or was it that I'd messed everything up, said the wrong thing, treated everyone like shit? I honestly didn't even know.

I felt like Catherine in *Wuthering Heights*, like a ghost, like something dead.

Except mine was a grave I had dug myself.

Twenty Four

I called Mum back the next morning. I'd only meant to give her a rough sketch of what had happened – that Ezra and Jonah were sleeping together behind my back – but before I knew it, I was crying down the phone like a child, struggling to keep all my words in order. Once I was finally able to breathe, I decided to tell her everything – not the sanitised version I'd told her before, but the *real* version of events, the one where I'd lied, ditched my friends, had sex with a boy who had never liked me. I waited for her to start shouting.

"Oh, Ashley," she said, faintly.

She didn't say anything else for a long time. I'd never been the type to get emotional in front of her, and I could tell she didn't know how to deal with it. Or maybe she was just shocked at how spectacularly I'd messed things up. She thought I'd been having a great time at uni – making friends, dating boys, being the most confident I'd ever been. But now she was forced to confront the truth. I was selfish, a bad friend, a person who didn't deserve to be happy.

"You're not a bad person," she said, "but you have to find a way to fix this. If you just explained to them why you lied in the first place, maybe then they'd see where you were coming from. This is all just one big misunderstanding."

"It isn't really," I said. "I tried to explain to Haz on the phone, but he didn't think they were being judgemental. He thought they were all just looking out for me."

"Well, maybe they were. You *have* always been very sensitive."

"Oh, right. So it *is* my fault."

"I didn't say that, Ashley."

"No?"

We were starting to sound like me and Haz.

"Just give it some time," she said after a pause. "If your friends care about you as much as they say they do, they'll come around eventually. Just leave them alone for a while. It'll give them time to cool off, and it'll give *you* some time to decide what to do."

"Maybe that'll work for Haz and Sam, but what about Ezra?"

"Yeah, that one's a bit tricky," she agreed. "Just leave him to it. He'll realise he's made a mistake before long. He'll come crawling back before you know it."

"And if he doesn't?"

Mum sighed, a little more deeply than I was expecting. "Just try not to worry too much. These things have a way of sorting themselves out on their own."

I nodded. "Yeah, you might be right."

But was she? I was hoping she'd know how to fix things, how to make me feel like I wasn't a failure, but she really knew as much as I did.

"Will you be okay?" she asked. "I hate thinking about you there on your own."

"Yeah, I'll be fine," I said. "Don't worry."

I sounded positive, convincing, but I was actually thinking something else.

Get used to it, Mum. I'm the most alone I've ever been.

My big plan for New Years was to fall asleep early. I wanted to be tucked up in bed well before midnight, trying to forget the fact that I had nowhere to be, that I had no one else to share it with. Over the Christmas break, I'd imagined me and Jonah on the roof of Dodge, watching the fireworks over London like we had on our first date – something I'd never get to do again. But how had my life come to this? Every choice I'd ever made, every decision in my life had led me to this moment: reading *Wuthering Heights* and eating a Pot Noodle alone in my room. Ezra was right. I *was* pathetic. I couldn't wait for the year to be over.

I kept telling myself not to stalk Jonah or Ezra on social media. I knew it would only upset me, that it would remind me of everything I'd lost. But I still kept looking twice a day, starved and vampiric, needing blood. I checked their feeds religiously, desperate for anything new to be posted, but they hadn't been active since Christmas Eve. I'd already checked their profiles four times today, sensing they'd post something for New Years. And then they did. At eight o'clock, Jonah had uploaded a new photo. It was a picture of Ezra on the roof of Dodge, wearing a black lace shirt and cat ears, a velvet choker with a silver bell. His lips had been painted a bright, rosy pink, and he was laughing, caught off-guard, like he hadn't realised he was being photographed. I hated how beautiful he looked. I wanted to make fun of him, to roll my eyes at his stupid cat ears, but he really *did* look like a model.

Underneath, the caption read, "happy new years u," followed by an emoji of a heart.

I wanted to be sick.

I checked Ezra's page too. Half an hour later, he'd posted a photo of Jonah in his room at Dodge. He was standing awkwardly in a blue sweatshirt, one arm raised like he was fixing his hair. He looked happier than I remembered, more natural, more at ease. It was kind of a goofy photo really, but I couldn't say it was unattractive. Ezra's caption was also more revealing. "This year has been a crazy one. Finished school, started uni, made some awesome new friends. And met THIS beautiful creature. Happy New Year, everyone!"

So, that was it. They were official. Apparently Jonah didn't have a problem coming out now he had a boyfriend as cute as Ezra. I knew it was something that never would've happened if he'd stayed with me. I could barely even keep him talking.

I tried to go to bed after that but I found it difficult to sleep. I couldn't think of anything except their photos, and though I hated myself for looking, I kept opening them again and again, watching the comments come pouring in.

"You guys are so cute!"

"So happy for you both!"

"Aw, this is adorable!"

I went back to reading *Wuthering Heights*. I'd always thought it was a romance, but it was a horrible book, depressing, filled with characters who hated everything. I was starting to understand how they felt. *All people are twats,* I thought, indignant.

It was midnight before I knew it. I could hear fireworks, people cheering, church bells ringing in the distance. I got out of bed and stuck my head out of the window, savouring the cold air against my face. I wanted to feel as though something had turned, as though something bad had been blown away. I was trying to work out how I felt but there was no discernible change. Though I hated to admit it, I felt just the same as I had before.

The next week was probably the worst week of my life. There was still no one around in Queensway, and since I had no friends anymore, I basically never left my room. I finished reading another book – the only productive thing I'd managed to do – but apart from that, I spent all my time watching *Xena*, silently wishing that I were dead.

People started coming back to Queensway that weekend. The corridors were suddenly filled with conversation; I could hear people talking about how great their Christmases had been, how happy they all were to be back. But this made me feel even lonelier. I was surrounded by people but had nobody I could talk to. I don't think I'd ever felt so isolated.

On the Sunday before term started, I was emailed my new course booklets. I scanned through the lists of names in the registers, but Jonah wasn't in any of my classes this term; I'd never be close to him ever again. I wasn't sure how I felt about that. On one hand, I was glad I wouldn't bump into him, or have to make awkward conversation with him about Ezra. But on the other, I knew I'd never get the chance to make up with him, to make him see how much he loved me. I wondered if I'd ever speak to him again. I'd gone from texting him all the time to acting like he didn't even exist. He felt far away from me now, unreachable. It was like he had moved to another country. It was like he had died and I couldn't mourn him.

I didn't have courses on Mondays anymore, so I stayed in my room to make a start on a new book. I ventured out to the shared kitchen to make lunch, and while I was waiting for the kettle to boil, I heard the door open slowly behind me. I didn't turn around; I wasn't in the mood to make conversation. Then I heard a familiar voice.

"Hey. It's Ash, right?"

I turned my head. Theo was someone I'd seen around Queensway before, but I'd never had any reason to speak to him. The only thing I knew about him was that he was gay too. He had brown hair, long on top and swept over to one side, and glasses that were made out of a bright, yellow acrylic. He was short and slightly chubby, but he was cuter than I remembered. Up close, I could see that there were freckles all over his nose, and his cheeks were red like he was permanently embarrassed. I realised that this was the closest I'd been to another person since my argument with Ezra. I suddenly didn't know how to act.

"Oh, hey. You alright?" I said.

My voice sounded flat, a touch disinterested.

"Yeah, thanks. Good Christmas?"

"Mm-hm. Yours?"

He nodded happily. He reached into the fridge and pulled out a fat-free yoghurt with his name written on the side. He checked it carefully, nodded again.

Like anyone would steal your yoghurt, I thought.

"I just wondered if you wanted to join Freedom this term," he said, rooting around in the drawer for a spoon. "I know you came to that Halloween party last year, but we need more members now. I thought maybe you and Ezra might want to join."

There was that name again, Ezra, always buzzing around like a mosquito. I could go my whole life without ever hearing it. One more time and I might start screaming.

"Oh, we aren't really friends anymore," I said, trying to sound nonchalant, laid-back. "Maybe you should ask him instead. He's much more fun than I am anyway."

"I wouldn't say that. Is everything okay?"

"Yeah, great, thanks. Fine. Why wouldn't it be?"

"I don't know," he shrugged, looking down at his feet. "I just assumed you were best friends. I mean, you *are* always together. I never see you around without him."

I nodded, pursed my lips.

"Well, I don't mean to pry," he said, "but…did you want to talk about it?"

"No. Thanks. I don't. Honestly, I'm fine."

"Oh, okay. Well, um…if you're sure?"

I nodded again. I was suddenly embarrassed of the Pot Noodle sitting open between us. It's not that I cared what Theo thought of me exactly, but I was instantly aware of how tragic I must've looked. Ezra had a boyfriend; I had dehydrated noodles. I didn't want him feeling sorry for me though. What good would that do me now?

"Oh, well…" Theo fumbled for something to say. "Maybe you'd want to join anyway? It might be fun. And maybe you could even make some *new* friends?"

God, are you my mother?

"I found it really helpful last term," he carried on, not sensing how much I wanted him to leave. "I was scared I wouldn't make any friends at uni, but all the guys there are really nice. And if *I* can make friends there, well, I'm sure anyone can!"

What was *that* supposed to mean? Was he trying to say that I was a lost cause, that I was someone who needed help? How much of a twat did he think I was?

"Anyway," he said, "no pressure, but we'd be happy to have you."

The kettle clicked and I poured the water into my Pot Noodle. I pulled out a fork and started stirring the contents, watching it turn a greenish-brown.

"Thanks, but I think I'm good," I said, turning around without even looking at him. "I'm fine as I am. Besides, I don't really want any more friends."

Theo sounded hurt. "Oh, okay. Well, you know where I am if you change your mind."

I felt bad for hurting his feelings – he was obviously a nice guy – but I didn't want any of his sympathy. Couldn't he see I was a bad person? I just wanted to be left alone.

I walked out of the kitchen, heard the door slam shut in his face.

Twenty Five

I was on campus three times a week, but I didn't hang around after any of my lectures. I came straight home as soon as I was done, not wanting to bump into anyone I used to know. I couldn't bear the thought of seeing Jonah around the English department, or Ezra, Haz and Sam all hanging out somewhere without me. I really had no idea how I'd act if I *did* see them. Whenever I imagined it, my breathing would change and I would feel like I was about to faint. I didn't want to give them the satisfaction of seeing how unhappy they had made me, how miserable I was without them. I didn't want them to know they had won.

I made it through the first week of term unscathed, and though nobody had reached out to see if I was alright, I knew it didn't really matter. Uni wasn't just about making friends. All I had to do was go to class and keep getting good grades on my coursework, then I could finish the year and work out what I wanted to do next. Lots of students didn't even live in halls, and I started wondering if I could move home after first year was over. I'd have to get the train in a few times a week, but that would still be better than the life I was living now, holed away in my room, depressed. At least I'd have Mum there when I was lonely.

But by the next Monday, I was starting to go mad from a lack of contact. I still didn't want to speak to anyone, but I needed to get out of my room and be around people my own age. I was beginning to feel claustrophobic, like the walls were closing in on me. So I decided to go to the library. I told myself I could do some research, make a start on another essay, but it was just an excuse to get some air, to leave my room for a little while.

I made the long walk to campus listening to the *Xena* soundtrack on my headphones. The music – all blaring drums and Bulgarian chanting – made me feel dangerous and heroic, like I was doing something important. It didn't really match my surroundings though. The sky was a flat grey, and everything looked dark, dull and depressing, the way it always does in the middle of January. When I got to campus, I stopped in the café next to the library to buy a can of Diet Coke. I kept my head down, not wanting to be seen if anyone I knew was around, but just as I was about to leave, I noticed Charlotte alone in the corner. I kept my eyes to the ground, hoping that she hadn't seen me. I paid for my Coke and turned to leave, but something told me I should go and talk to her. Whether I'd meant to or not, I knew I'd treated her pretty badly. She'd only ever wanted to be my friend. She'd never been anything but nice to me, and look at the way I'd acted! I was always blowing her off, trying to get as far away as possible. I felt I owed her an apology. I walked over to her without thinking.

"Hey," I said.

"Oh. Hey, Ash." She seemed surprised to see me there, but her voice was soft, a little concerned. It was like she was scared she'd upset me if she talked too loud.

"Um…can I sit?" I asked.

She nodded, moving her textbooks out of the way.

"Um…listen," I said. "I was hoping we could talk."

"Is everything alright? I heard about you and Ezra."

Christ, I thought, *does the whole world know?*

"Yeah, I'm fine," I said. "I was just thinking that… Well, I wanted to say I'm sorry. You've always been so nice to me, and I'm not sure I ever deserved it. I haven't been a very good friend to you, and…and I just wanted to apologise."

She chewed her lip reflectively, nodded her head. "It's okay."

"It's not really. I know I've been a bit of a dick."

"Well, yeah, but it doesn't matter now. I understand."

"You do?"

"You've had a lot going on. I know how hard it can be when you fall out with friends, and it's even worse when there's a boy involved."

"Yeah, you're telling me," I said.

"Are you sure you're alright though? You look terrible."

I laughed. I'd been avoiding the mirror in my room for weeks, and I hadn't exactly been taking great care of myself. She looked at me like I was a zombie in one of the movies Ezra liked so much. *The Evil Dead*. That was honestly how I felt.

"I'm okay," I said, quietly.

"Do you want to talk about it?"

I didn't want to make everything about me, but I sort of felt like I owed her an explanation for the way I'd been acting. I took a deep breath. I told her that I'd never had any friends before, and that I clearly had no idea how to be a good one. I didn't know how to be honest with another person, how to open up and express my feelings. I told her about wanting to be a better version of myself, and how I was scared the new Ash was worse than before. I finished by telling her how I'd been feeling more recently, about not wanting to make new friends, about wanting to drop out and go home. I said that it felt like my heart had been torn out, that I'd been spat on, thrown away, but I had no idea how to make things right.

Charlotte listened in silence, and when I was finished, she rested her chin on her hands and hummed thoughtfully. "That sucks," she said, "but you've got this all wrong."

"What do you mean?"

"You say your heart's been ripped out, but you've

thrown it away, Ash. You don't care about anyone anymore, not even yourself. I'm not trying to make you feel bad, but don't you see that you're closing yourself off? You can't live that way forever."

"No, I know, it's just…"

"I'm really sorry about Ezra. You didn't deserve that. But all of this self-pity will get you nowhere. It's *so* unproductive. It's just a massive waste of time."

I looked down at a spot on the table, too embarrassed to meet her gaze. Deep down, I already knew that she was right. I couldn't keep clinging to the past forever.

"But I…" My voice cracked. "How do I know that I'm not a bad person?"

Charlotte shook her head. "Nobody's a completely bad person, Ash. People fuck up, they make mistakes, they do shitty things to the ones they love. Stop blaming yourself and move on from it. You'll never get past it otherwise. Seriously."

I nodded, still staring down at the spot on the table between us. I wanted so badly to follow her advice, to let go and move forward, but – where to begin? I only knew one thing for sure: I couldn't ever go back. There was nowhere to go back to.

On Friday night I was in my room again, working on my first essay for the Brontë course. It wasn't due for a couple of weeks, but now I had no social life to maintain, I figured I might as well make a start. I'd read three novels for the course so far, and since *Wuthering Heights* had been my favourite, I thought I might find it more engaging. The question I'd settled on was, "Which is more important in the novel: love or hatred? How can the two be interconnected?" I was honestly asking myself the same thing. How could I hate Ezra and Jonah when I had loved them both so much? How could those feelings degrade so quickly?

Around nine o'clock, there was a sharp knocking on my door. I couldn't imagine who'd be wanting me so late, so I assumed that it must be a room inspection. I got up from my desk and pulled the door open. It was Charlotte.

"Hey," she said, waving. "What are you up to?"

"Oh, nothing much. Just writing an essay."

"On a Friday night?"

"Mm-hm."

She looked at me questioningly, waiting for me to say something. Then she pushed past me and sat down on my bed. "Get dressed," she said. "I'm taking you for a drink."

I closed the door and looked at her. "Huh?"

"You heard me. This is an intervention. You've been stuck in here since Christmas and I'm coming to rescue you. We're going out."

"But, I don't…I mean, I don't know if I…"

"We can stay in Queensway if you like, but let's go for a drink in the bar at least. Come on, it'll just be the two of us. We'll be a couple of hours tops."

I didn't know what to tell her. It wasn't that I didn't want to go, but I wasn't sure I'd be very good company, or that I'd have anything positive to contribute. Could I even maintain a conversation now that *wasn't* about Ezra or Jonah?

I was about to think of an excuse when I remembered what she'd said. I couldn't stay hidden away forever. I'd have to get out of here at some point.

I sighed. "Okay, give me two secs."

She smiled proudly but didn't say anything. I left her looking through my bookcase while I picked out a clean shirt. I wished I'd had time to wash my hair.

"Ugh, *Wuthering Heights*," she said.

"You didn't like it?"

"A bunch of awful people doing awful things to each other? No, thanks."

"Oh, come on, it's beautiful. Okay, the characters aren't exactly *nice*, but they love each other! They're only awful because they can't be together."

"I'll take your word for it," she said, doubtfully.

I was surprised at the way I was defending it. For someone who'd been going on and on about how sad the world was, I was certainly talking like someone who still believed in the power of love. *Maybe that's been her plan all along,* I wondered.

I glanced at my reflection in the cracked mirror. I looked tired, pale, less healthy than I had a few weeks ago. But I couldn't change that now.

"Okay, I'm ready," I said.

"Great! Well, let's go then!"

She led me out of my room and towards the bar next to the dining hall. I got us a table while she bought us a bottle of wine. I wasn't convinced I'd ever tried this kind before. It tasted acidic, a little like vinegar, but I could tell that it was strong too. The first sip went to my head, made my vision soft, unfocused. I tried to remember the last time I'd eaten.

"So, what's new?" she asked when she was sitting across from me.

"Nothing much," I said.

There was a long silence. Charlotte nodded but I was scared she was already regretting her decision to take me out. I'd have to make more of an effort, go out of my way to appear less dour, but I'd been alone for a bit too long. I didn't know how to start a conversation.

"Have you spoken to Ezra recently?" she asked.

"No. Why?"

"Oh, no reason. I just wondered if you'd been in touch. You guys used to be such good friends. I thought he might've apologised by now."

"I can't really see that happening, to be honest."

"No?"

I shook my head. "No."

I finished my first glass and poured another. The more I drank, the better the wine seemed to taste. I could tell Charlotte didn't know if she should tell me to slow down or encourage me to have some fun. I felt more relaxed than I had in weeks.

"What about you?" I asked. "Are you seeing anyone at the moment?"

"Oh, god, no," she said. "I think boys are terrible. No offense."

"But have you ever had a boyfriend?"

She shrugged. "There was a guy I was seeing in Sixth Form, but it wasn't serious. I just don't really want to waste my time, you know? I'm open to it if something comes along, but I'm not going out of my way. I don't really think it's that important."

"You don't?"

"Why should it be? We've got plenty of time for that later, Ash."

I suddenly thought about how desperate I'd been for Jonah's approval, how eager I'd been to please him, make him love me. God, I wished I was as self-possessed as Charlotte. I'd drop everything for any boy who gave me the slightest bit of affection. Was I really that insecure? I wondered if I'd always hated myself without knowing it.

I bought us another bottle of wine. I was definitely drunk now. I was making a start on my third glass when the air in the room seemed to change its shape. It was like electricity, a sudden tension; it felt like the sky right before it snows. Something made me look over to the door. Time seemed to slow down. Ezra and Jonah walked in holding hands.

Jonah was wearing a crop top underneath Ezra's leather jacket, and they had put on matching nail polish, a red so dark it resembled blood. Ezra had those fucking cat ears on again, obviously attempting to look cute. Then they turned around and saw me. They didn't laugh or speak or smile. They just stood there uncomfortably, unsure what to do.

I guessed that Jonah would be staying over. He'd come to Queensway to visit Ezra, and now they'd be spending the night in bed. They'd be having sex in a few hours' time. I suddenly felt sick. I heard Charlotte's voice but I couldn't catch what she was saying. I stood up, my chair screeching across the linoleum, and I ran out of the side door, past the bench where I'd first met Ezra. I wasn't exactly sure how it happened, but the next thing I knew, I was on my hands and knees like an animal, puking my guts out onto the grass.

I felt Charlotte appear behind me.

"It's okay," she said. "I'm here."

Eventually I stood up. I was unsteady, swaying backwards and forwards, and Charlotte had to hold me up, slipping her arms around my shoulders. My mouth tasted furry and I could feel tears drying on my cheeks. Had Jonah and Ezra seen me? I wanted to look back to make sure they weren't watching, but something in my head told me I shouldn't.

I looked at Charlotte. "I'm a mess."

"I've got you," she said. "I've got you."

We walked back to my room in silence.

This is my lowest moment, I thought, stumbling drunkenly against her. *I'm broken, unfixable. It can't get any worse than this.*

Twenty Six

That night, in a drunk haze, I dreamt of a house made out of flesh. Inside, Jonah was sitting on a chair of dark velvet – the colour of liquorice and red wine, the colour of plums and dried blood. I was sitting on the floor between his legs, bound at the wrists with an iron chain. I was kissing his feet, tasting them, feeling his skin against my lips. I raised my eyes to see him, but his face was as blank as the surface of the moon. There was no eye, or nose, or mouth that I could see – only deep blue craters where his features should have been. I was about to turn back to his feet when I felt something lodged between my lips, growing fat inside my mouth. I reached down into my throat. Trying not to gag, I started pulling up a string of fairy lights, icy blue then burning red. In the distance, Ezra laughed.

I woke up feeling more embarrassed than hungover. Charlotte had only been trying to make me feel better, to show me that I wasn't completely alone, and I'd just thrown it back in her face. Now I had something *else* I needed to apologise for. And what if Jonah and Ezra had seen? It was bad enough they'd been at Queensway together, but now I couldn't stop imagining them watching me, laughing at me being sick. They probably felt like they'd had a lucky escape. Thank god they didn't have to pretend to be friends with me anymore.

My mouth tasted disgusting. I slunk out of bed and brushed my teeth at the sink, trying to avoid my eyes in the mirror. I looked down and saw that Charlotte had left me a note. My memories were a blur after seeing Jonah and Ezra, but I vaguely remembered her bringing me back to my room. She must have put me to bed. Now I really *was* embarrassed.

Ash! I hope you're feeling better today! I left a glass of water by your bed, but hopefully you aren't too hungover. Please don't beat yourself up about what happened though. We've all been there! Text me if you need me, okay? Lots of love, Charlotte. xx

I couldn't believe she was still being so nice to me after everything I'd done. I wanted to climb back into bed, to stay in my room for the rest of the weekend. But then it occurred to me that if I really *did* want to make it up to her, I should start by following her advice. So, once I'd brushed my teeth and changed my clothes, I decided to try again, to take a step towards self-improvement. I had nothing else to lose. Things could only go up from here.

I left my room and started walking down the hall. I'd seen Theo coming in and out of his room a few times, so I already knew which door was his. I stood outside for a minute, breathing deeply, trying to think of something to say. I could hear Korean pop music playing inside, and very quietly, I thought I heard him singing along, making up the words that he didn't know. I chuckled softly to myself. I was jealous of how unselfconscious he was, how untroubled he seemed to be. I wondered how I could be more like him.

Eventually I knocked on the door. I heard a surprised little gasp.

"Just a second!"

I could hear him shuffling about inside, turning his music down and muttering under his breath. When he opened the door, he was wearing a *Pokémon* T-shirt: Pikachu angrily shooting off sparks. I thought he looked weirdly excited to see me.

"Hey, Ash!"

"Hey! Sorry to bother you on a Saturday. I was just wondering if it was too late to join the Freedom Society? I thought I might take you up on your offer."

"Oh, that's great!" he said. "It's not too late at all. We'd love to have you."

"Okay, cool. When's the next meeting?"

"Um, I think…" He screwed his face up while he tried to remember, then snapped his fingers so loudly I jumped. "Oh, I've got a flyer somewhere. Two secs!"

He disappeared into his room. I was left standing awkwardly in the corridor, holding the door open with my foot. While I waited, I peered inside.

Though the configuration was the same, his room looked completely different to mine. The bed was covered in anime bedsheets, and a vast army of stuffed toys – including bears, monkeys, sharks, and aliens – was standing watch against the headboard, staring out at me, protecting him. I would have cringed a few months ago, but now I thought it was kind of sweet. Theo was only being himself. He didn't need anyone's approval.

He reappeared thirty seconds later.

"Here it is," he said, handing me the flyer. "It's next Friday. You'll need to be signed in as a guest, but maybe we could go together?"

"Okay, sure," I said. "Why not?"

He clapped his hands excitedly. "Amazing! I'll come knock for you at seven then?"

"Yeah, no worries. See you later."

"See you!"

Halfway down the hall, I heard his music start up again, heard him dancing around his room. Only this time it made me sad, more alone than I'd been before. I tried to work out where it was coming from, but the source of this feeling – its essence and origin – seemed strangely distant, out of reach. Maybe I just wasn't meant to be happy.

On Friday night, I was far more nervous than I'd expected. I'd thought about finding Theo and cancelling on him, but

I already knew it would be a mistake. I was scared about meeting new people, about putting myself out there, but I couldn't let that deter me from trying.

I'd decided to wear the *Xena* T-shirt that Ezra had given me for Christmas. It had so many bad memories attached to it now, but Theo had inspired me to ignore other people's opinions. Even if everyone else thought it was lame, I didn't want to be something I wasn't. This was me, like it or not. And I had to learn how to like myself.

Theo knocked at exactly seven.

"Hey! Cool T-shirt!" he said, pointing at my chest.

"Oh, thanks. Ready to go?"

"You bet!"

He was wearing another *Pokémon* T-shirt and a yellow hoodie that matched his glasses. There was a huge purple rucksack on his back, and as he walked, he hooked his thumbs underneath the straps, like a little kid on his way to school. I was sure we looked like a pair of nerds, but for some reason I didn't care. He must've been having a good effect on me.

I spent the walk to campus asking him questions, trying to find out more about him. This wasn't exactly difficult. Theo was an open book, and every question I asked him prompted a long, excitable answer. I found out that he was from a small village outside Oxford. He had a brother and two sisters; a springer spaniel called Muffin;

and he was very close to his parents, who he spoke with every day on Skype. He was the president of the Anime Society – something I had no idea even existed – and he was studying computer programming so he could learn how to make video games. I'd never met anyone like him before, and though we didn't have much in common, we never ran out of things to say. He smelled a little bit like candy floss.

After he signed me in at Solutions, we sat with the other guys in the far corner, in the booth opposite the door. Theo introduced me to a few of his friends. There was Stephen, a guy so tall and broad he looked like a giant from a fantasy novel; Arjun, who had an *It Gets Better* tattoo on his left wrist; and Matthew, a trans man who was wearing a bright, rainbow hoodie. I immediately felt bad about the way I'd acted at Halloween. Okay, so I didn't have much in common with these guys, but they were all really nice people. And I'd written them off, thought I could do better. I was starting to hope I could make it up to them.

Although I was having a good time, I found myself thinking about Haz and Sam. I'd only had a few sips of my snakebite so I definitely wasn't drunk, but I decided to send one of them a message. I wasn't expecting a reply or anything, but I wanted them to know how sorry I was, how much I hated us not talking. I figured Haz was the safer option.

Hey Haz. I know it's random but I just wanted to apologise for everything that happened. It was all my fault. I guess I'm trying to say that I really miss you guys. I hope you don't still hate me. Anyway, send my love to Sam. Xx

I pushed my phone back into my pocket and re-joined the conversation. The guys were talking about some cartoon they'd been watching called *Inuyasha*. From what I gathered, it was about a demon-dog who liked collecting… sparkly gemstones? I couldn't keep track of the plot at all, but I was happy enough just listening. Theo kept looking over to make sure I was okay, to try and involve me in the conversation, but I would just smile and shake my head, letting him know that I was alright. I was genuinely having a really good time.

About half an hour later, I saw that Haz had text me back.

Ash! I'm really sorry too. Sam and I both feel terrible about what happened. We've been wanting to text but neither of us knew what to say. We miss you too! Anyway, we hope you're alright. Maybe we could all get together soon? xx

For a second, it made me angry. How could he say they'd been wanting to text me? It had been four weeks since we'd last spoken, four weeks where they had no idea how bad things had been, where they could've reached out to me but didn't. I needed to breathe, to let it go. I should be grateful he'd even replied.

Are you out tonight? I typed back.

We were thinking about it. Are you?

I'm in Solutions. Come if you want to!

A long pause. He must've been talking about it to Sam. Maybe it was too soon, or maybe we needed to talk more first. I knew I shouldn't have suggested meeting.

He text back a few minutes later. He said they were already on their way.

I explained to Theo who Sam and Haz were, and he was more than happy to sign them in. But waiting for them was painful. I knew they wouldn't be coming if they didn't want to be my friend, but I was still so nervous to see them in person. What was I even supposed to say? How could I possibly make things right? I considered talking about it to Theo but I thought it might be a bad idea. I needed to handle this mess on my own.

They walked in around twenty minutes later. Haz was wearing a cream turtleneck, and his hair was loose and fell in waves, as rich and brown as a chocolate ganache. Sam, dressed all in black, was even more witchy than I remembered. Wrapped in a scarf and a loose cardigan, it was impossible to tell exactly *what* he was wearing, where one garment ended and one began.

I stood up and waited for them to see me. They turned and raced over, pulling me into a three-way hug. I wanted to cry. I never thought I'd be able to be friends with them again, but here they were, just like they'd always been. How had I gone so long without them?

"It's good to see you!" said Haz, muffled by me and Sam pressed against him.

"God, you have no idea," I said.

They bought themselves drinks and then sat down in the booth beside me. We repeated our apologies – saying how sorry we were for not talking, for not texting, for letting things spiral out of hand – but once that was out of the way, we just decided to move on. There was nothing left to say, and if I'd learned anything in the last week, it was that dwelling on the past would get us nowhere. What mattered now was moving forward.

"Have you spoken to Ezra?" Sam asked eventually.

"Nope. Have you?"

Sam shook his head. "We had a fight with him on the phone, pretty much right after we talked to you. We haven't spoken to him since."

"What did you guys fight about?"

"Oh, you know," he said, choosing his words. "He was angry at you and was trying to get us to take *his* side. That's about it really."

I wasn't surprised. I wanted to ask them for more details, but I reminded myself that it didn't matter. Ezra was gone. Who cared how he felt about me now?

"I hope he's okay," Haz added, quietly.

"I know," I said. "Me too."

We spent the rest of the night catching up. I found out all about Haz and Sam's Christmases, about how they'd spent the last few weeks. I introduced them to Theo too, and Haz seemed to take to him immediately. They started bonding over *Animal Crossing*, bitching about Tom Nook and his evil, capitalist agenda. Sam and I, needing more drinks anyway, decided we'd better leave them to it. I was more nervous around Sam than I was with Haz. Sam would always tell you exactly what was on his mind, and he wasn't scared to be confrontational. I was afraid he was still angry that I'd upset Haz over the phone.

"Thank you for coming," I said while we were waiting to be served.

"Nah, thanks for inviting us," he said. "Haz has been a bit lost without you guys. I'm glad we can make friends again. Well, with *you* at least."

"Yeah, same. I thought I was losing my mind for a while."

Sam put his hand on my shoulder. He looked at me sadly and said, "I'm sorry about Ezra and Jonah. And I'm sorry if we didn't make things any easier for you."

I nodded, managed a smile. I didn't know what else to say.

We waited for our drinks in a comfortable silence. After a while, Sam glanced back at our table and nudged me gently in the ribs.

"So," he said. "Theo seems nice."

"Yeah, he is. I wouldn't have come if it wasn't for him."

"So you like him then?"

"Well, yeah. I mean, he's a great guy."

He nodded, wiggled his eyebrows. "I think he's into you, Ash."

"What? Theo?"

I turned around, glancing over in his direction. I guess he *was* kind of cute, but after the mess I'd made with Jonah, I couldn't imagine being in a relationship. It was like Charlotte had said – great if it comes along, but don't go out of your way.

"I'm not really interested," I said. "I think I've been scared off boys forever."

"Oh, come on. He's cute!"

"Yeah, he's fine, but I…"

"And he likes you!"

"I'm not interested, Sam!"

We both looked at each other and started laughing.

"Yeah, okay," he said. "Point taken."

But it was true. I *wasn't* interested. My love life had been a shambles so far, and all I wanted to do was focus on getting *myself* back on track. And besides, Theo didn't like me in *that* way. He treated everyone the same. He clearly just wanted to be my friend.

Didn't he?

Twenty Seven

The next day, I was just finishing up my *Wuthering Heights* essay when I got a message from Theo. We'd been texting about Freedom all morning – how to join, how often the meetings are – but I knew there was something he wanted to say. Then, out of the blue:

Would you wanna go out with me sometime? Like, on a date? I thought we could go for a pizza somewhere and then maybe go to the cinema?? No pressure or anything but I've been thinking about you a lot!! What do you reckon??

I wanted to tell him to calm down with the punctuation, but I was scared that he'd be offended. Should I make a joke? Play hard to get? Tell him I wanted to take things slow?

After speaking to Sam about him at the bar, I'd started to see Theo in a different light. I was coming round to the fact that I really *did* have a bit of a crush on him, and I could picture what it would be like to date him – the opposite of dating Jonah, I imagined – but at the same time, I was conflicted. I didn't want to stop myself from having a positive experience just because I'd been hurt before, but I still felt like I wasn't quite ready, that I still had some work to do on myself. I decided I should just be honest.

I really like you, Theo. Actually, I have a bit of a crush on you! But I'm not sure I feel ready to date right now. I was seeing a guy last term and it was bad. I mean, REALLY BAD. Could we maybe take things slow? Or just be friends for a little while first?

I hoped I hadn't upset him, but Theo text back straight away.

Of course! I've never even had a relationship, so slow works for me!! I'm sorry you had a bad experience though. Well, I'm kinda glad you did because it means I got to meet you, but I hope it wasn't too painful! Maybe we can still text each other??

I'd be mad at you if we didn't! I replied.

I wasn't used to this. Jonah always felt unattainable, out of reach, like I couldn't quite keep up with him. Theo was nothing like that. I was impressed with how upfront he was, how honest he was about his feelings. Maybe my luck was starting to change. I'd made up with Haz and Sam, I'd made new friends, and now there was a boy who liked me too. After such a shitty few weeks, it definitely felt like a relief. I was finally starting to turn things around.

I was even looking forward to washing my clothes. I normally dreaded taking my stuff down to the laundry room, but today felt different for some reason; I wanted everything in my room to be freshly cleaned, as good as new. Once I'd finished my essay, I stuffed all my clothes into a bin liner, filling the bag with dirty T-shirts, socks, and underwear. I locked the door and made my way down to the basement, but as I went, I couldn't stop thinking about Theo's message. I trusted him when he said he understood where I was coming from, but I wanted to show him that it wasn't an excuse, that I really *did* want to get to know him better. Maybe I'd ask him to show me one of the anime films he liked. I'd never seen one before, and I thought it might be a nice way for us to connect. I reminded myself to text him later.

I was so distracted thinking about Theo that I wasn't looking where I was going. As I walked into the laundry room, just as I was pushing the door open, I crashed into someone on the opposite side. I dropped my bag, spilling dirty clothes all over the floor.

I looked up and saw Ezra.

"Here, let me help," he said, already reaching out.

"No, don't! I can do it."

I crouched down and started stuffing my clothes back into the bag, but Ezra didn't even flinch. If I ignored him long enough, he'd leave. But why was he just standing there? He was literally watching me clean my mess off the floor. And it was all *his* fault anyway.

"Ash, please," he said. "I just want to talk."

"We have nothing to talk about."

"Yes, we do. Come on. Please?"

I looked up at him, scowling. He was wearing a Christmas jumper with a cartoon reindeer on it, green and itchy-looking, glittering, covered in gold and silver pom-poms. Where on earth had he found *that*? It was the ugliest thing I'd ever seen.

I glanced up at his face and saw that his eyes were red and watery. It looked like he'd been crying, or like he needed a good night's sleep. He smelled like beer and unwashed skin.

"Let me guess," I said, pushing past him. "You and Jonah have broken up?"

Ezra followed me into the laundry room. "Yeah," he said, softly.

"Too bad."

The washing machines were stacked on top of each other, covering one entire wall. I chose one at random and started shoving my things inside. Ezra sidled up towards me.

"I broke up with him," he said.

"Really?"

I sounded bored, disinterested.

"I liked him a lot, Ash. I thought I was in love with him, but he treats everyone like shit. You, me, everyone. He was always stringing us along, you know? Anyway, I'd finally had enough and broke up with him. I just couldn't do it anymore."

I shook my head. "If you came here for sympathy..."

"I didn't. I don't want you to feel sorry for me, or –"

"I don't."

I heard him take a breath. Why was he still here? Couldn't he see that I didn't want to talk to him? He was only running back to me now because Jonah didn't want him. But unlike the fight outside Dodge, I felt like *I* had the upper hand. I knew exactly what to say.

"Listen," he managed. "I just wanted –"

"No, *you* listen," I said, slamming the washing machine closed. "I trusted you! Okay, I wasn't honest with you and I apologise for that, but you had no right to do what you did. And the fact that you were doing it for weeks! You couldn't wait for me to walk in on you two. You were just waiting in his room for me like a spider."

"It wasn't like that. It's –"

"You were hurt that I'd lied to you, so you went out of your way to hurt me. That was so much worse than what I did to you. You say I wasn't being a good friend, but what kind of a friend does that to someone they care about? What kind of a person does that to anyone?"

I was expecting him to fight back, but he just sighed, looked down at his feet.

"I'm sorry," he whispered.

"Oh, no, you're not," I said, squaring up to him. "You don't care about anyone as long as *you're* alright. You're only sorry now because you don't have any friends left. And who's fault is that, Ez? Who's fault is that?"

I heard him sigh, saw his lip start quivering. *Oh no,* I thought, *that's not gonna work on me.* He turned his face to the ceiling, trying to sniff back his tears. He looked like a little boy in that ridiculous Christmas jumper, but I was still so fucking angry.

"Look, you can cry all you want," I said, "but it's not gonna make me feel sorry for you. You knew exactly what you were doing when you messaged him on Grindr."

"I know that. But if you'd just let me explain, I could…"

"And it's not even that you went behind my back, Ez. It's that I never realised how cruel you could be. The stuff you said to me that day when I…"

"I only did it because you hurt my feelings!" he shouted, suddenly angry. "I made a mistake and I'm dealing with that, but I can still forgive *you*! You have to forgive *me*!"

We stared at each other in silence, the machines whirring all around us. He looked pleadingly at me, desperate for me to talk to him. And then he burst into tears. He was clutching himself round the middle, trying to breathe, slowly turning a shade of purple. He looked ugly now, grotesque. I'd never seen him in such a state.

"I'm so sorry," he said between gasps.

"Ezra, stop it. Stop it!"

"Please, Ash. I *need* you to forgive me."

"No, I'm not buying it, Ez! Just stop it!"

"Please!"

"I said no!"

I wanted to turn back to the washing machines, but he looked so sad, so wounded that I didn't know what to do. I'd never hated anyone as much as him before. Jonah was just a boy; I could forgive him for not giving a shit about me, but Ezra was supposed to be my friend. I told myself I'd never forgive him. But then, suddenly, I realised *I* was crying as well.

"I'm so sorry, Ash," he whispered.

I sighed. "I am too."

We sat together on the rickety chairs, watching my clothes spinning round and round. Ezra told me all about what had happened with him and Jonah. After his birthday, Ezra had only replied to Jonah's message as a way of getting back at me, to prove he could hurt me like I'd hurt him. But Ezra had started developing feelings for Jonah, and by then it was too late. After I'd walked in on them, they had both felt guilty about everything, and their relationship was never the same. It wasn't long before it fell apart. The word Ezra used was *toxic*.

"He's been sleeping with loads of people since the start of term," he said, keeping his eyes fixed on the washing machines. "Even when he was with me, I knew he was sleeping with two other guys. I pretended not to care, but you can only do that for so long."

"Let's not talk about Jonah," I said, looking down at my hands. "We've wasted too much time on him already. I wouldn't mind if I never heard his name again."

"Do you still have feelings for him though?"

I thought about it for a long time. I'd always assumed I did. I still thought he was beautiful, and I'd had a good time with him on our dates, but I'd always known that it wouldn't last. And what was the point of loving someone who didn't love you back?

"I don't think so," I said. "He's hot but he's kind of a dickhead."

Ezra laughed. "He really is."

The machine started spinning with a renewed vigour, practically shaking the floor beneath us. When it started powering down, it made a sound like something falling.

"Do you remember when we met?" I asked.

"Yeah, of course I do."

"You were on Grindr, but you told me you were looking for love. You said it was the only thing that mattered. It's no wonder you'd risk everything for that."

Ezra sighed. "But I was wrong, Ash. All I've ever wanted was to find someone who loved me, but what I had with *you* was so much more important. I see that now. I can't believe I let some random guy get in between us."

"Yeah, but it's…"

"Don't make excuses," he said. "My friendship with you was the best thing I'd ever had. I trusted you. I *believed* in you. So when I found out that you'd been lying, I guess I just wanted to lash out. I know it was stupid of me, but I didn't know what else to do."

I nodded. "I'm sorry for bitching about you behind your back."

"It's no big deal. I get it. I know how annoying I can be."

"That's not the point though. I shouldn't have done it. I'm sorry."

The washing machine slowed and then stopped. It beeped to say that the cycle was finished, but neither of us moved. I hadn't realised how loud it had been. We'd adjusted our voices to the hum of the machines, but now the room was intensely quiet.

"I'm still kinda angry with you," I said.

"I know. I'm still angry with myself."

I looked over at him. His brows were furrowed and he was biting his lip, staring at the machines, trying not to cry. I couldn't forget about everything that had happened between us, but I also didn't want him to experience what

I'd been through in the last few weeks. I wouldn't wish that on anyone. It wasn't my job to make him feel less guilty, but that didn't mean I had to make it harder for him either. So – where did we go from here?

"Do you think you'll ever forgive me?" he asked, still avoiding my gaze.

I nodded, tried to smile. "I think I'm ready to give it a try."

Twenty Eight

The next day, Ezra came knocking on my door. Since neither of us had lectures on a Monday this term, we'd decided to try and hang out for a bit, to see what could be salvaged from the wreck of our friendship. He was dressed more like himself now, in a shirt printed with red roses, but I could see he was nervous to be around me. He could barely look me in the eye.

"Hey," he said. "What are you up to?"

"Not much. How's it going?"

"Yeah, okay, thanks."

He looked at me uneasily, pressing his weight against the doorframe. It was like he didn't want to come inside, like he was waiting to be invited.

"Is everything alright?" I asked.

"Oh, yeah. I'm fine," he said, shuffling his feet. "I just wondered if you wanted to go for a walk or something?"

"Right now?"

"Well, yeah. I mean, it's not very cold out. I thought we could go down to the woods behind the football fields. It's probably quiet during the week."

I had a sudden image of him luring me there to kill me. I guess I still had some trust issues to work through. We were awkward with each other, and I couldn't see things going back to the way they were before Christmas, but I really *did* want to try and be friends again. So why was I being so difficult?

"Um…well, actually…"

"You *can* say no. Or we can do something else. Honestly, it's up to you."

"Um…"

I didn't really have the energy to spend hours talking about our feelings. Then again, our friendship wouldn't just fix itself. It was something we needed to work on, something we needed to put some time into. And Ezra looked so nervous! He was so eager to please me now, so hopeful that I'd say yes, that I felt like I couldn't just turn him down.

"Okay," I said, sighing. "Give me a second to get my coat."

"Sure. I'll get mine too and meet you out front."

I watched him go and then grabbed everything I needed – my coat, my phone, the keys to my room – and made my way towards reception. But as I walked down the hall, Theo's door flew open suddenly. He was wearing flip-flops and carrying a laundry bag, one side crowded with Disney villains. I was appalled at how cute I was starting to find him.

"Hey, Ash!" he said.

"Hey! You doing some washing?"

He nodded gravely. "I hate it but it has to be done, right?"

"That's what I've heard."

"Did you wanna come too?" he asked, brightening. "We could watch some TV while we wait. I've got some great anime on my phone."

I actually *did* kind of want to go with him, but I'd already said yes to Ezra. I could always make an excuse, but Ezra and I weren't on steady footing and I knew I had to repair that first. Besides, what he had said yesterday was right. Boys would come and go, but my friendship with *him* was more important. I needed to make him a priority.

"Oh man," I said. "I'd love to, but I promised I'd hang out with Ezra."

"You made up?"

"Yeah. Well, only very recently. Things are still a bit tense, so we thought we'd go for a walk. You know, try and clear the air a bit."

Theo looked happy, almost proud, but I could tell he was disappointed.

"Aw, that's great," he said. "I'm glad you guys managed to sort things out."

"Yeah, me too. Maybe I could see you a bit later on though? You can show me this demon-dog thing if you want. I'm not against it."

"Oh, great! Okay, well, I'll text you later then."

"Cool."

"Have fun with Ezra," he said. When I didn't reply, he shook his laundry bag for emphasis. "You'll have more fun than *me* at least."

I laughed, gave him a wave, walked away from him down the hall. I was a bit worried that he'd lose interest if I kept blowing him off, if I kept finding excuses not to hang out. But then, that wouldn't matter as long as I made friends with Ezra again.

Right?

The conversation between me and Ezra – as we walked to campus – was abortive, unsuccessful. We'd avoided talking about Jonah, skirting over topics that seemed too likely to create friction. But with so many things off-limits, I didn't really know what to bring up. In desperation, I asked him about his Christmas. He shrugged, didn't say much, but I could already tell it had been disastrous. The only thing his parents had given him was that ugly reindeer jumper – a present so tragic he found it funny. I kept reminding myself not to feel sorry for him.

It wasn't a cold day, but the sky was flat and dull; I tried to remember a time when the sky hadn't been an ugly, featureless grey. The woods – if you could call them that – were on a small plot of land behind the football fields. I was pretty sure that students weren't allowed here, but everywhere I looked, there were empty crisp packets, cigarette butts, broken bottles, discarded condoms. I was starting to wish I had stayed in my room.

"Have you spoken to Haz and Sam yet?" I asked as we meandered down the path.

"Nope. Have you?"

I nodded. I told him about Solutions and how we'd managed to hash things out. He looked a bit upset that I'd been able to mend things, that I was friends with them now and he wasn't. But then he just shrugged, clicked his tongue.

"Oh well. It was fun while it lasted."

"Just text them," I said. "I'm sure they'd love to hear from you."

"I don't know. I mean, I want to, but we had a massive argument on the phone. I was being a twat really. I don't know *how* to make it up to them."

"Just give them a call. I felt the same way before I saw them again."

"Yeah, maybe."

He was silent for a minute, then added, "Did they ask about me?"

I paused, trying to remember what they'd said. "They told me about the phone call and said they hoped you were okay, but I think that was about it."

He pretended he wasn't upset. "Oh right," he said. "Fair enough."

We walked on in silence after that. Things were still a bit awkward between us and I didn't know how to fix them. I wondered if it was me. Once or twice I had to stop myself from asking him about Jonah. It sounded perverse, but I wanted to know more about their relationship, about their sex life, their dynamic. But why? I knew it would only end up hurting my feelings again. Was I getting off on being punished?

As I stepped over another used condom, Ezra suddenly turned to face me.

"Was I always a bad friend?"

The question caught me off-guard. "You were my best friend," I said. "You're *still* my best friend. I just sometimes wonder…"

"What?"

I didn't know what I'd meant to say. I was thinking about the fight we'd had in Queensway, about how annoying I used to find him. But that was my problem, wasn't it? In fact, now I looked back, he'd only *ever* been a good friend. He'd drawn me out of myself, included me. What had I ever done for him?

"To be honest," I said, "I'm not sure *I* was a great friend. I know I lied to you, but it's more than that. I used to find you really irritating. Like, all the time."

"You did?"

"Yeah, because I let things build up. I never told you how I was feeling, so I ended up getting more and more pissed off with you. I didn't know how to tell you that I needed more space, that I needed a bit more time to myself. I should've just been honest."

Ezra lit a cigarette and blew out a heavy cloud of smoke. I waited for him to say something, but he was reticent now, withdrawn. I hadn't meant to make him feel guilty.

"Maybe it's just me," I said, "but do you ever think that we don't really know *how* to be good friends? I mean, we were never close to people before uni. You're really the first friend I've ever had. Maybe it's harder for us to be honest with each other."

"I was always honest with you."

"Yeah, until Jonah."

I sighed, shook my head. I apologised immediately.

"Look, all I'm saying is that we haven't *always* been aware of each other's needs. Maybe it's something you learn with practise."

He seemed to consider this. "Do you think so?"

"Well, maybe. All relationships take work, don't they?"

Ezra shrugged, lowered his gaze. I was about to say something else when I felt my phone vibrate in my pocket. I pulled it out, saw I had a new text.

I already knew it would be from Theo.

Just finished my laundry and I want to curl up in bed and sleep for the next three days! I hope you and Ezra are having a better time than I am!!

"What are you smiling about?" said Ezra, watching curiously.

I hadn't even realised I *was* smiling. Should I tell him?

"Oh, it's only some guy," I said.

"Who?"

"Theo? He lives on my corridor."

"The *Pokémon* guy?"

I was starting to feel defensive. This was like the situation with Jonah all over again. I knew it was stupid, that it wouldn't happen, but I was scared his opinion would alter mine.

"I like him, Ez. Okay? He's a nice guy."

"Hey, that's great. So, are you dating him then?"

"Um, well, he *did* ask me out, but I told him I wanted to take things slow."

"Why?"

"Are you kidding? Because dating Jonah was a disaster! And all the stuff with you and him, and…" I took a breath. "I don't know. I just don't want to go through all that again."

Ezra stopped walking. He looked hard at me, assessingly, then turned away, sucked in his breath. "I'm sorry," he said, "about everything. But you can't let *that* get in the way. You should go for it if you both like each other. I mean, why not, right?"

"But…is it worth it?"

"It is if *you* think it is. And I'll support you no matter what."

I didn't need his permission, but I was glad he wasn't trying to stop me, or trying to convince me I was making a mistake. If *that* was even true, I wanted to find out for myself. But maybe not quite yet. I still felt I needed a bit more time.

"Thanks," I said, "but I already told him I want to take it slow. I want to fix things with you, and get my friendship with Haz and Sam sorted before I jump into anything else. I just don't think I'm ready for that yet."

"Look, it's fine to take things slow," he said, "but it doesn't have to be one or the other. I'm not going anywhere. Please don't stop yourself on my account."

I nodded, noncommittal. "I'll think about it," I said.

We came to the edge of the path, looped back, walked round again.

"Thanks for coming with me today," he said, stamping on the end of his cigarette. "I really appreciate you giving me a second chance."

"Hey, no mushy stuff, remember?"

He laughed, rolled his eyes, pushed me playfully away.

"I'm serious," he said. "I'm glad we're starting to be friends."

Starting to be friends? I wanted to ask. *Were we not real friends before?*

I decided to say nothing. I was certain I already knew the answer.

Twenty Nine

I went to see Theo later that night. We'd finished watching a few episodes of *Inuyasha* – which was actually pretty good – and now we were sitting on his bed in silence, trying to figure out what to say. I didn't know what had happened. Theo was normally so chatty when we were together, but now we were in his room, it was like he had no idea how to act. He opened his mouth, then closed it. He kept stumbling anxiously over his words.

"So," he said, hugging a stuffed monkey to his chest. "What now?"

"Um…I don't know," I said. "I guess we could…"

I suddenly noticed that our knees were touching. I quickly moved it away, but then caught myself and moved it back. I needed to remember that he wasn't anything like Jonah. He was a nice boy. Why was I so insistent on pulling away from him?

There was another long silence, but I tried not to think of it as uncomfortable. I didn't feel like I had to coerce him into opening up or talking to me. Even when he wasn't speaking, I knew that Theo liked me. I *trusted* him. At least, I was starting to learn how.

"I really want to kiss you," he said.

I looked over at him. "I do too, but…maybe we could just sit for a while?"

He smiled. "Yeah, of course! Take all the time you need."

He reached across to the laptop and started looking for something to watch. It suddenly occurred to me how lucky I was. Not all boys were as patient as Theo, and after the drama with Jonah, his appeal was becoming more obvious. I was starting to think that I might be okay. I didn't need to rush into anything. I had all the time in the world.

I hadn't ever been much of a Disney person before, but Theo wanted to watch *Mulan*. I said it was fine, told him to press play. I wanted to show him I was making an effort.

As the titles appeared on the screen, ink bleeding into parchment, Theo leaned back and gave a sigh. I reached across and held his hand.

"Thank you," I said.

He swallowed nervously. "For what?"

"I don't know." I shrugged. "For being you, I guess."

A faint blush spread across his cheeks. He looked like he was trying to think of something to say, but I just turned my face to the screen, letting him know that I understood. I didn't need him to say anything. I didn't need anything from him at all.

In the opening scene, the Huns invaded the Great Wall, throwing their grappling hooks over the battlements. I wondered if *my* defences had been breached so easily.

*

Over the course of the next week, things started to go back to normal. Ezra and I ate dinner together every day, and though he was more respectful of my need to be alone, we still spent every night in my room, just watching a film or listening to music. But something had definitely changed between us. Ezra was less performative now, less affected, and it was easier to gauge how he was really feeling. I couldn't imagine us falling out again; at least, not in the same way. I finally felt I could be myself. And for me, that was enough.

He'd even made up with Haz and Sam. I hadn't been there at the time, but from what I'd pieced together, he had called and opened up to them, telling them how sorry he was for everything. He'd gone to see them the next day, and though he'd invited me to come too, I thought it was best to leave them to it. That was another thing that had changed. I was always paranoid about being left out before, about things happening when I wasn't there. Now I understood that this was just part of being a friend – giving each other space, time to breathe. I didn't need them to reassure me. I wish I had learned that lesson sooner.

Once they'd made up, the four of us made plans to go out to Solutions together. I wasn't exactly sure where we all stood with each other now, but there was only one way to find out. And besides, I really *did* miss being around them. They were my best friends after all.

Ezra was already on campus that evening, working late in the library, so I said I'd meet them in Solutions at seven. I'd been distracted texting Theo – as well as stressing about to wear – so I didn't arrive until quarter to eight. They were sitting at the table where we'd first met, and the three of them looked relaxed, talking like nothing had ever happened. Haz and Sam seemed to be in the middle of a jokey argument, and Ezra was laughing, nodding his head. I stood and watched them for a minute, smiling. I never thought I'd see them like this again.

"Hey," Ezra said as I came over. "I got you a snakebite."

"Thanks, Ez. Hey, guys!"

They waved at me as I sat down, and after a quick summation of what we'd all been up to, Haz and Sam went straight back into their argument. Sam had apparently dropped Haz's favourite mug and was adamant he'd done nothing wrong.

"Well, who's fault is it then?" asked Haz.

"Yours! You're always leaving it right on the edge of things!"

"Oh, please. If you weren't so clumsy…"

"Clumsy?!"

Ezra and I were laughing at them, but I already sensed that Haz and Sam were playing it up, taking the heat off me and Ezra. None of us wanted to poke at old wounds, but I got the impression they felt things were tenuous, that we still might devolve into an argument. But *I* knew that it wouldn't happen. Ezra and I had changed since then. I was sure of it.

"Just apologise," said Haz.

Sam crossed his arms. "Oh, come off it. It was only a mug."

"But it was my favourite!"

"Well, I'll buy you a new one then."

"That's not the point!"

Ezra took a sip of his snakebite, then made a sound like he'd had a thought. "Why don't we go to one of those places where you can paint your own mugs?"

"Great idea," said Haz. "I can paint a portrait of Sam, all red-faced and knocking into stuff, and never apologising for anything."

"Oh, for fuck's sake," moaned Sam. "Are you a child? Just let it go!"

Laughing, I looked out across the bar. My eyes suddenly landed on Charlotte, all dressed up for a big night out. She was by herself, watching the door and sighing, then impatiently checking her phone. She was obviously waiting for her friends.

I stood up and skipped over. "Hey!"

"Hey, Ash! How are you doing?"

"Good, thanks. You waiting for someone?"

She looked down at her phone again. "Oh, just the girls from Queensway. I said I'd meet them here before the Union, but...well, you know what they're like."

"I can imagine," I said, picturing the nightmare scenario of Emily and Sarah getting ready. "But why don't you sit with us while you wait for them?"

She followed my gaze back to the table. She looked surprised to see Ezra there, but she didn't say anything, and she didn't ask about what had happened.

"Um...are you sure?"

I nodded. "Come and meet everyone. I mean, it's really because of you that we're all friends again. Did I thank you for that, by the way?"

She smiled, shook her head. I reached out and clasped her shoulders.

"Thank you," I said, "for everything."

She laughed and shrugged me off, looking down at her feet, self-conscious. Then I linked my arm through hers and led her over to our table.

"Guys," I said, "this is Charlotte."

"Hey," they all sang out in unison.

She sat down between Haz and Sam, and they both started interrogating her – how did she know me? What did she study? What house would she be in at Hogwarts? Ezra looked as surprised as Charlotte. I must've forgotten to fill him on what had happened while he'd been away.

All he knew was that I'd met her at the first night party. But it didn't matter now. What mattered was that I felt I owed this to Charlotte. I wanted her to know that I wasn't embarrassed of her, that I *wanted* her to meet my friends. She was one of the best people I'd met at uni, and she'd helped me more than she knew. I still hoped I could make it up to her.

"You're a Hufflepuff like me!" said Haz.

"And Cedric Diggory," she said, raising her eyebrows.

Sam threw up his hands. "God, I'm surrounded!" he wailed.

Ezra and I exchanged looks. It seemed like he wanted to tell me how happy he was we were friends again, but I just smiled, nodded my head.

I knew exactly what he wanted to say.

I had been thinking the very same thing.

After we hugged Haz and Sam goodbye, Ezra and I started walking home. There was a Full Moon Party at the Union tonight – a weird choice for the start of February – so there were lots of students still around, all in flower crowns and face paint. We were both a little tipsy, but I was really enjoying his company. It had been so long since Ezra and I had just been loose and silly with each other, and I'd forgotten how much fun we used to have before Jonah came on the scene. He was telling me about some

TV show he'd loved as a kid, something about a glamorous witch called T-Bag, when Ezra suddenly stopped walking. His face was frozen and his whole body become tense, like a fox stepping out in the road.

"Ezra?" I asked. "Are you okay?"

When he didn't respond, I tried to follow his line of sight. A few feet up ahead, and slowly walking towards us now, was Jonah. My heart jumped. He'd obviously just come from the Union. He was wearing a Hawaiian shirt, obnoxiously bright, but the glow of the streetlamps turned him pale. His face looked unhealthy, white as spit.

He paused momentarily, unsure if he should stop or just avoid us. I looked over at Ezra, hoping for some reaction or sign of life, but he was still frozen where he stood.

Oh god, oh god, oh god.

Jonah stopped in front of us, looking us up and down. "I see you two are friends again."

Ezra didn't reply so I could see it would fall to me. "Mm-hm."

"I wondered why neither of you had text me."

"Oh yeah, because you made such a good impression on us," I managed.

Jonah seemed amused for half a second, but then something else appeared in his eye. He looked at us both hungrily, alternating his gaze between me and Ezra.

"Do you guys want to come back to mine then? I've got some more drinks there. Maybe we could have a chat, get a bit pissed. Maybe even have some fun." He winked.

I couldn't believe it. Who did he think he was? I was about to tell him to go fuck himself when Ezra seemed to come back to his senses.

Don't say yes. Please don't say yes.

"Thanks," he said, putting his arm around me. "But we'd literally rather die."

Jonah was taken aback, but then he just scoffed and shook his head.

"Whatever," he said and pushed past us, walking away from us down the hill.

I turned around and watched him go, watched him slowly decrease in size. When he was gone, I turned back to Ezra. "You alright?"

"Yeah, of course," he said. "I'm perfect."

But I could see that he didn't mean it.

He reached into his pocket and pulled out his sunglasses, put them on. It was almost one o'clock in the morning; the only light was from the streetlamps; but I decided to let it go. He was allowed to be upset. He was as much of a victim here as I was.

As we carried on walking towards the main gates, I was starting to feel a bit guilty. I had Theo after all, and I *did* want Ezra to be happy. If he still had feelings for Jonah, was it really fair of me to get in the way? What difference did it make if they were together?

"You can go back to his if you want," I said. "Honestly, I don't mind."

Ezra turned to me in disbelief. He was looking into my face, trying to make sense of what I'd said, but then he cringed, cleared his throat. I wanted to see his eyes but they were hidden behind his glasses. I could see only myself, reflected darkly.

"Thanks," he said, "but no. We're way too cool for guys like him."

Thirty

Ezra started hanging out with a group of people on his course. He would only see them a couple of times a week, but every now and then, he'd go drinking with them on a Friday night too, often ending up at the Union. At first I was jealous. I had those old feelings of being replaced, of not being good enough for him, of being someone to get away from. But after a while, I started to see it as a good thing. Why did we need to do *everything* with each other? We didn't. I knew that Ezra and I were friends, but I was more introverted than he was, more comfortable being on my own. It also gave us other things to talk about. I liked it when he would come to my room the next day, pale and hungover, to tell me all about his night. It took the pressure off me a bit. He was still my best friend, but now I had the time away from him that I felt I needed. And *he* had all the drunken fun that we both knew I couldn't provide.

Though Theo and I were still technically dating, I was reluctant to make it official. We'd been hanging out more and more often, and though I liked him a lot, we still hadn't made it past first base. But that was alright with me. The affection between us was gradual, incremental. We held hands, then kissed, then started sleeping in each other's beds. We still hadn't done anything more than spoon, but I wanted to trust him before taking it further. And I was getting there. He was genuinely one of the nicest people I'd ever met. I wondered why I'd always seen that as something negative before, something boring, uninteresting. But I had learned from my past mistakes. Better to be nice than a total dickhead.

Ezra even started liking him too, though he was baffled by Theo at first. He didn't really understand his love for cartoons and manga – strange, I thought, considering that Ezra liked the Muppets so much – but after a while, they stumbled across a kind of mutual respect. Theo thought Ezra was exotic and exciting, and Ezra seemed to appreciate how earnest Theo was. I knew they'd never be close friends, but I was glad they were starting to get along.

One night, Theo asked if he could watch an episode of *Xena* with me. I'd been putting it off for a while, scared he'd make fun of it the way the others had. I knew I didn't *need* him to like it, but I was still scared I'd take it personally if he laughed, if he found it stupid. It was important to me, and secretly, I wanted him to love it too.

I gave him a few options to choose from. I thought he might prefer one of the comedies, something cute and romantic, but once he heard that Xena and Gabrielle get crucified by Romans, it was like his mind was already made up. I tried talking him out of it, told him it wasn't really his vibe, but Theo sensed I was only stalling. I hit play a little nervously.

Unlike Ezra, he was mostly silent the whole way through. He gasped or sighed from time to time, but I could tell he was getting into it. He was obviously expecting them to be saved at the last minute, and was shocked when they really died. He watched the whole crucifixion with his mouth open. He turned to me as the credits rolled.

"So, that's it? Xena's dead then?"

"Well, there's still two more seasons to go, so it's not like she's gone for good."

He squeezed his monkey tighter. "That sucks."

"You didn't like it?"

"No, I did. But I thought it was a kids' show! I wasn't expecting it to be so…*dark*."

I laughed. "I'm sorry! I should've warned you."

He looked at me and pouted, like he thought I was making fun of him. Then he turned back to the credits. "I don't get how Gabrielle's a pacifist though. Like, how can you travel around with Xena if you don't agree with violence?"

"Oh, it's a long story," I said. "She wasn't always a pacifist. She gives up violence halfway through the season, but it goes out the window once Xena's in trouble."

"Yeah, you're telling me."

Maybe I should've warned him about the scene where Gabrielle kills thirty Roman centurions after Xena gets taken down. It hadn't even crossed my mind.

"Their friendship's clearly the best thing about the show though," he said, sliding the DVD out of his laptop. "I like how different they are as people. I mean, they don't even have anything in common, but they're always there for each other. Even when it's difficult. *Especially* when it's difficult. It's like a real relationship, you know?"

"Yeah, that's what I like about it too," I said. "I'll have to show you season three sometime. Then you'll see exactly how much they go through."

Theo agreed, said he was up for it, but I suddenly thought about the boys. Before uni, all I'd wanted was a relationship like Xena and Gabrielle's. I thought that's what love was – something wild and all-consuming, a love so deep it could make you kill.

But maybe love was more gentle than that, more measured, slow-moving. It was no wonder I'd fallen for Jonah, but it was my friends who'd affected me most. And I'd almost thrown them all away, given them up for some random guy.

I shook my head, came back to myself. I realised Theo had been talking.

"Did you wanna watch another one?" he asked, scanning the back of the DVDs. "I wouldn't mind seeing how Xena and Gabrielle come back from the dead."

I was reminded then of Charlotte, of Theo pulling me out of my depression.

"Yeah, let's do it," I said. "It's a good one."

A few days later, Ezra and I were sitting on the bench where we'd first met. It was a Friday night, and he was about to head off to campus to meet up with his new friends from his course. He'd invited me to come with him, but I was happy to let him go.

"Are you *sure* you don't want to come?" he asked. "Haz and Sam said they might be up for it later. And you can always bring Theo too if you want."

"Nah, it's okay. I don't really feel like it tonight. But say hi to the boys for me if you *do* see them. Tell them we'll organise something soon."

"Are you going to hang out with Theo?"

I shook my head. "He's working on an essay, and to be honest, I just want an early night. I can't wait to hear about it tomorrow though."

He fumbled around for a cigarette. As he was getting one out of his pocket, I heard his phone go off, a little drumming sound. I knew what it was without him saying.

"Still on Grindr then?" I asked.

He looked at me uncomfortably, like he wasn't sure if I was judging him. But why would I be? I was happy as long as he was.

"Oh, it's bollocks really," he said, pulling out his phone and checking his message. I was half-expecting it to be Jonah, but when I peered over his shoulder, I saw a man in a white string vest, lifting weights in an empty gym.

"You should go for it," I said. "He's hot."

Ezra rolled his eyes. "You just want to hear the story afterwards."

"Ooh, yeah, I want all the details."

He nudged my shoulder with his and we both started laughing.

"Maybe I *will* hook up with someone though," he said, turning serious. "I *am* pretty horny, and why should I stop myself from having fun?"

"You shouldn't, but I thought you wanted love, not sex?"

Ezra sighed, turned his face to the sky.

"I don't know what I want," he said. "Sometimes I want something serious so badly, but then I worry about missing out. Do you know what I mean?"

I didn't know why he was asking *me*. I was pretty sure I'd proved that I didn't know anything much about love. Maybe none of us did. I had the feeling that all of us were just improvising, making it up as we went along. And maybe that was okay.

"I think you should do whatever makes you happy," I said, "and not worry too much about the future. I think we all need to worry a bit less."

He drew a breath, chuckled softly. "Yeah, I think you're right."

"Of course I am."

He laughed at me and lit his cigarette, blowing out the smoke in a blueish cloud. It had taken a long time but I'd learned to love his natural scent. It was like campfires and Parma Violets, like vintage leather and six pound wine. He always smelled like a Year 12 disco: a bit rugged, faintly dirty, but also comforting, nostalgic.

I wondered – if I stayed very still – if I could make these moments last, these fleeting seconds beside my best friend. But why did they have to be fleeting?

When I glanced over, Ezra was watching me.

"Oh, sorry," I said. "I must have zoned out."

"Are you alright? Do you want go back to your room or something?"

"No, I'm here," I said, and smiled. "And I wouldn't want to be anywhere else."

Thirty One

"Happy birthday, darling!"

I grinned. "Thanks, Mum."

"Now, I didn't send a present, but only because term ends in a few weeks. I thought we could go shopping when you're back at home. Maybe we'll get you a new pair of shoes?"

"Yeah, sounds good," I said. "I don't care about presents anyway."

Mum cooed on the other end of the phone. "Oh, you *are* a good boy, Ash."

I rolled my eyes. I was about to make fun of her when I realised what she'd said. It was the first time she'd called me Ash. I caught myself grinning even wider.

"So," she said, after a pause, "what are you doing tonight to celebrate? I hope you and the boys aren't planning on getting silly at the Union together."

Getting silly, I knew, was code for drinking until you blacked out. To be honest, I sort of wished I hadn't told her so much about my uni life. I was glad there were no secrets between us, but now she had the impression I was out drinking every weekend, snorting drugs, hooking up with guys. I was almost sorry to disappoint her.

"No, Mum, we're not gonna get silly. The boys wanted to go to the Union, but I wasn't really up for it. I just wanted to have a quiet one."

"Oh, well, if you're sure. I'll give you a call tomorrow if you're not hungover."

"I definitely won't be."

I could hear her smiling on the phone. "I'll check WhatsApp first anyway. Did you know you can see when someone was last online?"

"Um, yes?"

"Isn't it good? I sometimes look to make sure you're still alive."

I snorted, shook my head. "I'm hanging up."

"Okay, darling. Love you!"

But then I had a sudden thought.

"Oh, Mum, before you go, I forgot to say that I invited Ezra home for Easter. It'll just be for a week or so. I hope that's okay. I meant to ask you first, but…"

"Of course it is, darling! I take it things are back to normal then?"

"Yeah, we're all good now, thanks. I just wanted to check with you in case…I don't know, in case you had plans, or you'd rather not have guests or something."

Mum scoffed in mock annoyance. "What kind of mother do you think I am?"

*

Despite the boys insisting that we go out drinking, I really *did* want a quiet night in. My birthday always seemed like a bigger deal for everyone else than it was for me, and I hated being the centre of attention. I just wanted to hang out with my friends the way we always did – no presents, no cake and ice cream. Just a normal Friday night.

But that obviously didn't happen.

When Ezra and I turned up at Haz's room, it took all of my strength not to run away. The floor was covered in so many balloons I didn't know where to plant my feet. Garlands of fake flowers had been wound around the curtain rod, and strips of tinsel hung in the doorway, gold as sunlight, white as lightning. I couldn't believe they had done so much for me.

"Jesus, guys! You really didn't have to go to all this trouble."

"Oh, shush," said Sam, taking my elbow and leading me over to Haz's bed. "Now sit down and open your present."

"But I said I didn't want anything!"

"Well, it's a bit late for that now."

"Yeah, but guys…"

I couldn't even get the words out before a box was hurled into my lap. It was fairly heavy, wrapped in silver paper and tied with a length of purple ribbon.

"Happy birthday!" Haz said, beaming.

Ezra threw himself on the bed next to me. "Come on, open it, open it, open it!"

They were all staring, watching expectantly, and I could feel my face turning more and more red. I really wanted to save it for later, to take it back to my room, to open it with no one else around. But the boys had gone to so much effort and I didn't want to seem ungrateful, like I didn't appreciate what they'd done. It was so much more than I deserved.

I tore self-consciously into the paper.

Inside the box was a huge folder of *Xena* trading cards, all stored in protective pockets. Most were just screenshots from certain episodes, but at the back there were pages of shinies, iridescent as oil on water. I flicked through them open-mouthed. There was Xena as a Valkyrie, Gabrielle as a mermaid, Aphrodite in pink lingerie. There was a card for every episode, every character – a record of my life since I was ten.

"Oh, he likes it," said Sam. "Look at his happy little face!"

"Are they okay?" asked Ezra, peering over my shoulder. "The guy online said it was a full set, but obviously, *you're* the expert. I didn't know what he was going on about."

"Are you kidding me? They're perfect!"

"Are you sure? He said we've got fourteen days for a refund. I won't be offended if –"

"Ezra, stop. I love them. Seriously."

And I *did* love them. In fact, I knew exactly how much they were worth. I'd seen them for sale on eBay a bunch of times before, but they were always a bit *too* expensive. The boys must have pooled all their money together. I might not have made any of them *Xena* fans, but they knew how important it was to me. And that really meant a lot.

"Seriously, guys," I said, looking up at Haz and Sam. "It's all too much. You really didn't need to get me *anything*! I wasn't expecting you to –"

"You're welcome," said Sam, cutting me off.

I took the hint and started flipping through the cards again. Ezra, pointing over my shoulder, started asking me questions – who's that? What *is* she wearing? Who's the hunk with the fucked-up face? – and I tried my best to be succinct. I knew he didn't care about *Xena* really, but I thought it was sweet he was trying his best.

"Where's Theo tonight?" asked Haz, opening a bottle of prosecco.

"Just back in Queensway," I said.

"You should've brought him here. We wouldn't have minded."

"Oh, I know you wouldn't. It's just…Well, I've been spending a lot of time with him recently. I sleep in his room every couple of nights."

"Is that a bad thing?" asked Sam.

"Of course not. And I really like him. I just don't want to be the kind of person that can't do anything on their own, that has to bring their boyfriend along all the time. And you guys are important too. Theo wouldn't want to get in the way of that."

Ezra nudged into me. "Are you aware you just used the word *boyfriend*?"

"What? No, I didn't."

"You did! You just referred to him as your boyfriend, Ash!"

"I was talking hypothetically!"

"Oh, yeah, yeah," he said, closing his eyes and clutching his heart. "You guys will have the cutest wedding. *Pokémon*-themed too. I bet Theo would make a great Squirtle."

"Urgh, give it a rest, Ez," I said.

But I couldn't stop myself from smiling.

I kept on flicking through my trading cards as the boys started pouring drinks, started handing out prosecco. Eventually Haz appeared beside me.

"Speaking of cards, I have one more thing for you," he said.

He sat down across from me, folded his legs, and pulled out a yellowed deck of tarot cards. Ezra clapped his hands, but I still didn't know what was going on.

"You can read tarot?" I asked.

Haz blushed. "Oh, I'm not very good yet, but I've been teaching myself since Christmas. I must've been inspired by that *Xena* episode you showed us."

God, all that time I spent stressing about showing them *Xena*! If I'd just let them enjoy it on their own terms, we might've never fallen out. But what was the point of obsessing now? It had inspired Haz at least, and that was more than I'd expected.

"So," he said, handing the deck to me, "I want you to shuffle the cards and think of a question to ask. It doesn't have to be specific."

"Like, will he ever get married?" asked Ezra, winking.

Haz considered this a second. "Well, maybe a bit more vague than that."

I looked down at the cards. They were faded and old-fashioned, and had Renaissance-style artwork. And the words were in Italian too. *Il Matto, La Luna, La Regina di Bastoni*.

Ezra stood up to give us more room, standing next to Sam by Haz's desk. I started shuffling the cards, thinking about what I wanted to ask. But – what *did* I want to know about the future? I was finally happy as I was. I just wanted to stay here in the present.

I ended up thinking about the boys, about our friendship and what it meant. I guess it would be nice to know if we'd stay friends after next year, if the worst of it was over, if all the drama was in the past. But then I thought, *what if it isn't?*

I handed the deck back to Haz. He took three cards from the top and laid them out face-down in front of him. "Okay," he said. "You ready?"

He turned over the first card. It was an illustration of a heart, floating in a stormy sky and pieced through with three daggers. This wasn't looking good.

"The three of swords," said Haz, almost consolingly. "This card represents the past, so you've experienced heartache and rejection. Things haven't worked out the way you wanted them to, and you've had some feelings of disappointment."

Well, who hasn't? I thought.

"It's the past though," he went on, "so don't worry about it too much. See the storm clouds in the background? They're already moving, passing through."

I tried my best to keep my face neutral.

The next card was of a man in a cape, staring down at three spilled cups. His face was hidden, turned away, but he was obviously in mourning. Two goblets, full of wine, stood untouched on the ground behind him. It was a plaintive, ominous image.

"Ah, the five of cups," he said, nodding. "This is your present situation. You're still fixated on what you've lost and find it difficult to let go. You need to focus more on the good things, the positives, and not keep obsessing about the past."

Okay, that one was pretty accurate. I was definitely starting to move forward, but I was still holding on to some baggage. That was normal though, wasn't it?

"Cups are all about emotions," he said, gazing down at the cards between us. "You need to try and be less pessimistic, to not let your negative feelings take over."

"Kinda tricky after that first card though," I muttered.

Haz nodded, tried to smile. He made a point of not looking at Ezra.

He went to turn over the last card but I suddenly stopped him, raised my hands. Haz looked up me, concerned, afraid he'd offended me or something.

"Actually, would you mind if I didn't see the future card? You've got everything right so far – you're really talented! – but I'm not sure I actually *want* to know."

Haz smiled at me gently. "I get it," he said. "Don't worry."

"Well, let *me* look at least," said Ezra, grabbing the card and holding it up in front of his face. He showed it to Sam, then Haz, then clutched it tightly to his chest.

"Are you *sure* you don't wanna look?" he said. "Trust me. It's a good one."

I laughed, shook my head. I was happy in the present moment, just as I was right now, surrounded by all my favourite people. I didn't want to know the future.

But I couldn't wait to find out for myself.

Thirty Two

"You shagged him?"

"Don't say it like that," I said. "You make it sound so…
so *dirty.*"

Ezra was in my room, applying his makeup at the sink.
He'd been lining his lips with a purple pencil when I broke
the news about sleeping with Theo. I should've waited for
him to finish. He'd been so surprised that he'd messed
the line up, drawing halfway across his cheek. He started
fumbling around for a makeup wipe.

"Well..?" he asked.

"Well what?"

"How was it?"

I paused. How could I tell him it hadn't been great?

Having sex with Jonah had been all music and lights
and fireworks, and with Theo it had been…well, different.
It was much more intimate, more romantic, but also a
hundred times more awkward. I hadn't had a bad time; it
just wasn't as earth-shattering as I'd hoped. I didn't know
how to talk about it without making Theo look inadequate,
but Ezra could pre-empt what I wanted to say. He had a
sixth sense about these things.

"Oh, that's alright," he said, fixing his foundation. "The first time with a new person is always weird – even if you really like them."

"Even though it wasn't with Jonah?"

I immediately wished I hadn't said it. Four months had passed since I'd walked in on them in bed together, but we'd both stopped bringing it up. I couldn't remember the last time either one of us had said his name. But Ezra just shrugged, looked at me innocently.

"Who?"

I smiled until he turned away.

"Besides," he said, poking through his bag for a different makeup brush, "it doesn't mean you aren't compatible. Sex is just another part of your relationship. You have to work at it, figure out what you like. And everyone's different! You can't expect it to be mind-blowing right away. Keep practicing. You'll get there."

I rolled my eyes. "Thanks, Ez."

"You're welcome," he said. "Although I hope it's out of your system before next year. I don't want to hear you two rolling about like weasels every night."

Since it was the last week of term, the boys and I had decided to rent a house together in September. I had my reservations – it seemed like a big jump from only hanging out occasionally – but there was no one else I'd rather live with. Besides, the last couple of months had shown me how lucky I was to have them. I decided to think of it as an adventure.

"I'll keep that in mind," I said, scowling.

Ezra grinned at me. "Please do."

We were interrupted by a sudden knock on the door. It was Theo, looking especially cute tonight. He was wearing a *Jurassic Park* T-shirt – the yellow in the logo perfectly matched to his plastic glasses – and he was standing in the doorway with a bright, unguarded smile.

"Hey," I said.

"Hey!"

I pulled him in close and gave him a quick peck on the lips. I regretted it straight away. Ezra was watching us through the mirror.

"Ah! Young love!" he said, dramatically.

"Hey, Ezra," said Theo. He was still smiling but I noticed his face turning red, saw him shyly adjusting his glasses. I stared at Ezra with narrowed eyes.

"Ignore him," I said, closing the door. "He's just excited about tonight."

Ezra nodded. "Yeah, it's true. I'm on the hunt for my future husband."

I rolled my eyes again, but thankfully Theo started laughing. I'm not sure he understood Ezra very well, but I sensed he thought of him like a cat – cute and arch but unpredictable. I'd given up on trying to make them better friends, but actually, I quite liked their dynamic now. It wasn't perfect by any means, but they both knew how much they meant to me.

Could I ask for more than that?

"So, what's the plan?" Theo asked, sitting down on my bed.

I handed him a glass of wine. "Well, once Ezra's finished and the others are here, we'll have some drinks and then head to the Union."

"Others?"

"Just Haz and Sam. Oh, and Charlotte. I bumped into her yesterday and asked if she wanted to join us. Is that alright?"

Theo nodded. "I like Charlotte!"

But I hadn't thought about how small my room was before I'd invited people over. It was barely big enough for two people, and I could hardly imagine how three more of us were going to fit. Haz and Sam were already on the way, but I asked Ezra to text them, to tell them to meet us at the bar instead. There'd never be enough room in here for six of us, and I figured we could just as easily have drinks there. At least everyone would be more comfortable.

When Ezra was done, he turned towards us. Besides his purple mouth, the rest of his makeup was soft, subdued, more natural than I was used to. He looked like a saint in a classical painting, a sort of gothic Botticelli. His eyelids were dusted with silver powder.

"Okay, I'm ready," he said with a flourish.

"Gorgeous!" Theo exclaimed.

I grinned. I knew Ezra would appreciate the sentiment.

"Thank you, darling," he said, turning his face to catch the light. "What a discerning young man! Your boyfriend clearly has good taste, Ash."

"Obviously. He likes *me*," I said.

Now it was Theo who rolled his eyes.

About an hour later, the three of us – now joined by Charlotte, Haz and Sam – were sitting around the bench outside the bar, the one where Ezra and I had met. Sam had decided to teach us a drinking game. It involved a deck of cards and a bottle of a suspiciously green liquid, but he hadn't mentioned that you needed to be a neurosurgeon to understand. He'd explained the rules three times now, but I could still see that none of us knew how to play. Charlotte, breathing heavily, looked seconds away from a murderous rampage.

"Okay, I got an ace," said Haz. "Does that mean I have to drink?"

Sam rubbed his temples. "No, it means you have to draw another card."

"But I just did that?"

"No, you need another one."

"So, I put this one down here?"

"No, you keep it and pick one more. Fucking hell. It's not hard!"

Theo watched them nervously. "Um…maybe we could play a different game?"

"But this one's easy," said Sam. "Let me explain the rules again."

"No!" we all shouted in unison.

The rest of us started laughing, throwing down our cards and hoping the game was finally over. But Sam, tight-lipped and muttering, looked unmistakably annoyed. Haz put a hand on his shoulder, stroked him gently, calmed him down.

"Okay, I know an easier game," said Sam, shaking him off. "It's called *The Rules of Love* and it's really simple to understand. Let's play that one instead."

"Uh, I'm just going for a cigarette," said Ezra.

I quickly stood up too. "Yeah, um…and I'll help."

Laughing, we walked a little way off, downwind of everyone on the bench. As Ezra searched around for a cigarette, I leaned against the wall, listening as Sam tried explaining the rules. I let my eye rest on each of them in turn – Sam, then Haz, then Theo, then Charlotte – and I felt a surge of love like being car sick. Maybe I was just overwhelmed. As I looked at them, I couldn't stop thinking about how far we had all come, how much things had changed since the start of the year. And now it was nearly over. We'd have to come back for exams in a few months, but since they were staggered throughout the term, we couldn't say for sure when we'd all be around. This could be the last time I'd see them until September, and I didn't know how I would cope without them. They really were my favourite people.

Eventually I turned to Ezra. "What exactly *are* the rules of love?"

He shrugged. "Fuck if I know."

"Should we tell Sam to drop it?"

"Nah, he'll get the hint eventually. It's *your* fault for making friends with so many polite people. No one wants to tell him how boring his games are."

I laughed. "Yeah, that's true. But they're nice though, aren't they?"

"What? His games?"

"No, *them*! Our friends!"

He shrugged again. "Well, if you like that sort of thing."

"You know, I'm starting to think I do."

He nodded, grinned, made a little sound like laughter. He put his cigarette between his teeth and then reached out and touched my arm, rubbed it slightly, sudden and intimate. I didn't know what he was trying to say. We turned away from each other, embarrassed.

We lapsed into silence for a few minutes, looking up at the sky, the twinkling stars. Ezra glanced at me, glanced away. In the dark, his lips looked black.

"Do you think we'll all stay friends?" he asked. "I mean, we'll be living together next year, but...after that. Do you think we'll be friends for the rest of our lives?"

My gut told me to lie, to say that we'd always be inseparable, but how could I possibly tell him that? Besides, if I'd learned anything at uni, it was that you never knew how quickly things could change. It was a miracle we were still friends.

"I don't know," I said. "I hope so."

And this time, I really meant it.

Acknowledgements

Firstly, thank you to everyone who's given me advice, encouragement, or a shoulder to cry on while I was working on this book. Whether they knew it or not, their support always managed to keep me afloat when I was drowning in a sea of edits. Special thanks to Sina Sparrow, Jack Mason, Janet and Steve Richardson, Ollie Trickett, Lucy Edmonds, Aurimas Sabalys, Jack Firth, Maik Gräf and Alfie Speed (the two most beautiful boys in Hamburg), Andy Glancy, Marc Joss, Jess Mettam, Marcus Evans, and Martin Cornwell.

Thank you to the fabulous Candice Marshall, proofreader extraordinaire. When she finally finishes writing her biblical epic fantasy, I only hope I can return the favour.

I'm incredibly grateful to my parents for their many years of support, and I know that I couldn't have done it without them. I hope I've proved that all those hours spent watching Xena weren't wasted after all.

A huge thanks to Louise Richardson, my toughest critic. Louise was the first person I shared this story with, and her feedback on the earliest drafts made this novel into what it is today. She makes me work harder and always strive to be a better writer, and I'm very grateful to her for that.

Thanks also to Owen Johnson, the person who saw the value in my work when no one else did. I would never have attempted to write a novel were it not for his support, and his years of friendship have been a gift. For his willingness to help me out with marketing – and for writing the wonderful blurb on the back cover – I feel very lucky to have him on-side.

Without doubt, the person who heard the most about this book while it was being written was Laurence Hazel, who was always happy to listen to me bitching about it over the phone. Those phone calls became really important throughout the process, and Laurence was always able to convince me to carry on going, to trust my instincts, and not to throw myself into the Thames. So to him, a massive thank you.

Lastly, and perhaps most importantly, thank you to The Boys of South London – Alex Hambis, Ross Ingielewicz, and Sam Mason – without whom this book never would've been written. They served as the basic inspiration for the main characters in *Cold Like Ash*, and were all very accommodating when it came to stealing things they've done or said. Their thumbprints are all over this book, and I really, really hope they like it.

Max Deacon, January 2022

Max Deacon has a BA in English and Creative Writing from Royal Holloway University, and an MA in Creative Writing from Oxford Brookes. He enjoys cheap wine, scented lip gloss, and *Xena: Warrior Princess*, ideally all at the same time. He currently lives in London.

Cold Like Ash is his first novel.

@max.deacon.books

Printed in Great Britain
by Amazon

12777850R00189